Part 1: The Suffering of Jacob

Chapter 1

The Ostrich with Its Head in the Sand

"I want to talk about this Jacob. You can't just go into ostrich mode right now. Communication doesn't work that way."

She was right. Faith had coined the phrase "ostrich mode" for him years before, back when they were still in the earlier, more awkward stages of their relationship when they danced carefully around each other to avoid full disclosure of the idiosyncrasies that lay dormant just beneath the surface.

As their relationship progressed, however, Jacob's propensity for avoidance became all too clear to Faith. When she had first asked him about moving in together, Jacob had said he would "give it some thought" and then proceeded to say nothing about the matter for two full weeks. When Faith brought the matter to his attention once again, he tweaked his delaying tactics by suggesting "he needed more time to think about it," all the while both of them now conscious that he wanted nothing other than for the whole situation to simply go away, as if the words themselves had never been uttered.

Faith considered her next move deliberately. If she forced him on this issue, she might push him away from her, perhaps touching upon some ancient wound that she had not yet exposed. She had learned from her father, however, that problems unconfronted were just surreptitious demons lurking beneath the bed. Furthermore, she did not want to reinforce this trait in Jacob, especially when the precedents of their fledgling relationship were being set.

When Jacob returned home from teaching school that Friday afternoon, Faith was waiting for him on the concrete steps that led to his apartment building, holding the railing in a manner that was defiant yet compassionate. "I am here," she started, "because I refuse to let you bury your head in the sand like an ostrich. I want to walk through this life with you, Jacob, working on issues together, not pretending they don't exist. I can't promise to make all your problems go away, but I can promise that as long as we're together, I will be there to help you through them." As she said this, she handed him a worn and faded Get Out of Jail Free card from the game Monopoly, only Faith had crossed out the word Jail and written over it, Your Problems. "I want you to make a decision about the apartment. While I would love for us to move in that direction, I will not be offended or hurt should you feel that you are not ready for that yet. You can call me at home later tonight if you feel you need to talk about any of this. I do love you, you know?"

"I know," Jacob said, as he nodded his head unconsciously. "I know."

The next morning, Faith got her reply. Jacob and Faith lived in his Foggy Bottom apartment overlooking H Street for a little over a year until they were married and moved into the Georgetown home where he now sat staring out at the falling rain, that old Monopoly card secretly buried in his tight and anxious grip.

"Jacob, why are you so scared to bring a child into this world? Is it me? If it is, you should have told me some time ago."

Jarred back into the present conversation, Jacob seemed lost as he was beckoned from his quiet contemplation. He bent down to pet Samwise, the goofy but lovable Golden Retriever they had adopted last Spring, and then turned back from the window to see Faith resting on her slender arm against the entryway. Her hair was still wet and bedraggled from the short run from her car into the house.

"Of course it's not you," he whispered as he sighed with exhaustion. He knew that Faith had been getting warmer with her first question, but that she had suggested herself as the plausible cause only as a shielding mechanism, a polite excuse to pause without blame before commencing the acute incision into his inner psyche. "*Let the dissection begin,*" he decided to himself, as he prompted her by saying, "The issue lies with me, Faith. I just don't feel that I'd be the kind of father that I'd like to be. The dysfunctions I've inflicted upon myself are one thing, but to inflict them on a child- I don't know, Faith; that just seems selfish and indulgent."

"I think we both know that you'd make one hell of a good father, Jacob," she insisted with a look that was both pleading and reassuring. Being almost three inches taller than Jacob, Faith's chestnut-colored eyes peered down into the pools of blue and green that had so drawn her to him in the first place. "That's not the issue, is it? It's more than that. What is it Jacob? Talk to me. I feel like we've been having this same conversation for months now."

He looked intently at her now, and she seemed to him all that was left of what was good and true in the world. Her long brown hair reminded him of the rich, earthy soil from which his dreams grew. Her tall, supple frame was sturdy and athletic, but not extravagant. Her deep brown eyes calmed him and beckoned him to a home he had barely ever known. Peering deep into those eyes, he wanted to tell her what she wanted to hear, but the demons beneath the bed spoke instead.

"Faith, how can we possibly conceive of bringing a child into this world with the way it is today? Fuck today, ever! The world is a cruel and bitter place, Faith. Life is an uninterrupted series of losses and disappointments. Should we satisfy our own instinctual needs of reproduction only to wreak that havoc and misery upon another? I don't think that's fair, Faith."

"No, what's unfair, Jacob, is marrying me under the premise that you wanted to have children and then promptly changing your mind once I had made a commitment to you."

Faith was angry now, and the sharp lines of resentment cut across the delicate angles of her face. Her retort was biting because it rang true. He had initially told her that he had wanted children, but as the reality of it had been pressed upon him, he had grown progressively uneasy about the prospect. No, he had not been deliberately deceptive or manipulative; Jacob had believed it when he told Faith of his desire for children, but its palpable fulfillment now left him wary of the consequences. He had learned long ago that all which is given can just as easily be taken away.

"Listen, I apologize if you feel I have misled you, but you have to believe me when I tell you that I honestly meant everything I told you when I said it. I recognize that my retraction of those statements might be unjust and frustrating, but I have always tried to be honest with you, and now, maybe for the first time, I'm trying to be honest with myself." Jacob was entreating her now, attempting to play to her sense of compassion. His head, with its light brown hairs cropped neatly to the scalp, drooped down in resignation. He had gone where he had hoped not to go. "I don't want to watch my child suffer as I have." Swept away by his own confession, he began to cry lightly, and his body went limp before her.

Her glance turned more concretely into him, and she became concerned once again more for his uncertain happiness than her own. She pushed long stray hairs from her face to keep them from distorting her gaze and spoke to him directly, "But don't you see that life is more than loss and suffering, Jacob? Don't you see that? Don't you see that in us?"

"I see it in you," he thought to himself.

He turned his head back up to return her intent gaze. She was closer to him than he had anticipated, and it made him momentarily uneasy. "I...I need to know, Faith. Would you leave me over this?" He peered into her deeply, afraid of how she might respond. He knew he was asking more of her than she might be willing or able to give.

"What do you mean?" she asked.

"Would you divorce me if I decide that I am unwilling to have a child with you?" He averted his gaze from meeting her own.

She tried to find his eyes but could not. After a brief silence, she replied, "No, Jacob, I wouldn't." She let out a brief "humph" of exasperation. She had not intended to disclose so much. It left her feeling vulnerable, as if her final card had been played, and all she could do now was sit back and see how the hand unfolded. "So is that, I take it, your final answer?"

Jacob could not take his eyes off of her. In her moment of ultimate sacrifice, she appeared more radiant to him than she ever had before. Amidst all the pain and misery life could dredge up, here was a woman who proved that there was indeed some salvageable sanctity left in it also. Here was a woman willing to forsake her own aspirations and needs in order to satisfy his. Here was a woman who had pledged to never leave him and meant to see it through.

Again, he longed to placate her fears, not merely tell her what she wanted to hear, but to assure her that they would have a child together and that it would grow up to be strong and healthy and good. He wanted so very much to be capable of the same type of sacrifice that she was willing to make for him. Even more so, he wished that he could believe, really believe, that their child could grow up to be happy.

"I think I just need some time to think about it, Faith. I think I just need some time."

Chapter 2

The Feral Cats of Athens

Jacob and Faith moved into the brownstone at 3110 N. St. at the tail end of the summer of 1994, both of them knowing that they were fortunate to live there. It was a great neighborhood, relatively quiet for its proximity to the nucleus of Georgetown. Although it required Faith to commute almost twenty miles to the flower shop she owned in the suburbs of Virginia, Jacob could walk or bike the mile to Georgetown Catholic where he had taught English since graduating from nearby George Washington University.

It was Faith's beloved Uncle Charles, or so she and her older sister Trisha had called him since they were girls, who found their new home and helped them scrape together enough money for a down payment.

In truth, he was Faith's godfather, a friend of her parents since the couple had relocated to Fairfax from a small town outside of Roanoke back when her mother was pregnant with Trisha. After leaving behind most of their friends and family in Southwest Virginia, Faith's parents sought a figure of stability in their lives, a support system to give them emotional support in this city so far from their high school memories. That's where Uncle Charles came in.

They met him when Sam and Dottie were looking for an apartment. A hairdresser for the wealthy and prestigious in a city that had plenty of each, Uncle Charles had recently begun to dabble in the real estate market which would eventually be the more significant source of his wealth, if not his vocational pride. Not long before he met Sam and Dottie, he had purchased a number of duplexes in Fairfax that he intended to fix up and rent. He knew when he bought them that he would be able to command a top-end rent despite their outdated appearance and small, inconvenient floor plan, because they were close to the fashionable shopping district and had a view of the adjacent golf course.

When Sam and Dottie came to look at the place, Uncle Charles, in the time it took to show them the nine-hundred square foot apartment, discerned that this was a young couple with few financial means. He had examined the competing property rents in the nearby area before making his purchase, and he was aware of several available apartments that were both larger and more affordable. He wanted to inform them, but he also wanted to be sure not to insult them.

"Mr. and Mrs. Colms, I have to be honest with you. This is the only two-bedroom I have available in these duplexes. Unfortunately, I had a man in here the other day, and he told me that the unit has some significant termite infestation. If you can wait for a couple of months to occupy, well then I think this would make you a great, little apartment. If you are not in a position to wait, however, I would be happy to give you a few referrals for some other properties nearby that might be readily available. Of course, they wouldn't be this close to the golf course."

Only the first and last sentences of what he said had any truth in them whatsoever. While Uncle Charles was by no means a habitual liar, he was prone to falsehood if it meant sparing the feelings of others or avoiding confrontation. He was simply a pragmatist this way. Dottie was now quite close to term, and Uncle Charles instinctively knew, though he had not married or had children of his own, that no expectant mother would allow herself and her child to be thrust into a living situation held in limbo.

Sam knew enough about termites to know that it didn't take two months to spray for them. He also knew enough about human nature to know that Charles's deception was benevolent. Though Sam disliked pretending ignorance, he decided to make an exception.

"*He's a good man*," Sam thought to himself, a phrase Sam Colms did not take lightly.

In the course of their long friendship, neither man ever revealed their perspective of its beginning, each sitting back and grinning at the kindhearted deception they had pulled over on the other.

Faith first introduced Uncle Charles to Jacob in the summer of '93 while they were touring Europe. Jacob and Faith had been dating for almost a year when they decided that a month-long trek across the continent would be a measurable test of their relationship. Faith was taken aback when Jacob proposed at a mountaintop café overlooking Salzburg. She had anticipated but not expected the moment, and a trip that had up until that point been a much-needed break from the daily grind of the flower shop, now took on greater significance. Not only was this to be their first real trip together, it was now to be the excursion that bonded them together for a lifetime. And to think, she had never even left the country before.

Obscene overseas phone rates be damned, Faith just had to call her parents to tell them the news. When Faith finally hung up the phone, she looked over at Jacob. He had no one he needed to call. Once back in the States, he would call his longtime friend Tobin, his Grandma Tess, his friends Grace and Paula at work, but there was no one Jacob needed to call tonight. She knew this but spared him from the heightened awkwardness that would come from asking. Instead, she changed the topic.

"How do you feel about heading to Athens next?"

"Sure, if that's ok with you."

"Yes. Actually, you're going to get to meet Uncle Charles."

Faith had mentioned Uncle Charles to Jacob before but had been reluctant to introduce them until her relationship with Jacob was on a more solid footing. Though Jacob had worried that perhaps this was an indication of Faith's hesitancy to get emotionally involved, Faith had really done this to protect him. While Uncle Charles was by no means judgmental, his eccentricities rendered him an acquired taste. Although Charles lived only twenty minutes away, she had waited until she knew that Jacob was "the One". When her mother informed her that Charles was also in Europe and was headed to Athens for a few days, Faith felt that this was most definitely the time.

Two days later, weary and unwashed, they arrived early into Athens via the overnight train from Salzburg. When they checked-in at the front lobby, the manager informed them that their room had already been taken care of. Uncle Charles had also left them a hand-scribbled note that informed them that while his regimented itinerary of sightseeing had him occupied until the afternoon, he would enjoy taking them out to dinner that night, if they were available. "I'll be back by two, so stop by my room any time after that. That'll give me time for a nap, so I can keep up with you kids tonight."

As they retired to their room, a sense of weight seemed to lift from Jacob. His piercing green eyes had reawakened and shone with their accustomed luster. He still looked tired, but his spirits had been refreshed.

"I think I shall have a nap," he said as he disrobed.

"I think I shall have a shower and then a nap," Faith replied.

Peering back from the bathroom, where she had started the water running in the shower and then undressed, she saw Jacob out on the balcony, waving himself over the bustling city of Athens. She could not contain the childish amusement that spread across her lips as his naked member dangled and swayed for all to see. She loved this about him, his innocent recklessness and whimsy.

"Just what do you think you're doing out there?" she asked playfully.

"Waiting for you to join me."

She turned off the water, and then went out to the door of the balcony, not onto the balcony itself, and grabbed his wrist to pull him back into the room. Losing only a step or two in her initial tug, he, in turn, gripped her wrist and pulled her onto the balcony with him. She let him kiss her there, naked before the traffic below.

Back in the room, she made love to him with an unrestrained frenzy that surprised even her. Jacob seemed to bring out the best of her as he often did. She thirsted for the sense of oneness that came from the power of their love making. It felt so easy to give into that togetherness with Jacob, to let herself go in the embrace of another. She rode him rhythmically and passionately until both were satiated, full of the euphoria of knowing another that deeply. Falling back into his muscular arms and chest, she contemplated their life together- past, present, and future- before they both drifted off to sleep.

It was some time around four in the afternoon before Jacob and Faith made their way up to Uncle Charles's room. Still half-asleep, they knocked on the door and waited through some haphazard shuffling about before a middle-aged man opened the door, *USA Today* folded in his left hand and a smile forged from his wide, full lips. A bit disheveled, he appeared to have come from a lengthy stint in the john, his reading glasses pressed down towards the end of his nose.

Though she had not seen him in nearly a year, he was exactly as Faith had remembered him. Even now, in his mid-fifties, Charles had the complexion of a much younger man. A few laugh lines had begun to develop, but his skin was soft and rubicund, like the puffy cheeks of a cherub. He had perhaps put on a few extra pounds since the doctor insisted he start walking with a cane, but he truly seemed more plump than heavy. His skin tone was light, forcing him to avoid too much sun, but it also produced a rosiness to his cheeks that gave him a good-natured, jovial appearance. A stout man, whose slight curve forward detracted from his already short stature, Uncle Charles compensated for his height of just over five and a half feet with a bounce to his movement. While he now needed a cane to steady him from the curvature of his spine caused by his perpetual forward leaning, he would forever maintain a sprightly animation to him, a buoyancy to his steps as he shuffled to and fro like a child beaming from taking its first steps.

A man of routine, Uncle Charles generally wore the same attire (though he did, with much consternation, consent to wearing a tuxedo for Faith and Jacob's wedding). Never one to wear shorts, even as a child, he would wear nicely tailored, but loose-fitting, light colored slacks and a brightly-colored knit shirt, usually blue. The most distinctive components of his wardrobe, however, were his wide array of hats. Mostly they were tightly woven straw hats like some of the golfers wear on tour. He would wear them everywhere, rarely taking them off, lest he expose his bald dome to the elements.

"Well, please, come on in," Uncle Charles nearly shouted. "Welcome to my little abode on the road. I didn't know exactly when you were coming, or I probably would have picked up more. Please make yourselves comfortable. My hotel room is your hotel room; that's what I always say. Can I get you something to drink? Perhaps a refreshing *Fresca?*" he asked, adding a special Latin emphasis as he pronounced "Fresca" and giving a bit of a frisky wiggle with his hips.

"We'll split one of your 7-Up's which I know you must have a cooler of stashed somewhere around here," replied Faith, peering around the entryway to spy the red and white portable cooler that Charles took everywhere, always filled with ice and 7-Up's.

He took two cans of 7-Up out of the cooler and offered one to each of them. "Please, take a seat on the bed. You must be tired after that long train ride from Salzburg. Please, sit. Just throw that junk on the floor. In a glass or in the can?"

"In the can is fine," Faith answered.

"All right," Charles said as he smirked and headed playfully towards the bathroom, "but I'll have to ask you to please put the seat up when you're finished."

Jacob couldn't believe that Faith was laughing, but so she was. No matter how bad the pun or Uncle Charles's delivery, it never failed to make Faith laugh.

"We have some news for you, Uncle Charles," Faith said, redirecting the conversation.

"I know; your mother told me you two got engaged a few days ago," Uncle Charles responded as he re-entered the main room with their drinks.

"Darn her," Faith said disappointedly, "I wanted to tell you myself."

"Well, sweetheart, the beauty is in the details. Those she apparently left to you to tell me. How did our young friend here propose?"

As Faith finished telling him about Jacob's romantic proposal from a few days before, Uncle Charles revealed his indelible smile and turned his attention to Jacob, "Rumor has is it that you teach English, correct?"

"I do."

"Where at?"

"Georgetown Catholic. It's a small high school for girls near the university."

"Yes, I know it," Charles responded, nodding his head agreeably, "Several of my clients send their daughters there. Quite a good school, by its reputation anyway. Don't mind me asking, but are you Catholic?"

"I don't mind you asking, if you don't mind the answer. I do not happen to be a Catholic." It was a question he was asked often, and yet no matter how many times he answered it, he still felt uneasy about his response. Truthfully, he did not know much *what* he, in fact, was. Raised by his mother as a part-time Episcopalian (at one point, he even rode his bike the eight miles to the plain white church on High Hill Road when his mother was too sick to make it herself), his father's family had been Jewish until they gave up their religion after narrowly escaping pre-World War II Germany. Upon coming to America, both of his paternal grandparents forsook their Hebrew past only to become Christmas Eve Christians. He remembered a chilly October morning in his sophomore year at George Washington University when a school-owned van full of students pulled alongside him as he hurried on his way to class.

"Hey, Jacob," the driver of the maroon-painted van yelled out impatiently of the partially rolled-down window. "Are you Jewish? A bunch of us are going down to the temple on Wisconsin Ave. for Rosh Hashanah services. You wanna go?"

He stopped to consider what had prompted the driver to think that he may, in fact, be Jewish. Did his facial features appear Jewish? Though a bit crooked, his nose was more his mother's than his father's, and he could recollect no other telltale signs of Hebrew genetics. He recognized the driver as a student from one of his Philosophy classes; maybe he had deduced it from this experience. It might also explain the driver knowing his name.

"I'm half Jewish," Jacob replied noncommittally.

"Which half?" According to Christian tradition, a child's religious doctrine is decided by the father, while Judaism reserves this role to the child's mother. Ironically, therefore, Jacob was essentially wanted by neither faith. As a child, he had turned to God for answers and there had been none. What can God say to explain the unexplainable?

"On my father's side..." Jacob barely managed to eke out before the driver stepped on the accelerator so forcefully that the van made a squeal against the pavement. "Oh," was all the van driver had said. Even now, as he answered Uncle Charles's question, this was how Jacob thought of himself: a religious outcast, a squeal of tires against the pavement, a misfit without a home.

"So they don't mind?" Uncle Charles asked reassuringly, "Or don't they know? None of their damn business if you ask me, even if they are a Catholic school."

A smile returned to Jacob's face. "That's right. None of their damn business. No, I'm just joking. They know."

"You may find me strange, but I've never been much of one for organized religion *per se,*" Uncle Charles said as he leaned in towards Jacob, a gesture both aimed at and achieving a heightened sense of familiarity and camaraderie. Uncle Charles was a master of employing gesture for intended psychological effect. Having grown up in Savannah, he had retained just enough of the southern accent to be melodious in his speech. "Don't get me wrong, I consider myself to be spiritual, but I feel that the path towards God must be a path each person walks on their own, though sometimes a soul mate can help us in this pursuit." He pointed his elbow towards Faith for Jacob's benefit.

"Well said," rejoined Jacob. "I believe much the same myself."

Leaning back, Uncle Charles nodded his approval. "You're going to make Faith a wonderful husband."

"I'm sure going to try."

"Oh, I have a feeling you're going to do much better than try."

Later that night at dinner on a hillside terrace overlooking one of the commercial areas of Athens, Uncle Charles and Faith, to the unspoken but discernible horror of the proprietor and staff of the restaurant, fed scraps of their meals to the throngs of feral cats from the local alleyways that soon congregated around them. The two giggled together covertly, giving each of the brazen beggars a name from Greek mythology: Adonis, Hermes, Aphrodite, and so on. Faith was particularly fond of a scrawny, gray-haired cat, whom she named Hercules and whose paws had small patches of white. More than anything, she was pleased to see Jacob witnessing a fraction of her past.

Uncle Charles's salon, Cuts by Chaz (as he was known in those circles of D.C.), was located a few blocks Southeast from the Capitol. While his stylings were generally pragmatic and straight-forward, like a strong power tie, they resonated with a voice of authority. His clientele even included two former presidents, though both opted for on-staff hair cutters once they had actually made their way into the oval office.

From the time she was twelve, Faith would spend most of her summer vacations riding the orange line Metro to Union Station where she would then walk the remaining five blocks to Uncle Charles's salon. While she had gone under the auspices of gainful employment, Uncle Charles imploring Sam to let him hire his favorite "niece" to assist with the bookkeeping and general cleaning duties, for Faith it had really served as an escape from spending her summers at a home that had become increasingly unbearable.

The main room of the salon had three antique barber chairs along one wall and three porcelain sinks along the other. A small waiting area in front held four black leather chairs and a low glass coffee table covered with magazines long since past the date of publication or cultural relevance. The dichotomy of these two parts of the room was further enhanced by the flooring: while the waiting area was covered in a low shag, gray carpet, the rinsing and cutting area was a parquet wood floor. In between the two areas was an old-fashioned cash register with metallic buttons and a large lever.

A long black curtain separated the floor of the salon from Uncle Charles's office in the back. Here Uncle Charles gave Faith piano lessons in between clients on the antiquated Steinway upright he kept kitty-corner from his desk. Although she would eventually become an accomplished pianist in her own right, she would often just listen to him play, a hobby he had tinkered with since boyhood. Though his hands, like the rest of him, were stout, they were, also like the rest of him, nimble and deft. Flitting across the keyboard with ease, they produced fanciful melodies and chord structures that would manifest themselves in Faith's life-long passion for the instrument.

On an early morning soon after she started working there, Faith was taking a bag of trash out to the bin located in the alley behind the salon. As she opened the door that led from the office into the alley and stepped beyond the threshold, her foot sunk into what she feared was a mushy pile of dog crap from one of the strays of the neighborhood. What she discovered, however, was a bowl of cat food neatly placed on the left side of the entrance beside a matching bowl of milk. Saying nothing, Faith merely moved the bowls to the right side of the entrance. The next day, she noted that they had been re-filled and put back in their former position, so she moved them back to the right once again. Sure enough, the next day, they were re-filled and back on the left. When she finally confronted Uncle Charles about his clandestine feline feeding, he confessed to her that he had been doing this since he first moved into the salon and saw the homeless cats that wandered the alley. In Savannah, cats had a home; someone took care of them. From that day forward, there were two bowls of cat food and two bowls of milk outside the back door. None of the other employees ever knew about the two nuts who fed the neighborhood alley cats.

Even though Faith had recounted this story to Jacob on more than one occasion, and he had seemed to consider it humorous, she sensed his reticence to be associated with their feeding of the cats as appalled onlookers fixed their intent gaze upon them. Later on, he might consider the episode to be funny, but as the spotlight shone, he wanted no part of it.

"Where are you off to next?" Uncle Charles politely asked, noticing Jacob's discomfort as well.

"A few days here and then back up to Zurich for our flight home," Jacob replied. "And you?"

"The group leaves for Italy the morning after tomorrow. I sort of like these group tours; they give you a little piece of everything, so you know where to come back to when you have more time for just one place. Still, the main tour guide is this uptight, little British bitch, Ms. Haverford. She's so damn meticulous and punctual. She has every minute planned for us like we were back in boarding school."

Jacob asked, "What places do you plan on coming back to?"

"At my age, I'm not sure I can *plan* on making it back anywhere, but in a way, that's also the beauty of it. Time reminds me that I had better do what I can while I can do it. I'll tell you one thing: I would sure like to make it back to Lucerne. That's as beautiful a place as I've ever seen. I can't remember exactly what he said, but Twain once wrote about the statue of the lion in Lucerne. I'll tell you where I won't come back to, though, and that's this place. The Greeks can be so rude; just the other day, I had a museum guard yell at me in front of the whole group I'm traveling with just because he said I got too close to the ruins. It was unnecessarily embarrassing. Yes, Greece is one place I will not come back to."

"So what do they have planned for you to see tomorrow?"

Uncle Charles leaned towards Jacob covertly, as if someone might hear. "I was thinking of ditching the sightseeing tomorrow and taking a cruise for the afternoon. You guys have any interest? You know, in joining the old fart for an afternoon on the Mediterranean?"

"Sounds great to me. Faith?"

Faith agreed. "I'd love that! Where does the cruise go?"

"Oh, just a day trip to some of the local islands. Mostly old people probably, but I'm sure we'd have fun. We'll have to elude that Ms. Haverford, though. She'd give me hell if she caught me ditching the day's tour."

The waitress, a younger, slender woman dressed in traditional Greek attire to attract the tourists, interrupted to ask them if they cared for dessert. She seemed in a hurry, and when she had no takers for dessert and only one coffee amongst them, she appeared disgruntled and annoyed at the inconvenience. The entertainment of traditional music and dancing was about to begin, and she likely hoped to usher in another table of paying customers before they started.

Moments later, as Charles sipped the coffee that he complained was too hot, the music started, and dancers began to urge customers onto the stage in the middle of the terrace. Clumsy tourists were given impromptu lessons of Greek dance, while their dining compatriots watched and laughed, hoping not to be dragged up next. Faith noticed Jacob, whose seat was adjacent to the makeshift dance floor, slowly angling his chair away from the dancers.

"You two should go try that," Uncle Charles urged. "Looks like fun."

Faith said to Jacob coaxingly, "Yes, Jacob, let's give it a whirl, cut a rug, do the tango, if you know what I mean."

Pleadingly, Jacob turned to Uncle Charles, "Would you like to dance with Faith?"

"Can't I'm afraid, my boy. Doctor's orders," Charles protested, pointing to his cane. "But you two go have a good time."

As Jacob stepped onto the wooden planks of the dancing arena, he gave a glance back towards Uncle Charles who was smiling brightly. Beginning awkwardly, Faith and Jacob did the best they could to fall in step with the other dancers. After a while, Jacob began to feel more comfortable, and while his dancing got no better, it did become more lively. He leaned into Faith and whispered, "Your uncle is a hell of a guy."

"I'm glad you think so," she whispered back.

While they were each, in their own way, attractive people, the disparity in their heights made for a humorous, disjointed appearance as a dancing couple. Only a couple of inches shy of six feet, Faith merely accentuated the two or three inches she already had on Jacob by wearing heels. He attempted to spin her through two pirouettes, failing miserably each time. Still laughing at his own incompetence, he espied Uncle Charles who was beaming even more than when he had last looked. Far from wrenching himself in self-pity at his own inability to participate, Uncle Charles seemed content to share in their frolic. Jacob had always considered the potential joys of living vicariously through another to be complete and utter bullshit, but here was a man who had proven him wrong. Uncle Charles took his happiness where he could get it, knowing that it might, indeed, be fleeting. At that moment, Jacob knew he would come to love this man.

The next morning, Jacob and Faith met Uncle Charles in the hotel lobby shortly after six. Though the boat would not be leaving until eight, Uncle Charles wanted to have breakfast at the hotel and then "skeedaddle before that cranky old witch discovers us in the lobby."

After a breakfast of pastries and coffee, the only beverage Uncle Charles ever drank other than 7-Up, the three of them discreetly made their way out of the restaurant and around the corner past the hotel convenience store. Suddenly, Uncle Charles saw her and pulled both of them back behind a large marble pillar.

"Shit! There she is, right in front of the entrance."

"Who?" Faith asked curiously.

"That witch, Ms. Haverford."

Ms. Haverford, or Betsy to the rare few who knew her well enough to call her so, was the type of uptight, snooty Brit that fueled the unfair stereotype of the sexually repressed Anglo. Her thin, wiry hair, speckled with gray and a diminishing presence of light browns, was drawn back into a bun pulled so tight that it must have exerted enough force to serve, if correctly harnessed, as propulsion for a miniature sailing vessel set upon a parkside lake. Ms. Haverford's figure was small and compact; her skin seemed stretched as though it were holding in the massive tension that kept her so tightly wound. Her glasses lay at the end of her sharply-sloping nose, affording her the possibility of literally looking down at everything she saw. The lines of her face were pronounced and declared the verdict of her age and stress.

There had been a time when Betsy Haverford might have even considered herself to be easy-going, to proclaim that she was "happy." This, however, would have been quite some time ago, before she walked in upon the one love of her life, Mr. Stanley Haverford, mercilessly and furiously penetrating her sister, Ethel. Shocked by the rawness and passion of the act as performed in this manner and unable to comprehend why her husband may prefer this to her own bland and benign brand of sexuality, she divorced him and disavowed all forms of sexuality except for her increasingly infrequent trysts with her straightforward, white dildo. Now, as Uncle Charles pointed his figure skeptically towards her, just long enough to avoid being discovered, Ms. Haverford, in her overly-starched, bright blue guide's uniform, looked like a small parrot perched on a high branch straining out for the calls of her fellow birds.

"Why can't we simply walk past her?" Faith asked, failing to see why Uncle Charles, a full-grown man, could not do as he pleased.

But Charles was a man who invariably wanted to please others and shirked from open conflict, and so he insisted, "Oh, but if she were to see me, she would want to know where I am going, and then she would get quite upset when I told her that I was skipping out on the tour for today."

"But it's *your* vacation, not hers!"

"I know, I know, but it would just be such a hassle, so much trouble to best be avoided."

"Do you want *me* to go tell her that you're coming with us for the day?"

"Oh dear, no! Then I'll just hear about it for the next several days."

Finally, Jacob interjected himself into the conversation, "Uncle Charles, didn't you mention that you had been chewed out by a museum guard the other day?"

Faith was already beginning to lose her patience, "What the hell does that have to do with the price of tea in China?"

Jacob turned his head towards Faith and smiled smugly, "If the price of tea is low enough, even a tight-ass like Ms. Haverford will buy it." He returned his focus back to Charles, "You did say that, right?"

"Well, I hate to admit it," Uncle Charles acknowledged sheepishly, "But this one guard at the archaeological museum next to the Parthenon kept yelling at me for coming too close to the exhibits. I didn't touch them, mind you, but he kept yelling at me to keep 'my grubby American hands' away from the exhibits. I'm not dumb enough to touch stuff like that, but he still kept yelling at me."

"Perfect. I'll take care of this dilemma with Ms. Haverford, and you'll never have to explain a thing. Wait right here for a moment. I need to go up to the room for a second."

Jacob was only gone for a few moments, but when he came back, he had removed his t-shirt and swimming trunks and donned the formal suit he had brought with him for the sole purpose of proposing to Faith. The t-shirt, swimming trunks, and a towel were rolled up into a tight ball which he handed to Faith.

"Ok, we're all set. Now when I go over there and start talking to Ms. Haverford, be ready to bolt. I am going to take her around the corner to the hotel restaurant for a cup of coffee. I'll be sure that she's seated so that she cannot see you, so head out the door as soon as we sit down. Go out the doors and turn right. Walk for two blocks, and I'll meet you at that corner in fifteen minutes or so. Got me?"

"Just what are you planning on doing, Jacob?" asked Faith incredulously.

Uncle Charles, however, seemed entirely comfortable with Jacob's ability and was quite willing to leave the matter entirely in his hands. "If you say so, my boy."

Jacob leaned towards Faith and whispered, "Trust me." It was far from the first time he had said this to her, and he had proven true to his word up until now.

"All right, but don't get yourself in trouble, Jacob."

"I won't. See you in fifteen minutes." He gave her an affectionate peck on the cheek, straightened his shirt, and then walked directly towards Ms. Haverford. At first, she appeared startled by his approach, but Jacob extended his arm so as to lead her towards the café he had mentioned, seemingly without reservation.

"I'm liking this fiancée of yours more and more by the day," Uncle Charles whispered to Faith as he nudged her towards the front entrance of the hotel and out towards the pre-arranged meeting spot.

When Jacob had not arrived a full twenty minutes later, Faith began to fret. *"What could be taking him so long?"* she wondered, at first to herself, and then, as the time stretched to twenty-five minutes, aloud.

"I'm sure he's fine," Uncle Charles reassured her. "Ms. Haverford is a hag, but she certainly couldn't do much harm to him, after all."

Finally, Faith spotted Jacob walking down the crowded city street packed with early morning delivery people. "Well, there you are. Where the hell have you been?"

Jacob ignored her irritation and got to what he saw as the more significant point, "I don't think we'll have to worry about Ms. Haverford today."

"Did you beat her unconscious?" asked Uncles Charles with a gleeful, mischievous smile. Never one to wish genuine harm on anyone, he was, however, amused at being a part of Jacob's devious plot.

"No, nothing like *that,*" Jacob beamed back coyly, mostly to Uncle Charles who was obviously more amused by his endeavor than Faith was. "I simply told her that I was with the American Embassy..."

"You told her you were with *whom?*" Faith interjected, but it was a losing battle; Uncle Charles and Jacob were merely egging each other on at this point.

"You told her you were with the American Embassy? Oh, this is a great story, my boy!"

Regaining his composure after a laugh with Uncle Charles, Jacob continued, "I told her that we had taken you to the embassy for the day because we needed to question you regarding an incident at the archaeological museum."

It was already beginning to be another hot, arid day in Athens, and Uncle Charles, who was laughing to the point of genuine physical exertion, had to remove his hat and wipe his brow with his sleeve before he could ask, "Wait, you told her this was all about that guard yelling at me at the museum?"

"I explained to her that the Greek government does not take this sort of thing lightly. I told her that they suspected you of trying to smuggle artifacts out of the museum and that your room and all of your bags must be thoroughly searched before you were allowed to rejoin the group. I almost lost her there; she didn't seem too sure about the Americans allowing one of their citizens to be held on so little evidence."

In the blatant pause Jacob left dangling there, both Faith and Uncle Charles, almost simultaneously, had the time to inquire, "So how did you convince her?" Faith then added, "Didn't she ask you for some sort of identification?"

"I told her that there had been numerous reports of an American art thief who would go on escorted tours and use them as an opportunity to case the museum, often intentionally evoking a guard's response to get a feel for the security measures being employed. I said that Uncle Charles fit the profile, both physically and otherwise, of this thief who has supposedly stolen works in Madrid, Budapest, and Vienna. I had hoped that this somewhat fantastic story would appeal to the lonely romantic in her, the one that curls up on that couch alone at nights and dreams of a life with anything that doesn't require batteries. As it was, she bought it- hook, line, and sinker."

Impressed and amused, but still somewhat irritated by the delay, Faith then asked, "But what then took you so long?"

"Well, I had to keep up the act by asking her about any information she might have about Charles, anything suspicious that might have suggested that he was not who he said he was," Jacob replied, this time directly to Faith.

This piqued Uncle Charles's curiosity, who abruptly stopped laughing to ask, "Well, what did she say to that? Did she note anything *suspicious* about me?" His complexion was now flushed red from laughing. You could even see a few clusters of capillaries that lay close to his nearly translucent skin.

"She implied that your hats were conspicuous, a sign that you were trying to hide something. Moreover, she found it odd that you traveled alone and yet were so fastidious in your daily regimen. Lastly, she thought that your accent was fake, that perhaps you had assumed a different dialect to throw people off on your origins." At this, Jacob could no longer contain the straight face that had made this retelling of the story so funny. He knew that he had won over Uncle Charles for life. His full lips parted, he turned back to Faith to measure her expression, and then he permitted the bright smile of laughter withheld to come forth.

For her part, Faith shot him back a look of knowledge and appreciation. Gone now was any semblance of irritation. She looked deeply at Jacob and adored him. She knew that adventurous moments like this were difficult for Jacob to muster, but she also marveled at how much he reveled in them when he did.

Uncle Charles, though, being quite proud of his Southern roots, was peeved by the final insinuation elicited from Ms. Haverford. "She thinks that I have *assumed* this dialect? Why, if that stuffy British wench wants to hear a faked accent she should tape herself and listen to the pretentious crap that comes out of her mouth. For crying out loud, you'd think she was having tea with the Queen Mother herself."

A year later, when they moved into that brownstone on N St., that would be the joke they played on Charles. As with most gag gifts, the motivation for the all-inclusive lessons arranged with one Betty Sue Thompson, originally from Macon, Georgia, for Charles to "Improve Southern Dialect and Etiquette," was purely for their own amusement.

Chapter 3

When Life Throws You a Curveball...

They met at a Red Sox game. Not that the game itself was played at venerable Fenway Park- no, this game took place at Camden Yards, home field to the Baltimore Orioles since 1992. Still, if you had asked Jacob, he would have said it was a Red Sox game nonetheless. Such is the nature of being a sports fan; perhaps such is the nature of life: We can only see from the one perspective that we have been given.

Jacob's perspective as a die-hard Red Sox fan was one of the few things his father was able to leave him before he passed away. Walter Hartman, though a dedicated and earnest parent, spent many of his weekends traveling for the sports memorabilia sales job he was forced to take after his own mother disinherited him for marrying Jacob's mother, Elizabeth, citing the relatively sizable discrepancy in their ages as the reason for her reproof. Once the prodigal son destined to ascend to the throne of the family paper business, Walter promptly told his overbearing, contemptible mother to go fuck herself and never turned back.

Though Walter swore to himself to work hard in order to afford himself this costly liberty from filial servitude and not subject his son to fiscal sacrifice, in the end it was Elizabeth who really paid the price, for years later, after Walter had passed and the insurance money had run out, Walter's mother was sure to provide for Jacob's needs, as long as none of the funds went to Elizabeth's expenses. "Life isn't always fair," Jacob's mother used to like to say, and as if to prove her point, the "Miserable Miser," as Elizabeth used to refer to her, managed to triumph in the end, though the victory itself was certainly hollow.

So while their times together in those early years of Jacob's life were sporadic, his moments with his dad held a sacred reverence even then as an eight year old unaware that his father would be dead before he was nine. It was early June in the summer of 1975 when Walter bust through the door of the modest apartment they had rented in an aspiring middle-class neighborhood. Blatantly overjoyed, Walter ran over to where Jacob was planted on the sofa watching television and hoisted him into the air. At that age, Jacob still loved it when his father would toss him into the air and snare him just before he hit the ground. He loved the uncertainty of it, that lift and then drop in the pit of the stomach, and he would ask for more until Walter's arms grew numb from Jacob's incessant demands. It would not be long, however, until he dreaded, even went to neurotic means to avoid, the exact same sensation of uncertainty.

"*You*, my young friend, are skipping school tomorrow!" Walter pronounced as he caught Jacob's head perilously close to the hardwood floor of the entryway.

Jacob tried to respond, but he needed to catch his breath, and by that time Elizabeth, disrupted from cooking pasta in the kitchen by all the initial commotion, had come in and demanded to know, "Just *WHAT* is going on in here?"

"I'm taking Jacob to his first baseball game tomorrow," his dad exclaimed, righting Jacob upon his feet and straightening his shirt.

"And what about school? He does still have school for a couple more weeks, you know."

Walter implored, "But Beautiful, Joe got two tickets in for tomorrow's game, and he told me to take the day off and use the tickets to take Jacob here to the game. It's his way of saying thanks for all the extra hours." A gifted man of his trade, he now walked over to his wife, dragging hopeful Jacob behind, and put his arm around her for the final sales pitch, "Plus, honey, he goes to school every day. How often does he get to see a ballgame with his old man?"

In fact, that Wednesday in the early summer of 1975 would be the one and only time.

The next morning, as Jacob awoke, he was surprised by his dad's absence. His mother seemed to be uninformed as well, saying only, "Your dad said that he forgot something at the office."

As Jacob was getting dressed in his room, however, his dad walked in with his hands behind his back and said to Jacob, "I've got a present for you. Guess what it is."

"A talking giraffe?" responded Jacob.

"No, silly. Look at this." From behind his back, Walter produced a baseball bat and handed it to Jacob. Bewildered, Jacob was amazed at how much larger it seemed in real life than when players wielded them on television. Even more confusing was what he was expected to *do* with it. Did this mean his dad had somehow made arrangements for him to *play* in the game?

His father turned the bat over in his hand and pointed to the signature that laid along the thicker end of the bat. "That bat was signed by Fred Lynn, Jacob. He's a player for the Red Sox- granted a rookie, but he's having a heck of a season so far. In any case, he gave my boss these tickets and this bat as a favor, and my boss gave them to me."

Jacob took the bat in his hands and tried to give it a thorough inspection, but it was too heavy and cumbersome for him, and the thick end of the bat thudded to the floor. With the handle still in his hands, however, Jacob rolled it over to see the signature. "What did you say his name was? It's hard to read on the bat. He has very messy penmanship. He would definitely get an 'Unsatisfactory' on his report card for penmanship."

"His name is Fred Lynn. You're going to get to see him play today."

Up until this moment, Walter had been Jacob's favorite baseball player. Though his dad had never played beyond his college days at Bowdoin, there were pictures of him playing second base for the Polar Bears back in the early 60's. Jacob had often watched baseball games on television with his dad on weekends when Walter was home, but he never knew any of those players by name. Without encouragement from his parents, Jacob had magnified the extent of his father's playing experience to the point where he thought Walter had himself played professional baseball for years. As he now gazed at the bat and his dad's eager expression yearning for acknowledgement, Jacob gleaned that this Fred Lynn was in a whole different league than his father had been.

"Thanks, Dad."

"You're welcome Jacob. I knew you would like it," his dad said, clearly overjoyed at having won his son's approval. "Now don't forget to bring your glove today. We're going to be in prime foul ball territory."

"Gotcha, Dad."

On the drive up to Boston, Walter drove more quickly than Jacob's mother would have liked had she been there. Her absence always brought out the speeder in him, as he quietly but irritably accepted her demands for him to slow down in her presence. The family had but one car, the tan Volvo sedan Walter's mother had purchased for him when he had graduated college ten years earlier. This made moments without Elizabeth in the car an opportunity to re-establish his will, even if furtively. Still, with Jacob in the car, he could generally be trusted to at least keep it under seventy-five.

As they drove through Sturbridge and left I-84 for the Mass Pike, Walter started to test Jacob's knowledge of various baseball statistics.

"After all, son, baseball is predominately a game of numbers. It is a game that can be understood, discussed, argued, and managed largely by a few key statistics. It's mathematical probability at its finest. Have they taught you about mathematical probability yet at school?"

Walter, while an involved father, was often a relatively oblivious one, particularly in this case where Jacob, still yet to finish third grade, had barely gotten past rudimentary arithmetic. He gave his father a puzzled look and shrugged. "I don't think so."

"Well," his father continued, dismissing this revelation as entirely inconsequential to what was obviously the larger point at hand, "that's what baseball is all about is numbers. But what makes baseball so amazing are those times when numbers fail, when, despite all mathematical probability against it happening, the incredible, the magical happens." His father stared past the windshield and shook his head in disbelief, noticeably recapturing a moment from his youth in the daydream just beyond his reach.

Abruptly, he turned to Jacob and asked him, "Do you know what we call that Jacob? Do you know what we call it when we believe in something even though logic says it really shouldn't happen?"

Caught off guard, Jacob looked at him blankly and shook his head. "No."

"'Faith.' That's what we call 'faith', Jacob." Jacob could not immediately grasp everything his father was saying at that moment, but he could tell that it was important to him. His father, slightly taller than six feet, was, even seated, physically awe-inspiring to him. Jacob tilted his head to the side and nodded to convey some sense of understanding and subsequent rumination.

This prompted Walter to continue, "Do you know when the last time the Red Sox won the World Series was?"

Still somewhat overwhelmed, Jacob again shook his head in the negative.

"1918. For chrissakes, that's the year your grandpa was born, Jacob. *Fifty*-seven years! That's a long damn time, Jacob, a long damn time. And, for all we know, it might be another fifty-seven years before they finally do win it." Walter's demeanor became more animated, and despite fairly heavy traffic on the Mass Pike, he centered his attention squarely on Jacob. "But that's the beauty of it all! As a Red Sox fan, you believe each and every year that *this* is going to be the year. You scout the roster, you invest your time and energy watching the games, and you *believe*, heart and soul you believe that *this* is going to be the year. And each year, right when they've got 'ya really thinking that they just might have the team to do it this time, they go and screw it up; they blow it somehow, usually to the Yankees." He paused after a sigh of resignation before concluding, "But then the next year comes, and you believe all over again. Now that's faith Jacob."

"You mean you think they're gonna win, even though you know they're going to lose?"

"Exactly!" Walter exclaimed as he frolicked with his hand in Jacob's hair, leaving it tussled.

Jacob had never been so confused when he was supposedly so correct, but his dad's indefatigable zeal was reassuring. He leaned back into the gray vinyl seats of the Volvo and watched contentedly as the pavement and the cars and the power line poles went rolling on by.

Jacob would remember this not only as his first baseball game, but also as his first experience with an actual city. Growing up in the suburbs of Connecticut, everything around him seemed so manufactured, so insular, so falsely safe. Even as he stepped from the car, he felt an unrefined frankness here, a vitality that gripped him with the sense of being alive. As they made their way by foot from the side streets of the university neighborhood, tucked in between the highway and the Charles River, and onto the more traveled thoroughfare of Brookline Ave., the crowd around them accumulated, growing denser as they went. It was a one o'clock start on a weekday, and so the crowd heading to the game consisted chiefly of middle-aged men with distinguished beer bellies and neglected stubble that left them unlikely to rectify their bachelorhood any time soon and college students blowing off class for an afternoon of sun and a few beers at the ballpark. All of them seemed to be engaged in a scholarly discussion of the in's and out's of manager Darrell Johnson's choice of lineup, the health of the starting rotation, and the possibility of finding any effective relief pitchers. Interspersed amongst these baseball die-hards were those who worked in the neighborhood and were on their way to eat lunch. Mostly dressed in suits, they stood out from the rest of the crowd but were nonetheless included in this dialogue. People would chime in on the general conversation around them, each adding their own theory as to what would doom the team this year.

The crowd drew tighter as they crossed the bridge over the highway. You could now see the backside of the legendary Green Monster, the left field wall which had made and broken the career of many a big league ballplayer since Fenway Park was opened in 1912. Even as a young child, to whom everything seems old and past its allotted time, the ballpark resonated with a sense of hallowed nostalgia. Jacob couldn't have explained it, but he felt it. He felt like there were ghosts there, friendly ghosts that called to him, wanting to share their story. He pointed his chubby right index finger in that direction, but it was Walter that spoke.

"There's Fenway Park, kiddo. Almost there. You still got your mitt, don't you? Show me your move for catching that fly ball."

Jacob thrust his left hand into the air and clasped the glove shut, enclosing an imaginary foul ball, just as his dad had taught him in the limited time Walter had in the evenings after work.

"Nice job!" Walter exclaimed.

Proud as could be and beaming with excitement, Jacob hustled down the other side of the bridge. As they turned left onto Yawkee Way, there were people moving in every frenzied direction. Vendors called out, offering, "*Hot* dogs, *Braut*wurst, *Polish Saus*ages," or "Pretzels, nuts," or "Programs *Heeere!*" Walter guided Jacob over to one of the booths and asked the man for a t-shirt and cap, a red one with a blue B on it and an adjustable size strap in the back. Only once Jacob was sufficiently decked out in Red Sox regalia could they pass through the red brick entryway and the lime green ticket gates into the park.

Their seats were located out in right field, so they had to walk for a while in the dark concrete walkways that ran underneath the stands, but as they started up the ramp towards the field, sunlight filtered in like a train emerging from a tunnel, and the pungent, accumulative smell of beer, roasted peanuts, and moist grass beckoned to young Jacob. As they hit the top of the ramp, an old man with a sun visor and a towel for wiping seats asked to see their tickets so that he could show them where they were sitting, but as Walter started to follow the usher, Jacob stood there mesmerized, unable to fully digest the immensity of it all- its sheer size, the greenness of the grass, the overwhelming variety of sounds. Walter reached back and picked him up underneath the arm to carry him along the way.

The usher showed them to their seats and folded down the hard, green plastic chairs. They were about fifteen rows off the field in a short row that was inside the right field foul pole. Seated next to Jacob was a portly, middle-aged man wearing a threadbare Red Sox shirt that had seen better days. His stubbly beard was grizzled and unkempt, and a matching cap hid what was sure to be a nearly bald dome, though a few stray puffs of wild, black and gray clumps of hair did protrude from underneath the cap, particularly near the ears. Next to him was a younger man, who appeared to be his son. Now grown, his attire was far more stylish than the other man's, as he wore a pair of tan khakis and a light blue polo shirt. This look was accentuated by his thin-wired glasses which gave him an air of competence and professionalism that the other man so noticeably lacked. Despite this discrepancy in their attire, however, there was an unmistakable similarity in the sharp angle of their noses and the fullness of their lips.

"How you boys doin' today?" the older gentleman asked them shortly after they had been seated.

Jacob, usually reticent with strangers, willingly responded, "Great!" Jacob hesitated there and turned back around, leading the man to believe that this energetic statement was going to be limited to one word, but Jacob abruptly added, "I'm missing school today!"

To Jacob's surprise, the man appeared to be as excited about this as he was, "Well, aren't you lucky! Seeing a ballgame with your dad, I assume?"

Walter leaned over from his seat at the end of the aisle and said, "It's his first game."

"Well," the older man chortled, "That's a special occasion now, isn't it? My son Jonathan and I have been comin' to Sox games since the days of Teddy Ballgame. We don't get out to many games anymore; he lives with his family out in Chicago now, but we still usually get to at least one game a year. Name's Ernie, by the way."

Still eager, Jacob interjected, "I'm Jacob, and this is my dad. Who's Teddy Ballgame?"

"You don't know Ted Williams?" the elder man asked incredulously. Seeing no recognition in Jacob's face, he explained, "Just the sweetest hitter to ever play for the Sox. He's the last man to hit .400 for a season, but that was even before I started bringin' Jonathan and his brothers. Back in '41 I think it was." He scratched his head near where the few remaining hairs held on for dear life, soon to join their departed brethren.

Though Jacob had no clue what hitting .400 meant, he was duly impressed and nodded his head in order to impart a sense of this to Ernie.

Before his father could get on even more of a roll, Jonathan asked Walter, "So, where you boys from?"

"Just west of Hartford," said Walter, glad to see his often reserved son so engaged.

Nothing Jonathan could do, however, could dissuade Ernie from his beloved topic of baseball. "Well, should be a good game. The Sox have got 'The Spaceman' going today."

This commentary made no sense whatsoever to Jacob, but he liked the man's manner of speaking and was anxious to replicate his banter, "Does that mean they're going to have Neil Armstrong playing?"

Ernie chortled again. His laugh was earthy and calming despite its intense volume. "No, son. 'Spaceman' is the nickname for Bill Lee. He's pitching for the Red Sox today."

At this point, Jonathan leaned over and spoke directly to Jacob, "My dad loves baseball stats. He keeps score for every game, even when he watches at home."

"Can you show me how?" asked Jacob.

"Of course I can," replied Ernie, as he drained the remainder of his oversized Coca-Cola and put it aside. With infinite patience, Ernie then gave Jacob a crash course on how to keep score for a baseball game.

By the time the crowd stood in respect for the singing of the national anthem, Jacob was hankering for play to begin. Walter had to remind him to remove his cap for the duration of the anthem, which he did begrudgingly only after noting that everyone else in the stadium had done likewise. As the heavy-set singer drew the anthem to a close, she dramatically held the note for "brave," signaling the crowd to burst through its finely-held decorum with an eruption of applause that droned in and out like an ebbing tide. Jacob was overcome by the sheer enormity of it all.

With the game ready to start, the crowd remained standing much like the parish waiting for the priest to instruct them to be seated, only here the Blessed Sacrament came with the delivery of Bill Lee's first pitch. As Lee started with what was for him a rare fastball for a strike on the outside corner, it made a crack in Carlton Fisk's glove that reverberated even up to their seats in right field. With that cue, the crowd gave a contented clap, along with a few high-fives and pats on the back, and settled into their seats for the game. From there, Bill Lee would go on to retire the side in order.

"'The Spaceman' is on his game today," said Ernie after Bobby Darwin swung and whiffed at Lee's final offering of the at-bat.

In the home half of the first inning, the Sox opened with back-to-back singles before Carl Yastremski walked up to the plate.

"Hey, he wears number eight too," said Jacob to his dad energetically.

Walter nodded, pleased with his son's enthusiasm. Ernie, overhearing the comment, leaned over to Jacob and informed him, "Yeah, they call him Yaz for short."

"I wear number eight on my little league team. We're the Firebirds."

"Well, you could do a lot worse than hitting like Yaz, that's for sure," replied Ernie, and with that, Yastremski promptly nailed a sharp line drive into right-center field, leaving runners at the corners and Jacob's newest hero, Fred Lynn, coming to the plate.

As the young center fielder strode towards the batter's box, Walter nudged Jacob with his elbow amidst a mounting fervor in the park. "All right Jacob, that means Fred Lynn is up. Have you shown Ernie and Jonathan here your bat yet?"

As Jacob did so, both Jonathan and Ernie went out of their way to show Jacob how impressed they were with the boy's cherished treasure. "You hold onto that now," said Ernie. "He's going to be a big star in this league. That's going to be worth quite a lot some day."

Lynn took Dave Goltz's first pitch, an outside curveball, and stepped back to ready himself for the next offering.

"Good eye, Freddy, good eye!" yelled someone a few rows back so loudly that Jacob swore that Fred Lynn must have heard him.

Goltz's second pitch, also a curveball, was a bit outside, but this time it was too enticing, and Lynn swung and missed for strike one.

"That's all right, Freddy! Don't swing at that weak crap!"

On the next pitch, however, Goltz misplaced a fastball that was intended to be on the inner half of the plate but was instead right down the middle, knee-high. Fred Lynn pounced on the mistake deftly, like a leopard seizing its prey, and hammered it off the legendary Green Monster in left field, scoring the Sox's first run of the game.

Upon contact, the crowd surged and rose to their feet, cheering wildly. "That'a boy Freddy!" yelled Ernie, punching his right fist into the air. Then he turned to Jacob and, high-fiving him, proclaimed, "See there Jacob, it must have been that bat of yours there."

Even as a young boy, Jacob was riddled with intense self-consciousness, but for once, he perceived himself letting go, allowing himself to join the communal jubilation, a jellyfish carried along by the waves of excitement. How he had yearned for such a moment. He jumped up and down repeatedly, each time thrusting the bat into the air for everyone to see.

"That's right, Freddy! Rough 'em up, Freddy," he shouted. While Jim Rice would subsequently ground into an inning-ending double-play to short, Jacob's intent interest had been piqued.

By the time Fred Lynn came to the plate for his third at-bat in the seventh inning, the Red Sox had relinquished that lead and were trailing 3-2. Bill Lee had pitched brilliantly but had given up a three-run homer in the top half of the seventh. The crowd was deflated, but the traditional singing of "Take Me Out to the Ballgame" put them back in better spirits and had them hoping for a comeback after Yastrzemski strode to the plate and led off the home half of the seventh with a sharp liner to left for a single.

As for Jacob, he had been swept up into the newness of this raw emotion. He looked over his left shoulder and was further reassured by his dad smiling back at him, clapping him on the shoulders and goading him to cheer even louder. Glancing back over his right shoulder, he noted that Ernie and Jonathan were engaged in their own moment of father-and-son bonding that Jacob would spend most of the rest of his life envying.

"Crank one outta here, Freddy!"

"C'mon now Freddy. Big base hit here!"

"You can do it, Freddy!"

Lynn swung at the first pitch, a fastball that he had seen in each of his previous at-bats, but now Goltz's heater had lost some of its velocity, causing Lynn to mistime his swing and launch the ball foul deep into the seats of the left-field side. The crowd, fully aware that Lynn had narrowly missed a golden opportunity, groaned audibly.

Goltz knew he couldn't go fastball again; it was too dangerous, and Lynn clearly had a keen eye for the pitch. He had to go curveball, but his fatigue had likewise made him a bit erratic, and he threw back-to-back pitches that trailed outside for balls. When a third straight curveball then nearly hit Lynn for a 3-1 count, the excitement in the crowd became palpable; they knew Goltz would have to come back with a fastball or else risk walking Lynn with power threat Jim Rice looming on-deck. More importantly, Lynn knew it.

The entire crowd jumped to its feet as they witnessed the fluid swing of Lynn's bat making impact with Goltz's outside fastball, immediately followed by the sharp, penetrating crack that reverberated off the hallowed walls of Fenway Park. Lynn started his swing just a bit early, so he pulled it out to right field, but the contact was recognizably solid. Goltz immediately threw down his cap in disgust; he knew his night was over.

From the instant that Lynn hit the ball, Jacob could tell that the ball's trajectory was bringing it in his general direction. What he could not accurately determine was its longevity of flight. As the ball kept coming towards him, he wondered if it were really coming straight at him as it appeared or if it was just his hyper-vigilant imagination wishing for it be true. He was prepared, though, and as the ball soared above him, he thrust his left arm, glove still intact, into the air to catch it.

At first, Jacob was unaware that the ball, in its considerable velocity, had skimmed off of the webbing of his glove and shot into the seats two rows behind him. When he felt the impact the ball made on his glove, he assumed that he had caught it. When he reached into the glove to extract the prized ball, however, he found it lamentably empty. He looked behind him to see the frantic melee that had already ensued as people attempted to scoop up his loss.

Somehow what should have been a moment of triumphant joy in celebration of Lynn's home run had been transposed into one of regret. Jacob looked helplessly at his father.

It did not take long for one of the combatants to raise his hand in victory, claiming possession of the ball he now clutched tightly in his fist. He was a tall, muscular kid with his BU sweatshirt tied around his waist to expose his well-developed chest. He shouted back to his group of four buddies, each also shirtless, who were still standing at their seats three rows behind him. The TV camera zoomed in on him as the rest of the crowd cheered wildly that Lynn had given the Sox back the lead.

"Hey!" Walter yelled up to the guy with the ball in his hand, "Why don't you give the ball back to the kid over here? He deserves it. He almost caught it, for chrissakes."

The college kid raised his eyebrow incredulously and stared intently at Walter as though he were astonished that anyone would even make such a suggestion. "'Almost' isn't good for much, is it Pops?" He looked back at his friends with a hearty laugh.

"Oh, come on, lad, have a heart." Walter implored. "It's the kid's first game. Don't you remember your first ballgame?"

A few of the members of the surrounding crowd had now grown aware of the developing situation and entreated the young college student, either verbally or visually, to relinquish the ball.

The college kid's glare softened, and he let out a resigned sigh. "Ya betta turn inta a real Sox fan there kid," he said in a thick, Southside Boston accent. "I mean it kid, a real chowda' head, you hear me? I want to see you dressed in Red Sox footie pajamas. All right, here ya go." He leaned over the back of the seats to toss Jacob the ball. "Ya hear that old man? Ya betta make sure that kid turns into a real Sox fan."

Ernie smiled back at him and with a flick of his wrist, said, "Hey, I appreciate the gesture. You did the right thing. Now if ya were to do that without so much balkin' ya just might get one of these girls around here to lay ya."

Later that evening on the long drive back home, Jacob would ask Walter what "to lay" meant in Ernie's context

(Walter would, in a half-deception, tell him that it meant to "sleep with someone"), but for now he merely turned to his father and grinned at what this day had brought him. Walter returned the look with a smile of his own and said to him, "That's a pretty special ball you got there, Jacob. You be sure to hold onto it. You're a real Red Sox fan now."

"I will," Jacob replied and rubbed his hands across it as if he half-expected for a genie to magically appear, but then, after all of this, what more could he have wished for?

If he had, however, been granted those three wishes, he probably should have requested some bullpen help for the Sox, for while Dick Drago would come in and pitch a perfect eighth in relief of Bill Lee, he would once more surrender that lead to the Minnesota Twins in the ninth on a base-clearing double by Rod Carew, and the Sox would go on to lose, in typically heart-breaking fashion, 6-4. Still, the loss did not deter Jacob one iota from his newfound devotion. If anything, it merely gave him a heightened appreciation of the dramatic ups and downs that came with supporting the Red Sox. As he admired his coveted ball, he left as probably the only contented fan in the building, knowing that he would unquestionably fulfill the promise to the young man who had given him the ball.

That moment would have probably had a fundamental presence in Jacob's memory regardless of the circumstances that would befall him shortly thereafter, but they certainly heightened the significance, for it was a mere two weeks later that Walter would pass away, leaving Jacob fatherless. Jacob should have felt that cold wind of fortune swirl and shift directions behind him, but he was too young yet to decipher the pattern of disruption that would mark his later years. He was still naïve enough to believe that happiness in this life could be anything more than evanescent.

Two weeks later to the day, Walter was driving home down I-91 South from Bradley Airport. His flight back from a sports memorabilia auction in Montreal had been delayed by over an hour due to weather, and he was trying to make it home before Jacob would be asleep. The day at the ballpark with his son had been memorable for him as well. That afternoon had been one of the first times he had gotten to experience Jacob as a person in his own right, to enjoy his company as an end in itself, not the distinctly separate reward of a parent appreciating his child's development. He liked who his son was becoming and looked forward to more such moments ahead. Anxious to get home, he started to pass an 18-wheeler that was struggling in the right-hand lane. The sudden rain was collecting in the roadway, and the virtual tidal wave created by the truck's splashback caught Walter off-guard. He never got a moment to think how to rectify his fatal error, however, as the Volvo hydroplaned violently out of control into the truck on the right and then slammed tragically into the guard rail on the left.

When his Grandma Darcie led Jacob in to see the rabbi before the elaborate service she had arranged for her son, Jacob could not get an answer to the one question he wanted to understand: "Why?" The rabbi looked as utterly lost as

Jacob did. He felt an empty solitude and begged his mother to let him go home.

The following Sunday, Jacob stayed after the service to talk with the minister. A loving man with infinite patience, he consoled Jacob by telling him that his father had gone to "a better place".

"But what about me? Why did he take dad from me?" Jacob lamented.

The minister dropped his brow weightily and raised his eyes towards Jacob, "I cannot tell you what plan God has for you, Jacob, but I can tell you that this is part of it."

Jacob thanked the minister for meeting with him, but the words rang hollow to their breath. Where was God now? Why would God want him to feel this way? What possible *plan* could God have that would take his father from him?

He thought about what his father had said about faith. Is that what God wanted? Faith? As a young boy left without a father, Jacob could not make any sense of the tragedy that had befallen him, and if God was giving any answers, it certainly wasn't coming from his appointed representatives here on Earth.

For years afterwards, and even sometimes in his adult life, Jacob would be watching a Red Sox game, and he would envision his dad sitting next to him, slapping him on the knee or giving him a high five. He would get swept away in the memory and feel his dad loft him into the air to carry him back to the car, exhausted and satiated, just as he had that one June evening. As the illusion would dissolve, he would reflect on it as one of the few examples of his life when he remembered being truly happy, and he would yearn for a similar experience in his present life, thinking that if he could once again have such a moment that maybe, just maybe, everything would finally be ok.

Being a Red Sox fan in the suburbs of Hartford, Connecticut, ground zero for the Yankees-Red Sox Cold War, was never easy. About two hours from either city, his school had kids with allegiances to each side, setting up a modern-day Hatfields and McCoys feel to the lunchroom bravado in the inevitable discussion of baseball. For the most part, each kid was a byproduct of their parents; whomever their old man rooted for, so did they.

What was really noteworthy, however, were the socio-economic and cultural disparities that echoed through this seemingly meaningless choice of a favorite baseball team. The Yankees fans had parents with more pronounced ties to New York; some of them even had a dad who commuted there, if only a couple of times a week. These people had money, though it was commonly new money. They were often powerful businessmen who ran important and successful companies that traded in commodities they knew little or nothing about. For them, winners won at all costs, crying was for losers, it was a dog eat dog world, and the ends always justified the means.

Conversely, the Red Sox fan was burdened with the ethos of the New Englander. Most lived there because their families had lived there for generations before them. They believed in hard work that generally went unrewarded. Whether professionals or blue-collar workers, they had the sense that suffering was more than just a necessary rite of passage; it was somehow ennobling.

The Yankees fans, of course, had the decided advantage in the verbal confrontations of the lunchroom. There was no real angle the Red Sox fans could take to credibly suggest that their team was superior. The Yankees had won more World Series and won them more recently. The Yankees, like their fans in Jacob's area at least, were consummate winners; they had become so ingrained with the idea that they would somehow find a way to win that the arrogance seemed etched onto their smug faces. The Red Sox players, meanwhile, kept the look of those truly cursed, like dead men walking amongst the living. No matter what the odds, the Sox would find a way to lose, and their fans knew it.

Jacob's best friend in those years was fellow Sox fan, Tobin Crowder. Tobin was a quiet, athletic kid who became more and more popular as the years went on. When Jacob first met Tobin in the seventh grade, their only common denominator was their willingness to defend the Sox to their dying breath. Tobin, himself a pitcher with a formidable arm that eventually garnered him a college scholarship, knew all the intricacies of the game and thus made for a knowledgeable counterpart in the debate. As a middle-schooler, Tobin had not yet grown into his six-foot frame; he was lanky and had a glaring case of acne. Jacob enjoyed

Tobin's company because Tobin was the first person his own age who accepted him unconditionally. Since Jacob's mom never let him have friends over after his father died, they spent most of their free time over at Tobin's house, where Tobin's mom made them snacks and let them play in the large, unfinished basement of the house. There they traded baseball cards, listened to 70's rock albums, and watched Red Sox games on the old television that had belonged to Tobin's grandfather.

Even after Jacob moved to D.C. to go to George Washington University and Tobin headed to upstate New York to pitch for Union College in Schenectady, the two remained close friends and planned at least one day trip each summer to Boston to watch their beloved Sox play. Shortly after college, Tobin moved to Boston to work for a corporate investment firm downtown. Jacob, however, never left the D.C. area, taking the job at Georgetown Catholic immediately after college.

Now in their twenties, Tobin and Jacob would take turns going to D.C. or Boston respectively to take in a game. Jacob would ride the train up to Boston in early June once school was out for the summer and stay with Tobin for a game at Fenway. Later in the summer, when the Red Sox would be playing the Orioles at Camden Yards, Tobin would drive down, and the two would catch a game there. Although Jacob relished any opportunity to watch the Red Sox play, he rarely went without Tobin, and he would look forward to these ventures as soon as he saw the fresh grass of spring on his morning runs.

In early July of 1992, Jacob was especially craving some quality time with his long-time friend. Jacob had mounting concern regarding his nagging inability to approach women in the two years since his break-up with Lynne, the nice Jewish girl from Houston he had dated for the final two years of college. Why couldn't he just loosen up and talk to women like most men did, or at least seemed to? When he encountered a woman he thought he might be interested in, he would stare blankly at her from across the bar, creating fantastical scenarios for approaching her. His tortuous anxiety would compel his best friends from work, Grace and Paula, to embolden him to at least talk to her. "What's the worst that can happen?" they would suggest.

But that was just it, wasn't it? What *was* the worst that could happen? He could unalterably close what was meant to be a life-defining chapter of his life. With one fell swoop of the tongue, he could change future events destined to be, saying the wrong thing one more time. Or he could have one of those rare moments where he was what he liked to think himself to be: a more refined, comfortable version of himself, where he spoke perhaps too profusely, but at least he did so with self-confidence. What then? Would he trip blindly down that emotional circular staircase, plunging headlong into an unforeseeable abyss? Would he allow himself to give his heart to another just to have them ripped from him just as his father had been? Isn't that what his whole life had been teaching him? There are no keepable promises of tomorrow; everything once given can be taken away.

After nearly two years of sharing an apartment with Lynne, she had just left, packed her stuff into a U-Haul and never came back. He left messages on the only phone number he had for her, but it was to no avail; she never called back, not once. He thought that he would have liked to have heard her voice one last time, to ask her, simply, "Why?" Perhaps she could provide insight into the subtle character flaws that left him perpetually alone. But he thought of that question much like he thought of the dirt flying off the back of the rented U-Haul he envisioned her driving across the dustbowls of Oklahoma, dirt that whirled around in the air, only to settle silently on the receptive pavement.

Jacob was hoping he might find some answers, some peace of mind, from Tobin. Who else could he talk to about such matters? When he had gone to Boston in June, Tobin had been largely preoccupied with his new girlfriend, Heather. This was a first for Tobin. Having grown into his physical features to become a ruggedly handsome man, women never held much sway with Tobin, and though he was considered quite a catch, they seldom stayed long. Tobin made for a charming date, but he was far too wedded to bachelorhood to make the incremental adaptations of lifestyle that every woman wants to see as the eventual path to some estimable form of domesticated salvation.

This woman, however, was different for Tobin. Heather, who radiated not only a dark Greek beauty but also a sharp and analytical intelligence, seemed to have Tobin wrapped around her finger. After the game at Fenway in June, instead of hitting a few of the bars around the park and then heading back to Tobin's for a night cap of video games, as had become their custom, Tobin insisted they rush home so that they could watch the episode of *Friends* Heather had taped in Tobin's absence. "I could care less about watching it, to tell the truth," Tobin said, poking Jacob in the ribs playfully with his elbow, "but Jacob, man, I don't wanna be in the dog house for this one, you know what I mean?"

Jacob nodded and feigned understanding but instead wondered to himself if it was his inability to comprehend Tobin's predicament that was precisely the source of his own current misery. *"Perhaps this is how normal relationships function,"* Jacob thought to himself. Perhaps if he had acted like this towards Lynne she never would have left. Perhaps.

They had chosen to meet at Woody's, a fairly non-descript sports bar down by the Inner Harbor district that was only a short jaunt from Camden Yards. Jacob had thought that he would be the one sipping down a cocktail waiting for his friend, as he was at least fifteen minutes early, but as soon as he strolled through the entryway, he spotted Tobin's shaggy mop, seated at a barstool and making conversation with a tall, vivacious redhead, with a tight, white sweater who was seated next to him but leaning in ever so flirtatiously.

"Hey Tobin!" Jacob thundered, slapping his hand down onto Tobin's shoulder, not wanting to interrupt, but feeling that if he had to do so, it would be better if it be done quickly.

He followed up the brazen act with a reserved posture, pulling back moderately so as to give Tobin some space. Tobin kept the exact positioning of his torso and pivoted instead at the neck, inviting Jacob in and shutting him out at the same time.

"Jacob, you're early! That's great. Hey, this is Audrey. We've just been shootin' the shit here while I was waitin' for ya." Tobin smiled at Jacob profusely. It felt good to be smiled at like that, like being in a dark movie theater and walking out into the daylight to be bathed in the sun's warm rays.

"So, how long have you been here?"

"'Bout an hour. Fortunately, Audrey here's been keepin' me company." Tobin now returned his interest to Audrey. Subconsciously or not, he had up to this point maintained connection with her by keeping his torso pointed in her direction, but his subtle gesture of swinging his head invited a comfortable three-party discussion. This had always been Tobin's great gift: the ability to make everyone feel like a welcome addition to the party.

"Are you heading to the game, Audrey?" Jacob asked.

"No, I have to catch a train to New York in about an hour, but I hope you boys have a good time. Tobin here tells me you're quite a Sox fan."

Jacob laughed and clapped Tobin solidly on the back. He then turned and tried to get the bartender's attention so that he could order a beer. As he waited, he could not help but notice the oddly-matched couple next to him. She was strikingly beautiful, her tall, slender frame accentuated by the straight brown hair that flowed down to her mid-back. Her eyes were set deep against the soothing backdrop of her soft white skin.

He, meanwhile, was fairly short with a slight but athletic build that could not have allowed him to weigh more than a hundred and thirty pounds. His head was shaved bald, which seemed to be a fitting and attractive look for him, but it did reveal a pronounced vein that ran along his brow and left him appearing perpetually concerned and agitated. This effect was exacerbated by his large, round eyes that strained from his head as if he were an owl searching for mice at night. His clothes- a sleek, tapered purple shirt with the cuffs rolled to the elbows and tight, black jeans- were pristinely pressed.

"Can I grab a Sam Adams when you get a chance?" asked Jacob as the bartender made his way over.

"I don't know," the bartender replied sarcastically, "You gonna take off that Sox cap in here?"

"That's right, Charlie," chimed in the woman to Jacob's right, her thin, red lips curled into a cunning grin, "Don't be serving those dirty Sox fans in here."

While Jacob was pretty sure the bartender was joking, he did not know how to take her comment. He stood there silently for a moment.

"Oh, we're just joking with ya," she said spiritedly as she slapped him on the back and took a sip of her beer. "Charlie, put his first round on my tab." The bartender shot Jacob an amicable smile and headed off to get his beer.

"Well, thank you. Given your generosity, I'm going to guess that you are an Orioles fan rather than a Yankees fan."

She took another long draw from her bottled beer and said, "I guess you could say that. To be honest, I don't really pay much attention to baseball, but I've been promising to take Gary here to a game since Mother's Day."

"Why Mother's Day?" Jacob asked perplexedly.

"Oh, I run my own flower shop, and Gary helps me with the arrangements. Mother's Day is crunch time for us, so I promised to take him to a game for all of us his extra hustle. Aren't I a nice boss? Well, you know, minus the two month wait. He doesn't care much about baseball either, but he wanted to check out the new ballpark scene."

Jacob felt a cautious optimism but wanted to ask a question that would provide further clarification without divulging his interest. "Is that weird dating one of your employees?"

Caught off guard by this, she erupted in laughter and spewed some of her beer into the air like a Hawaiian water spout. Once she had recovered, she grabbed Gary's shoulder to turn him around, even though he was busy talking to a fair-faced younger man on his other side. "Gary, you've got to hear this. Our new friend over here thinks we are dating!"

"Oh, darling," said Gary in an effeminate voice that clearly delineated his sexual orientation, "You couldn't handle *me*."

"No, you couldn't handle *me*," she replied with equal sass.

"Maybe not, but I'd sure like to try," he said as he pinched her rear playfully. To this, they raised their bottles of beer, and Gary promptly returned to his promising conversation with the fair-skinned young man on his right.

"Hi, I'm Faith," she said as she stuck out her hand with a formality that was entirely incongruous with the previous exchange.

"I'm Jacob," he said as he took her hand in his. As he did so, he swore he felt her give his hand a barely perceptible squeeze, as if to let him know she was there.

"So what do you do, Jacob?" she asked, leaning towards him.

"I teach English at Georgetown Catholic."

"Isn't that the all-girls' school?"

"That's the one."

"So do they all wear those plaid mini-skirts? You know, the little schoolgirl outfit?"

"Afraid so."

"Do you ever find yourself turned on? They are pretty sexy." She was being intentionally provocative. Gary had put her in that mood. He always did.

"You're talking about my students," Jacob replied matter-of-factly.

Faith wanted to see what would happen if she teased him further, "So..."

Jacob relaxed and decided to play along. "Well, you know, sometimes. Just the really hot ones."

It was their first shared laughter, and she pulled him into a friendly but meaningful hug.

Their conversation flowed easily and naturally like two old friends sitting on a park bench recounting former times.

"What got you into owning a flower shop?" Jacob asked.

"I really love to watch things grow, to take the sprigs of life and see how they flower into something beautiful. It's the great mystery of life played out before me each and every day. What about you? What got you into teaching?"

Jacob thought for a moment before responding, "In some ways, the same thing I guess, but on a somewhat different level, right? I mean, what I love is watching young people mature into the person they will become and being a part of that process, of helping them become who they want to be."

"That's somewhat profound," she said with a lack of intonation that made it difficult to ascertain if she was still joking or not.

Although Jacob was somewhat self-conscious that she was at least two inches taller than he was, he felt confident, assured, and relaxed. She brought out the best of him; she brought out who he really was when the defenses and insecurities finally waned.

Faith was drawn to the luminous green of his eyes that stood out in such dramatic contrast to his olive skin. Somehow he was both man and boy with an allure that was nuanced and, she speculated, probably overlooked by most. His set chin and wrinkleless complexion suggested that while he had endured hard times, he remained a benevolent soul.

A few moments later, with Audrey having gone to the restroom to freshen up before departing to catch her train, Tobin returned his focus to his friend and the woman Jacob had met in his absence. "So Jacob, who do we have here?" He extended his hand and cocked his head slightly.

As Faith introduced herself, she seemed mildly irritated by the interruption. "I'm Faith, and this is my friend, Gary."

When she pulled Gary away from his conversation, however, he seemed anything but annoyed once he had an opportunity to glance at the tall, strapping Tobin. Instead, he beamed and took Tobin's hand confidently. "Pleased to meet you, I'm sure," Gary said suggestively with a wink that was hardly inconspicuous.

Tobin, instantaneously repulsed by Gary's homoerotic undertones, forced his visual attention elsewhere, making an effort to show that he was earnestly seeking for Audrey amidst the crowd. With his head overtly turned in the other direction, he barely muttered, "Yeah, same here."

Gary's father, a powerful lobbyist who bought the embarrassment his son brought him out of his life with a one-time cash payment of one-hundred thousand dollars that he used to justify dissolving all ties with his son whatsoever, had taught Gary all he needed to know about homophobia. He readily noticed Tobin's discomfort and knew the darkness that lay behind it. He decided to indulge himself at Tobin's expense.

Using an exaggerated falsetto, even for him, Gary intoned, "Well, you know, I should correct myself. I say that I am pleased to meet you, but what I really mean is that I would be pleased to *eat* you, or that it would be a pleasure for me to please you, whichever double entendre does the trick for you."

Tobin stood tall and pushed the stray ash-blonde hairs from his face. He turned his nervous attention back to Gary who was staring at him intently with the eyes that bugged out from the marked bone structure of his face. "Hey man, I'm sorry and all, but I'm not gay."

Gary smirked at him lasciviously. "Oh, not yet you're not."

Tobin then stumbled upon what he thought was a moment of blind luck as Audrey returned from the restroom, saying that she needed to leave. Grabbing Audrey by the waist and pulling her over to him, Tobin uttered the comment he thought for sure would bring the conversation to a screeching halt. "I'm sorry, Gary. I don't mean to interrupt, but let me introduce you to my girlfriend." Audrey was noticeably caught off guard by this but offered no resistance or denial.

Gary, however, was non-plussed. "Well, I don't mind if you bring her along, honey, but I'm not sticking *my* dick in her. I don't do vaginas."

Tobin was left speechless. He put his arm around Audrey's shoulder and escorted her to the door. When he returned, all he said to the general company was, "Hey man, we better get going if we want to catch first pitch." Then Tobin leaned in to whisper but spoke audibly enough for Faith to hear, "You can get fag hag here's number and call her later."

Jacob exploded on Tobin as he had probably never done, "What the fuck was that, man? Since when did you become a fucking homophobe?" Jacob apologized profusely on his friend's behalf, but it was too late; the damage had been done. Although he and Faith still did the perfunctory number exchange, it was clear that Faith's attraction to him had been deflated by the "company you keep" theory of asshole detection.

As Tobin would point out on their walk to the ballpark, "You know she gave you a fake number and that she's not going to call, right?"

"What the hell makes you say that?" Jacob replied indignantly.

Tobin, however, spoke from a position of knowledge. "She hesitated before she wrote down her number. Chicks always do that when they're giving a fake number. It gives them time to think of a number that won't seem fake."

Still crisply irritated, Jacob shot back, "Well, she wouldn't have given me a fake number if you hadn't made that stupid 'fag hag' comment, asshole."

"Whatever, dude. There are a thousand more just like her. Stop worrying about it."

But that was just it; that was why Jacob was so upset about it: he knew that wasn't true.

Opened only a few months earlier in April of 1992, Camden Yards was one of the first of a series of newer ballparks meant to echo the stadiums of baseball's past. Hearkening back to places such as Wrigley Field in Chicago, it replaced the cookie-cutter approach taken to ballparks built in the 70's and 80's with a nostalgic aesthetic that included numerous odd angles and varied dimensions. While it was certainly no Fenway Park, with Jacob now living miles away in D.C., it provided him a reasonable surrogate, especially when his Red Sox were in town.

The seats Jacob had purchased were in the upper deck outside the left field foul line, not optimal for viewing the game but well within the modest budget afforded by his teaching salary. He stopped for a moment to breathe in the summer air and recall with whatever force his lagging memory could deliver that day with his father so many years before.

Before Jacob could even sit, however, a young boy behind him poked him on the shoulder and loudly informed him, "Excuse me, sir! Do you mind sitting down? I don't want to miss a fly ball if it comes this way. I brought my glove so that I can bring back a baseball for my mom!"

Jacob smirked to himself at the overeager fan who was worried about catching a foul ball even before the game had started and turned to look at the boy who could not have been more than six or seven. His wiry blonde hair stuck out from his newly-purchased Orioles baseball cap, and his numerous freckles were even more pronounced as he beamed without restraint. While his cap may have been a recent acquisition, his once white Orioles t-shirt with Cal Ripken's name and number on the back had enough wear holes and mustard stains to evidence significant use even though it was still two sizes too big for him.

"Well, all right little dude! What's your name?" Jacob asked.

"I'm Tommy, and this is my mom's boyfriend, Frank," the boy said as he gestured with his left hand with the glove on it.

"Nice to meet you," said Frank, leaning down to offer his hand. Muscular, with a dark complexion and even darker strands of fine, straight hair, Frank had a thick Boston accent that suggested he might be an Italian 'Southie.'

As it turned out, Frank was indeed from the South side of Boston but moved down to Baltimore a few months ago after meeting Tommy's mother in an on-line chat room.

"I told Tommy's mom here that I would take the kid to a game but only when the Sox were in town," Frank said as he munched down on a foot-long hot dog with mustard, relish, and onions. Frank explained how Tommy's real father had up and left shortly after Tommy's birth and lived with a different wife and kids somewhere in California. When Tommy tried to explain his missing dad's choices, Frank merely shook his head in disbelief.

When it was Jacob's turn to get more beer, he took a brief detour so that he could purchase a magazine with a scorecard for Tommy and teach him how to keep score, much as Ernie had done for him nearly seventeen years before. As he sat down and handed the two beers over to Tobin, Jacob extracted the scorecard from his pants and passed it along to Tommy who was overjoyed even before he was entirely sure what it was that he was receiving. Over the next several innings, Jacob taught Tommy how to keep score while Frank and Tobin discussed corruption on the police force, local Massachusetts politics, and, of course, the ever-struggling Red Sox. It soon became apparent that Frank was hardly an heir apparent in the fatherhood department and viewed Tommy mostly as the extra baggage that came with his relationship with Tommy's mother.

"So who's your favorite player?" Jacob asked the essentially fatherless child, a bond that Jacob could not deny drew him closer.

"Definitely Cal Ripken. He hasn't missed a game since 1982!"

"Good choice. He's going to break Lou Gehrig's record in a few years if he keeps it up. He's up second next inning, you know," replied Jacob.

"I know," said Tommy proudly pointing to his scorecard, "I've got the lineups right here."

Then, Tobin, rising from his seat, broke in, "Hey, Jacob, you need anything while I'm up? I gotta take a leak."

"I don't think so, but thanks for the informative update. I feel much better knowing," Jacob jested with him.

Tobin laughed then slugged him in the arm. "Funny, asshole. Seriously, do you want another beer? You'll probably be finished with that one by the time I come back."

"Sure, ok. You know you don't have to hit me that hard," Jacob said as he rubbed his arm where Tobin had hit him.

"Whatever. Don't be such a puss," Tobin responded dismissively as he started down the stairs.

When Cal Ripken came to bat during the next half inning, the crowd's interest had already begun to wane under the weight of a 5-0 Red Sox lead going into the bottom of the sixth. To make matters worse, center fielder Mike Devereaux had just popped out to second base, making it twelve straight batters retired by Boston pitcher John Dopson who was making the usually potent Baltimore lineup appear woefully anemic. With many of them here simply to soak up some warm rays while drinking a few cold beers, the crowd seemed resigned to an Orioles defeat.

The first pitch was a fastball high and inside that sent Ripken diving to the ground: clearly a message pitch. Ripken, however, merely stood up and dusted himself off. As he positioned himself back inside the batter's box and readied himself for the next pitch, the only change in his affect was the steely resolve he emitted as he glared intently at the Boston hurler. Dopson, seeing the look in Ripken's eye, knew that he could not come back with the fastball; he would be waiting on that. Instead he threw an off-speed pitch to disrupt Ripken's timing. Ripken anticipated the pitch selection but not the degree of its slowness. He swung for the fences, but fractions of a second to early, as he made solid contact but pulled the ball foul.

Although baseball can often feel as though it drags on at a snail's pace between moments of consequence, what keeps fans on the edge of their seats is the brisk and dramatic way that those game-altering moments can suddenly arise. In an instant, a baseball can come screeching at you from out of nowhere, so you better be ready. Fortunately, Jacob was.

The ball rocketed off Ripken's bat with an upward trajectory that had little arc to it. Jacob barely had time to process that the ball was headed straight towards them before it was already upon them. Had he not stuck out his bare hand in desperation, there is no telling whether or not the ball would have struck young Tommy and, had it done so, what damage it might have done. The fact is that Jacob did stick his hand out and somehow, unlike seventeen years before, managed to catch it and not let go.

Despite the pain that reverberated throughout his lower arm, Jacob was unsure that he had indeed caught it, thinking it might have bounced off his hand and caromed into the seats behind him. Even he had to glance up at his hand to assure himself of its continued presence there. With the realization, however, came an overwhelming sense of elation. He could not believe his luck or the fact that he had actually caught the opportunity that had been cast his way. He looked around to share his joy and triumph with those surrounding him.

But Tobin was still off at the bathroom, or getting beers, or god knows what. Instead, as he looked around him, the first person he saw was Tommy. He flashed back to the incident at Fenway Park student seventeen years before and remembered that the last time he had felt such joy was when Ernie had insisted that the BU student give that ball to him. Instantly, Jacob knew what he needed to do.

What he did not know as he turned and placed the ball into Tommy's glove was that his spectacular barehanded catch had already caught the attention of the stadium camera crews and that his beneficent gesture was being broadcast on the Jumbotron in centerfield. He was too focused on the rapturous surprise on Tommy's face to concern himself with anything else. Only when Frank tapped him on the shoulder and directed his attention to the giant screen did he recognize that for the past several seconds he had become a public persona that had melted the hearts of the entire crowd with a rare act of random kindness and human goodwill.

When Tobin finally made his way back to the seats, two beers in hand but one of them already halfway consumed, the first thing he managed to say to Jacob was, "Please tell me you didn't really give the ball to that kid."

Jacob merely smiled and patted Tobin on the shoulder in commiseration, being sure to snag the beer that was still nearly full.

Meanwhile, in the lower section above the first base dugout sat Faith and Gary. As Cal Ripken had come to the plate, Faith had started to rummage through her purse in order to find enough singles to buy each of them one last beer. Her head buried beneath the seat, she almost missed the opportunity that changed her life.

Because Faith had, in fact, written Jacob off. As it was, however, Gary grabbed her thin, bony arm and pointed excitedly. "Hey, isn't that your boy from the bar up there?"

At first only casually interested, she looked up and noted, "Yes, I think it is."

Then she saw the unsolicited gesture, and something awoke inside of her. She knew that her first impression had been right.

"Maybe he's not a douche bag after all," said Gary.

"Maybe not."

That night, when Jacob got home, there were two messages waiting for him on the answering machine. The first was from Faith. It said, "Hi. This is Faith from Woody's before the game tonight. I saw you on the big screen giving that ball to the boy behind you. That might be the sweetest thing I have seen from another person in a long time. Call me. I don't want to sound like a freak or anything, but I think…I think I might have fallen for you at that moment. Well, anyway, call me, ok? Ok, bye."

The second message was also from her, "Oh, um, I'm sorry, but the number I gave you after your friend called me a 'fag hag'- yeah, that was a fake number. My real number is…"

Chapter 4

The Gift of Music

In the year since they had first met, Jacob and Uncle Charles had fostered a meaningful relationship of their own, independent of their mutual fondness for Faith. Uncle Charles would often call Jacob shortly after school ended when he knew that Faith would still be working at the flower shop. These calls usually had no specific purpose except Uncle Charles's desire to chat with someone who would listen to his stories and at least feign genuine interest. For Jacob's part, he truly enjoyed the stories, although even he would have acknowledged that something was lost in their numerous retellings. Perhaps he found in Uncle Charles something akin to the father figure he had been searching for since his youth.

So, when Uncle Charles called on a Thursday afternoon in late April, Jacob was hardly surprised. "Well, good afternoon, my boy. How are things shaking today?"

"Things are going quite well, Uncle Charles, though I must admit there's not a whole lotta shaking going on."

"Ha, Ha- nicely played, my boy. Go after the old man with a Chuck Berry reference. Well done indeed."

"Actually, Uncle Charles, 'Whole Lotta Shaking' was Jerry Lee Lewis." Although Jacob's forte was not 1950's rock n' roll, his knowledge of all types of music was extensive, a trait inherited from his mother before the nervous breakdown from which she would never recover.

Uncle Charles's musical repertoire, meanwhile, was limited to show tunes and jazz standards prior to the second World War. He hated to admit, however, that he was out of touch. "That's right, of course. Jerry Lee Lewis- didn't he marry his cousin or something like that?"

"I think so. Something like that anyway. So what are you up to Uncle Charles? No trouble with Interpol I hope."

"Ha! No, no, my boy, nothing like that. I was just calling to see if you and Faith could join me for dinner tomorrow night at the Monocle. I have something of an announcement," Uncle Charles managed to say, his voice trailing off for the final sentence.

"I'll check with Faith when she gets home, but I don't see why not. What time do you want to meet?"

"How about seven? Oh, and stop by the salon first, ok? We can walk over from there."

Jacob had not heard Uncle Charles quite so pensive before. Though he tried to dismiss it, it worried him somewhat. "Sure, we'll see you there. Is there anything we can do for you in the meantime, Uncle Charles?"

"No, but it will be good to see you kids, probably our last dinner together before you two are officially hitched."

"All right," Jacob said with hesitation, "if you're sure."

"I'm retiring," Uncle Charles announced stiffly almost as soon as they entered the salon. Then he breathed deeply as if he had been waiting to remove this weight from his chest and could finally breathe again.

"Retiring?" Faith asked with a touch of melancholy.

Jacob, however, said, "Good for you, Uncle Charles. You deserve it."

"Well, thank you to both of you," Uncle Charles began, "I'm sure you know it's been a tough decision. It's never easy to admit to yourself that it's time to hang it up and move on."

"You don't need to look at it like that Uncle Charles," Jacob encouraged. "Think of it as your time to do what you want to do in life. I think it's great."

Faith, now over her initial shock, added, "I agree. I think this is going to be wonderful for you, Uncle Charles. I think you're going to be really happy. I sure am going to miss this place, though."

Uncle Charles nodded thoughtfully. "I know. Lots of memories here, especially for you and me. I will miss this old place, but that does bring me to why I asked you to come over here tonight." As he said this, he led them into the back room where the old Steinway upright still sat, though it had seen some further wear since Faith had seen it last. "I want you to have it, Faith. I don't have room for it in my little bachelor pad, and it would be perfect in your new place. I was thinking right outside the dining room, but I'll leave that up to you. One way or another, I wanted you to have it, if you think you'd enjoy it, that is."

Seeing the look of expectant joy on Charles's face, it was clear that any protest would be futile.

"That's mighty thoughtful of you Uncle Charles. It's a gorgeous piano, but what are we going to do with it? Neither of us play," Jacob finally said.

Uncle Charles glanced over at Faith quizzically. "Have you never told Jacob here that you play?" he asked her.

"I thought I had, but I guess not," she replied.

"You told me Uncle Charles used to play for you, but you never told me that you played," Jacob responded.

"He used to give me lessons," Faith said.

A coy smirk emerged on Uncles Charles's lips. "Oh, it didn't take long for this student to outshine her teacher, I'll tell you that."

Jacob turned to Faith and implored her, "Why don't you play something? I'd love to hear you play."

Faith sat down and ran her fingers over the keys that were cracked and mildly discolored. The chestnut wood veneer finish was streaked and uneven. Several of the keys were chipped or fractured, and the wood frame had a distribution of dings along the surface. While it was clear that the piano had once been a magnificent instrument, its current state of disrepair and neglect made it difficult to imagine exactly what it may have looked like way back then.

Faith, however, felt right at home, as if she were curling up inside her favorite blanket, the one that was frayed and worn but all the more comfortable for the effect. She let her fingers run lightly over the black keys before stretching them and letting them fall into place in chord structures that anticipated what she would play.

As she started into Beethoven's "Moonlight Sonata" (always her favorite piece to play with its sweeping melodies and powerful harmonies that resounded long after the song was over), it was at first difficult to discern if the lack of aural cohesion was due to her playing or the current state of the piano. As Jacob watched her hands move rhythmically across the keyboard, however, it became apparent that the fault was by no means hers. Although Jacob himself had never learned to play an instrument, he had a vast appreciation for those who did, particularly those who could demonstrate mastery of the piano. Although the sound quality was entirely lacking at the moment, Jacob could easily see Faith's technical flair for the instrument.

"I'm sorry that sounded so terrible. I really do play better than that," she said longingly as she finished abruptly and closed the keyboard cover.

"No need to apologize. Your playing was lovely. It's the piano that sounded terrible," Jacob reassured her.

Faith then looked ruefully at Uncle Charles and said, "I'm afraid it's true, Uncle Charles. It really does need a lot of work. I would love to take it, but I don't know if we have the resources right now to repair it. I hope you understand."

"Oh trust me, I know," replied Uncle Charles. "It has needed a tuning for some time now."

"I'm afraid it needs a lot more than that," said Jacob, knowing without any further investigation much of what would be required to restore the piano to playable condition.

Uncle Charles looked at him curiously then said, "Well, I have done some research, and there's a place up in Beltsville that restores old pianos. I wanted to see if you actually wanted the piano first, but let me call them and get an estimate of how much it would cost to fix up the old lady. As long as it's reasonable, I'll cover the cost."

Faith protested immediately, "We couldn't let you do that, Uncle Charles!"

"No, no child, I want to…"

"Uncle Charles, I don't mean to interrupt," said Jacob, "But I'm not sure if you realize how much that is going to entail. We're talking thousands of dollars."

Both Uncle Charles and Faith now focused on Jacob as they wondered how it was he seemed to be speaking with such authority on the subject. Jacob sensed this and explained, "I used to fix up old pianos with my grandmother during the summer. How about you let me take a crack at restoring it? I'll have to get inside and see whether or not the soundboard is still intact, but I think I can fix it."

Now it was Faith and Uncle Charles's turn to stand in amazement at recent revelations.

"Do you really know what you're doing?" Faith asked him.

Jacob turned to Uncle Charles. "When are you giving up the shop?"

"The end of June, my boy."

"Perfect," replied Jacob, "I'll come in on weekends. I should have it done by then."

"But we have a wedding to plan for," Faith reminded him.

"We've got almost everything taken care of," said Jacob coaxingly. "I can help you with the planning during the week and do this project on the weekends. Plus, I would really like for this to be my wedding present to you."

Faith thought about it for a moment and then asked, "Well, what do you think, Uncle Charles?"

"I say, 'Let's give it a shot, my boy!'"

Jacob had learned to restore pianos while living with his "Grandma" Tess in Maine during the summer of 1978 while his mother was institutionalized following her second nervous breakdown. "Grandma" Tess was actually his great aunt, the sister of Elizabeth's mother who drank herself to death while Elizabeth's father was serving in the Korean conflict.

Elizabeth would always remember her father as the tall, kind-hearted man that he was prior to his tour of duty overseas, but when he returned, he was a changed man. Gone was the affable, easy-going father who had read to her before bed every night until she was seven. In his place was a belligerent drunk who would never discuss the nightmares he had witnessed but would instead reenact their brutality upon Elizabeth and her sister Margaret in a nightly ritual that soon made it evident that he was not capable of raising two girls by himself. Margaret would be sent off to live with a distant cousin in Wisconsin, while Elizabeth moved to Maine to live with her Aunt Tess and her husband George. Having recently discovered that they themselves were incapable of producing offspring, they were all too happy to bring young Elizabeth into their home and raise her as their own.

It was natural then, when Elizabeth herself proved temporarily incapable of fending for Jacob, that Jacob, in turn, go to live with Tess, who insisted that he call her "Grandma". With George having passed from a sudden heart attack several years earlier, Tess was now one of only two direct family members he had left outside of his mother. The other was Walter's mother, "the miserable miser," and while Elizabeth was desperate for assistance, she would have had to have died before she allowed that woman to be responsible for her only child.

Tess was, on the surface, a tough, rugged woman, made so by the many years of harsh Maine winters and the unending tasks required to endure them. This stern exterior, however, belied her immense care and compassion for both Elizabeth and, in turn, Jacob. While it took both Jacob and Elizabeth many years after her care to fully appreciate what she had done for them and why, Tess was severe and unforgiving because she had experienced many of the brutal hardships of winter in Maine and recognized that life was that way too. She was callous in order to harden them for all the pain she knew awaited them.

By the time Jacob came to spend the summer in her blue and white Victorian a full five minutes outside of town and perched upon a hillside overlooking the Saco River, she had begun to hunch over as her spinal column capitulated to the gravity imposed by her sturdy frame and ample bosom, a tendency that would only magnify itself in her later years. Despite this, she got along quite well, moving about with surprising dexterity. Her hands, though slightly curled from the early onset of arthritis, were thick and capable. Determined not to let them impact her performance of her daily work, Tess merely scoffed at their deteriorating condition and went about her business.

When she and George started their piano restoration business back in the 1950's, she knew little of carpentry or musical instruments. It was George who had been taught to work on pianos since he was a boy growing up in southern New Hampshire. While she originally handled the finances for the fledgling business, she was not the type of woman to let that stand for long. She demanded to learn the trade, and George was all too happy to indulge her. By the time George passed away, she was as well-versed in the fine art of piano restoration as he was.

Not having had a dad to teach him how to be handy, Jacob showed no immediate interest in learning the trade. That, however, would not sit with Tess, who demanded that he make himself of use if he were going to stay the summer. It was not that Tess needed the assistance, but she would not suffer a young man who could not make himself serviceable in some capacity or another. She worked him hard, but her praise was effusive, and it instilled in him a confidence he had not previously known and a desire to know even more.

Thus, over the course of that summer and many more to come, Jacob learned, through Tess's harsh but supportive tutelage, to take even the most ravaged piano and turn it into a functioning, even aesthetic, musical instrument.

In some ways, Jacob could not have imagined a better opportunity for applying his talents to a project destined to awaken Faith's own artistic potential. When he had heard her fingers run across the decrepit keyboard to produce melodies that were fractured but still lovely, it had inspired him. Each Saturday as he rode the Metro down to Uncle Charles's salon so that he could continue his work on the old Steinway, he would envision the beauty of the final project, only this time, unlike with any other piano he had restored, the allure centered on its eventual destination. That he would be able to actually hear the manifestation of his work in the hands of Faith thrilled him with a fervor that poured itself into his craftsmanship. Somehow they would be united in that piano, drawn together into an artistry that both belonged to each of them as individuals and yet brought them together in the creation of something elegant and indelible.

It really was a fine piano, one of the most spectacular specimens he had yet had the good fortune to restore. Though he generally preferred grand pianos to uprights, this was a classic, full-size upright, a somewhat rare find in any condition. Built in 1896, it had, despite its significant wear, held up rather well. Although his initial investigation revealed that it needed new hammers, damper felt, and bridle, he was pleasantly surprised to discover that the pin block, soundboard, and bridge were in suitable condition. Though he had known it would require a pitch raise from the moment he heard Faith play it, he had come to realize that it would also need to be re-strung and have tapes put on the action. It would be a costly venture but one well worth the price.

Although the faded coloring suggested that the original hue was something of a chestnut brown, he decided to use a cherry-red stain that would complement the dining room hutch Faith had inherited from her grandmother. It required more coats than he ever would have guessed, but when he was done several weeks later, the piano had a luminous shine to it that permeated a dimly-lit room.

All throughout the process, Jacob refused to permit Faith or Uncle Charles to view the progress of his work, not wanting them to see it until the finished product. He had politely moved all of Uncle Charles's bookkeeping materials into the waiting room of the salon. In the open doorway between the salon and the back office, he hung a large, white sheet to create a makeshift screen that hid the advances he was making. He had to trust, of course, that Uncle Charles would not sneak a glimpse during the work week while he was not there.

He finished it the second week of June, only two weeks before their wedding. School had gotten out a week before, so he was able to take two days during the week to finish up the project that had been more exhaustive than he had predicted. Finally satisfied with every minute detail, he scheduled a mover for Wednesday and then called Uncle Charles to invite him to a dinner at their house to celebrate the occasion.

As soon as Uncle Charles entered, his gaze sought out the piano, but he was vexed to note that Jacob had covered it in the sheet that had thwarted his curiosity for weeks now.

"Well, when are we going to get to see this piano of yours anyway?" he insisted to know in a manner that was at least a little irritable.

"After dinner," Jacob said. "I figured we would let Faith provide us with some post-meal entertainment." Appreciating Jacob's gesture to heighten the impact of the moment, Faith walked over and placed her right arm around his shoulders while taking his hand in hers and giving it a subtle squeeze.

"All right, well, let's get on with it then," Uncle Charles replied.

When dinner was done and Jacob did at last remove the sheet to reveal the fruits of his labors, Faith was visibly shaken, actually falling to her knees as a thin strain of tears fell unrestrained from her warm, brown eyes and down her soft and supple cheek. She could not believe what he had managed to accomplish. He had taken something she had already loved and brought out its true beauty, revealing its latent potential for all the world to see, like a sculptor who discovers the magical and the poetic within a brick of stone.

"It's stunning, Jacob, simply stunning." This was all she could muster to say as she held her thin, trembling hand to her mouth in wonderment and awe.

"It really is Jacob. Well done, my boy," rejoined Uncle Charles.

Jacob put his firm arms around Faith's waist and drew her into him. "Will you play it for me, Beautiful? Will you bring my heart to its epiphany?" he whispered softly into her ears as he leaned his head towards hers and felt the warm tears as they ran from her cheek to his.

When she was finally able to pull herself from him, able to draw together the strength to act as an independent body once more, she sat upon the accompanying piano bench and took a moment to regain her composure. She giggled nervously before beginning to play "Moonlight Sonata" once again. This time, the music was transcendent, lifting both player and listener into a state of euphoria that seemed to exist not as an abstract concept but as a tangible, physical place. The notes created a space where they were able to merge into one as their souls united in the common language of music. Jacob walked behind her and placed his hands ever so lightly upon her shoulders, solidifying the connection without speaking a word. She played on as if his hands had been there all the while.

As she brought the piece to its inevitable crescendo, each of their chests heaved a mighty breath and exhaled with the self-satisfaction of mutually fulfilled lovers. Her head tilted forward in resignation to an emotion that had entirely overwhelmed her. "Thank you, Sunshine," she said to Jacob.

"Thank *you*, Beautiful."

"I don't know about you, Samwise," Uncle Charles said discreetly to the affable Golden Retriever at his feet, "but I'm beginning to feel a little uncomfortable in here. How about you and I go for a walk?"

Chapter 5

The Blossoms of the Dogwood Tree

"Why do you never speak of your mother, Jacob?"

The question had been a long time coming. All Jacob had told Faith about his mother was that she had been institutionalized after a series of nervous breakdowns. The back story had gone unspoken. While Jacob wore his father's death upon his sleeve, he was mute on the subject of his mother.

Though Faith had several nights earlier conceded defeat in her battle with Jacob to have children, she had not abandoned the war altogether. By acknowledging that she would remain with Jacob even if he was unwilling to have children, she had inadvertently given him carte blanche to ignore the topic altogether. That did not, however, deter Faith. She knew that she was going to have to dive deep into his psyche and extrapolate a reason for the fears that held his belief in life captive. What was it that made him so hesitant to embrace all that life had to offer? Why was he so convinced that the world was such a harsh and hostile place?

She thought that she might find an inroad to answering those questions by delving into Jacob's past. Did his relationship with his mother mask a long-dormant wound that Jacob had suppressed? Was it a scar that ran too deep?

"What do you want to know?" Jacob responded casually, as he poured himself a glass of orange juice and then walked back into the living room, his shoulders slumped.

"What happened to her Jacob? And why don't you ever talk about her?" Faith questioned. She stood to her full height, tall and elegant in the open passage between the rooms, like an ibis stretching in the morning sunlight.

Jacob, to her surprise, seemed unaffected, as if she had asked him what movie he wanted to see. "I told you this already. She had her first breakdown a couple of years after my father died when I went to go live with Grandma Tess, but she always teetered on that line of instability. She was a very fragile egg, was all my life. Then about a month after I left for college, she lost it altogether, couldn't cope anymore. We didn't have any choice at that point."

"'We' Jacob? Who was the 'we' making this decision?" she asked curiously, making quotation mark gestures with two curled fingers on each hand.

"My grandmother and I," he said matter-of-factly as he sat down into his armchair.

"Wait, your mom's mom was already dead. Do you mean Tess?"

"No, not Tess. She really didn't have anything to say on the matter."

"Then who?" Faith asked impatiently.

"My Grandma Darcey."

"But she was on your dad's side. Why was *she* making decisions about *your* mother?" Faith asked perplexedly.

That was the nerve. She had stumbled onto something. Jacob stood up out of his chair, brushing past her as he went back to the kitchen under the unuttered pretenses of refilling his half empty glass of orange juice. Her head pivoted with his movement and followed him as he strode into the kitchen. He refilled the glass and took a sip before speaking. "She was the one with the money."

"The one with the money?"

Jacob let out a sigh and then turned and faced her, placing his back against the kitchen cabinets, "When my mom lost it, I mean lost it for good, no going back, we had to put her somewhere. Without any money, she would have been placed in the state facility. Those places are soul-sucking dungeons. Grandma Darcey came up with the money to have her put in the Institute of Living in Hartford. It had gardens the patients could walk through and staff that actually cared about the patients. It wasn't perfect, but it was a hell of a lot better than the state facility. I signed the papers, and that was that."

"You had to sign the papers to put your own mother into a mental hospital?" Faith asked with sympathy as she walked into the kitchen. She wanted to go over to him and embrace him, swaddle him in her arms like a newborn baby. Jacob's body positioning, however, was defensive, and she could not be certain whether he wanted contact or not.

"Yes. Who else was going to do it?" he said resignedly.

"When was the last time you saw her?"

Jacob merely slouched further against the cabinets. Unable to speak, he buried his head into his hands.

Faith went to him and put her long arms around him and rested her head upon his, like a giraffe eating from an acacia tree. She whispered softly to him, coaxingly, "When was the last time you saw her, sweetheart?"

"The day…they admitted her…to the hospital," he managed to say, as if he were drowning and barely able to get the words out between desperate breaths.

An uncontrollable sadness took over him. It gripped his body and froze it motionless in time. All the embittered and suffused sorrow welled in his soul and took the form of a tear that ran delicately down his cheek until it fell upon his shirt and was no more.

Faith squeezed him tighter now, as if the harder she squeezed the more she could wrest away the grief from his forlorn heart. "Why haven't you seen her, Jacob? Why haven't you visited her at the hospital?"

"I couldn't stand to see her like that. Not like that."

"But why, Jacob? I thought you said this Institute of Living was a nice place."

"It is," he started, but then drifted off into his own thoughts for a moment as the conversation stood there, suspended in the heavy air of tragedies that had long ago attempted to be forgotten but would not drift away. Finally, he continued, "I can't stand to see what has happened to *her,* to see what she's been reduced to. I can remember my mom before my dad died, and it was too hard to see what life had brought her to. The guilt is just too much."

"Why guilt, Sunshine?" she said trying to reassure him, "You had no role in your mom's breakdown. You don't need to feel guilty for that."

"You don't understand," he said pulling away, "Her final breakdown came when I left for college..."

"But you can't hold yourself responsible for that," Faith interrupted, "You had to lead your life, too, and go off to school."

Jacob turned away entirely. A cloud of darkness enveloped him. "Faith, my mother's nervous breakdown came because she didn't even have a way to live. The one fear she had had since she was a kid with no real parents finally came true. She was poor and destitute. Once I left the house, my grandmother shut her off completely, left her totally high and dry, told her that she was a hussy that had been living off of her for long enough.'

"Oh, but she was more than willing to pay for my school- tuition, books, housing, everything- as long as she could write the check directly to them and thus be sure that none of it ever went to my mother. And I took it; I took it, Faith. I took her blood money and went to college while my mother went insane with fears for her own survival. And a few short months later I just signed the papers and shipped her away."

Faith let him have a long moment of silence, a reprieve from his confessional.

"We're going to see her, Jacob."

Faith called the Institute a few days before their visit to let them know that they would be coming in on Saturday morning. Dr. Thompson, a genial, deep-voiced man, told her that he would be pleased to meet them on the steps of the Center Building around nine.

"Hard to miss it with the dome on top and all," he said loudly enough that Faith had to hold the phone away from her ear. "It will be good to see Jacob again. I know his mom will be glad to see him."

"You remember my husband? But it has to have been almost ten years!" Faith said amazed.

"Oh, I remember everyone, Mrs. Hartman, part of my job, I guess," he said with a folksy New England accent, "But your husband was a particular case. He seemed like such a lost soul, a lot like his mother really, a lost soul trying to find some peace and comfort in this world, merely wanting to know that the world is not as bleak as it may seem at times."

"You seem to know my husband quite well, sir," Faith remarked, stunned by the doctor's insight.

"That's my job, Mrs. Hartman."

Surprisingly, Jacob had acquiesced without much objection. It was as if he had known he needed to do this all along but required someone to push him in the right direction.

For the rest of the week, as they prepared to take off for the weekend, Jacob slept poorly, waking frequently to visions of a mother he no longer knew.

Faith asked Gary to close up the flower shop on Friday afternoon so that they could leave as soon as Jacob got home from school, but their drive was impeded by the typical beltway traffic and a consistent rain that developed soon after they passed Philadelphia. By the time they had veered onto I-84 and entered the Nutmeg state, the drizzle created a mist that hung in the air like a funeral shroud, concealing the New England countryside behind it.

The Marriot in nearby Farmington was something of a luxury they could not afford, but Faith had booked their room there because she wanted Jacob to feel relaxed. She rubbed his shoulders as they lay in bed but could tell he was distracted, even as she ran her nails down his back. "What can I do for you, Sunshine?"

He looked back at her and smiled appreciatively. Then he turned his mind back inwards, playing out a thousand scenarios of tomorrow in his mind, mental dress rehearsals for the day ahead. "You've already done everything, Beautiful. You've done everything for me."

After a long night of fitful sleep, Jacob woke strained, worn, and anxious. He was a frayed rubber band pulled taut, ready to snap at any moment. As he lifted himself from the oversized bed, Faith rolled away from him and returned to an angelic, undisturbed sleep. He pulled on his pants from the night before and grabbed a fresh t-shirt from his bag that was still by the door. Putting on his shirt and shoes in the hallway as he closed the door quietly behind him, he felt compelled to take a morning walk.

By the time he re-entered the room, Faith was standing at the mirror, drying her hair from a shower. Jacob took a deep breath of the air around him and found that she smelled of the Earth. He kissed the back of her neck delicately as he disrobed in preparation for a shower of his own.

"You know there's a reason my mom's in the hospital, right?"

"I didn't think she was there on vacation," Faith quipped as she smacked him playfully with her towel, fully exposing herself.

Jacob reached around and gave her a good smack on the ass. Faith jumped a little and then chastised him sternly but affectionately, "Not in the middle- only on the cheeks." She gave him a good one herself, for demonstration purposes only of course.

"All right," Jacob said, "Don't say you weren't warned."

"About your mother or your directionally-challenged spanking?" Faith asked him light-heartedly.

"Both." Then Jacob looked at her more seriously. "Just realize my mom's not all there. She will say some crazy shit at one point or another."

"What is her official diagnosis anyway?" Faith asked.

"Acute grief. At least that was what Dr. Thompson called it."

Faith's look showed real sorrow, a commiserate pain in her heart. "*Acute* grief? Plain old grief sucks bad enough as it is, but *acute* grief? That just sounds miserable. I'm so sorry." Faith ran her hand along his arm as he stepped into the shower and pulled the curtain.

"Thank you, Beautiful," he said from behind the curtain. Then remembering something, he poked his head back out from around the curtain and added hastily, "Oh, and don't ask her about schools."

"Why?"

"Just don't ask her about schools."

The Institute of Living, actually representing a number of buildings and various programs surrounding psychological well-being, resembled a university campus. This was not quite what Faith had been expecting. The tree-lined walkway leading up to the Center Building where they were to meet Dr. Thompson was framed by a stone and marble sign surrounded by azaleas of a variety of different colors. The greens surrounding the buildings were neatly mowed to a consistent height, and there was even an identification chart and map for the number of rare trees to be discovered in the over thirty acres of imminently walkable grounds.

"I think I could live here," Faith said with a note of unhidden surprise. "The azaleas are simply beautiful. This isn't exactly what I had in mind when you said your mom was in a mental hospital."

"It really is a nice place," Jacob said somewhat contented. "It reminds me a lot of GW but with more grass."

"So why did Darcey spring for this? I thought she hated your mother."

Jacob grinned. "Oh, she did and she does. Of that you can be sure. But that was the deal I made with her. I would sign the paperwork, but I got to choose the place and no matter what, she had to foot the bill until my mom died."

"I'll tell you what, Sunshine, you hooked your mom *up*!" Faith exclaimed, trying to lift his spirits.

"It's still a mental hospital, Faith," he responded soberly, "She doesn't leave unless it's an outing with the staff. I did the best I could for her, but it's still a fucking mental hospital."

"And what if that witch dies first, as she presumably will?"

At this question, Jacob looked up towards one of the buildings across the campus. "Then I'll have her money, and I will come back here and get my mom out of this place."

The Center Building, which was flanked by the like-themed Fuller and Todd Buildings, was a colonial, red brick building with a simple but stately gold dome atop it. Built in the early 1800's, it belonged to the stately neoclassical design school that marked New England architecture built before the Victorian Age. The marble steps leading up to the Center Building were, like the rest of the facility, flawlessly spotless.

On these steps sat a thick fellow whose husky knees were pressing into the substantial girth of his belly. His light blue dress shirt unintentionally revealed a bit too much, as the wear from many years of service rendered it powerless to hide the hair-covered chest and back of its abundantly-proportioned owner. The man wore a multi-colored knitted tie that hung down only to the second to last button on his shirt, as if it were desperately trying to stretch itself to proper length but was rudely prevented from doing so by the midriff that hung in its path. His unkempt beard seemed unable to decide if it was gray or black as the two hues were intermittently dispersed without any recognizable pattern. Though his posture suggested contented relaxation, his short, fleshy hands were furiously scribbling and erasing on a newspaper crossword that was stretched out across his lap. Given his prominent position in the middle of the stairs, it was evident that he was waiting for someone but had become so enrapt in the puzzle that he failed to notice Faith and Jacob as they approached.

"Dr. Thompson?" Faith asked, extending her hand in greeting.

It took him a moment to remove his attention from the crossword puzzle, but then he gathered his thoughts, grasped her hand, and used it to help pull himself up from his seated position. As he rose to his full height, or lack thereof (he was easily four inches shorter than Jacob even), he took on the shape of something akin to a human bowling ball. His manner, however, was bright and endearing. "Why, yes, and you must be Faith Hartman."

Taking his cue, Jacob shook Dr. Thompson's hand. "Thank you for taking the time to meet with us Dr. Thompson."

"We're glad you came to visit your mother, Jacob," said Dr. Thompson with a subtle tone of implied guilt. After a moment of awkward silence, Dr. Thompson changed the topic and went on. "Well, I had you meet me here because the building is so easy to find. Your mother is actually over in Donnelly where the inpatient services are. I can lead you over there, and we'll get you registered for your visit. I explained to Elizabeth that you were coming so that she would expect you, and she seemed quite excited about your visit."

As they walked down the stairs and followed the path through the interspersed trees, Dr. Thompson tucked his notebook under his arm in an effort to keep its numerous scattered papers from being blown away by the stiff wind or getting wet from the rain that was redeveloping. He hurried in the direction of the most modern looking building at the facility, but his stocky legs were only capable of propelling him at a certain rate of speed. He ducked his head and pushed forward, making, as he was accustomed to, the most of a bad situation.

The four-story Donnelly Building was made of concrete and glass. The contrast of this contemporary structure amongst the quaint colonial architecture and immaculately landscaped gardens was lessened only by the fact that it was set off to the side and isolated from the main grouping of buildings behind them.

This was, of course, an intentional construct, as the Donnelly Building was the sole housing for long-term inpatient care. Its symmetrical, functional design was more than simply aesthetic; it afforded the building the pragmatic purpose of being divided into four separate but adjoining "pods", each housing a distinct demographic of the inpatient population. Although each pod had its own identity, the concept allowed for flow from one pod to another, giving the patients an enhanced sense of restrained freedom.

Donnelly South 1 was home to geriatric patients generally diagnosed with Alzheimer's disease or chronic age-related dementia. These folks could often tell you in great detail what they wore to their uncle's wedding in 1925 but had nary a clue as to where they left their favorite belt or what they had for breakfast. They were usually harmless but frequently frustrating to the counselors who had to constantly remind them of what they were doing and why, like some scene out of an absurdist drama. Donnelly North 1 was the only pod with more significant restrictions and safeguards as it housed the long-term schizophrenic patients who could be of danger to themselves or others. Donnelly North 2, meanwhile, had generally short-term patients who had recently experienced a trauma or crisis of some sort. As such, the monitoring in this pod was continual, but there was a general freedom of movement. Here is where one would find young people who had slit their wrists with razor blades or anorexics trying to kill themselves off in a slower sort of death. Though this was the pod with the greatest hope for spiritual appeasement, for a reunification with the world of peace and light, it was also the pod with the darkest, most disturbing realities that must have often left the counselors who worked there wondering at night how they could ever help these unfortunate souls to get there.

"Your mother is in Donnelly South 1," Dr. Thompson said as they approached the entrance. "Most of the people in her pod are here for cognitive behavior therapy. They are stricken with a compulsion, addiction, anxiety, or pain so acute that they are unable to function in daily life. The goal of our program is, of course, to help these patients develop the coping skills and mechanisms for returning to a healthy, stable life in the outside world. But your mother, even though she participates fully- even eagerly, perhaps too eagerly- in our group therapy sessions, she simply cannot seem to make any personal progress. Her grief is so deeply embedded, so engrained, so *damned* persistent that she continues to maintain these essential fallacies to protect the defense mechanisms of her subconscious."

They arrived at the registration desk just as Dr. Thompson was concluding his diagnosis. His attention momentarily shifted towards the secretary at the front desk, Dr. Thomson did not hear Faith ask, "What fallacies?"

Instead, he introduced them to Mrs. Wagner at the front desk and expeditiously led them through the registration process so that he could take them to the lounge upstairs where they would wait for Elizabeth while Dr. Thompson went to fetch her. While the décor here was somewhat dated and bland with tweed striped upholstery done in muted earth tones, the furniture was well kept and showed few signs of wear or use. What the room lacked in any sort of aestheticism it made up for in comfort. A number of relaxing chairs in mixed styles were thoughtfully placed throughout the room to allow for a myriad of different conversation dynamics. One felt soothed here, instantaneously at home. *"These shrinks sure know what they're doing,"* Faith thought as she considered the deliberate choices that had been made in fashioning this space.

Jacob, however, was absorbed in contemplating the possible scenarios for the encounter that was about to take place, even though it was far too late for any further preparation. He stared out at the door through which Dr. Thompson had left them as he walked down the hall to beckon the woman Jacob had once seen every day but who had now been absent from his life for nearly a decade.

When Dr. Thompson finally returned with Jacob's mother on his arm, seeming to almost clutch at him, the figure was unrecognizable to him. Elizabeth, who had always been a petite, slender woman, had lost weight and with her cheeks shrunken in, appeared more like an apparition than an actual human being made of flesh and bone. Her thin hands displayed the misshapen bones and joints beneath her wrinkled skin. Her disheveled hair gave her a bewildered, frenzied appearance despite her obvious efforts to apply make-up and put on special clothes for what she ostensibly deemed a rather important occasion.

As she entered the room, her thin, wiry lips were pressed tightly together in a look that lacked any expression whatsoever. When Elizabeth saw her son, however, she absolutely beamed for what Dr. Thompson would later inform them was the first time in months. A color rose into her previously pallid cheeks, and she raised her head so that she might meet Jacob's gaze and stare deeply into the one set of eyes she had had a hand in creating.

"Oh, sweetheart, you've come to see me! Thank you so much! It is so *good* to see you!" Elizabeth proclaimed with a voice that stood in stark contrast to her physical deterioration. She shuffled towards him excitedly with steps that were short and hurried.

Jacob stood motionless but opened his arms as wide as he could in order to welcome Elizabeth to him. His arms, though, were stretched far wider than needed given the unsubstantial, threadlike form that approached him. As she reached him, Jacob reached around to engulf her and pull her towards him so that he might feel her tangibly against him.

Although Jacob was clearly shaken by his mother's rapid physical transformation into the body of an old woman, they immediately fell back into a pattern of speaking with each other that was both comfortable and revealing. Faith was mesmerized by their fluid and rhythmic dialogue centering on a variety of topics ranging from politics to Aunt

Tess to which of the staff were friendly and which were not. Moreover, Faith could not detect any of the mental instability that warranted Elizabeth's placement in an institution.

"Now you, Dr. Thompson, you are one of the nice ones," Elizabeth said as she patted him on the arm familiarly and shot an impish, conspiratorial glance towards Jacob.

"Well, thank you, Elizabeth," Dr. Thomson replied politely, "Now I am going to excuse myself as long as you feel safe here with Jacob…"

"Of course, I feel safe with Jacob," she interrupted curtly. "He's my son for crying out loud! God, are you a mother hen. I'm fine, thank you. You're dismissed, Jeeves." As she said this, she bent her wrist and shooed him off with the back of her hand.

Dr. Thompson, however, had been in the business far too long to be insulted. He said calmly, "All right, Elizabeth, you have the whole morning with your guests. I'll be back at lunchtime, but remember we have group sessions this afternoon."

"Ok, Mr. Goebbels."

"Mom!" Jacob cried out with admonishment.

Like a reprimanded but still recalcitrant child, Elizabeth tugged nervously at the purple and white blouse that draped off of her and turned to Dr. Thomson to apologize, "Ok, ok, I'm sorry Dr. Thompson. I should not have compared you to an evil Nazi propagandist." Dr. Thompson merely nodded his head in acceptance of the apology before going about his other business.

"He's a good man but very uptight. He's wound tighter than an ass-clenching frog," whispered Elizabeth as she attempted to pull something from her entangled hair.

"What the hell does that even mean, Mom? Why would a frog need to clench its ass anyway?".

"Well, I'm sure there are homo frogs out there, smart guy. How's the frog supposed to protect itself from the homo frogs? They don't have guns, you know." Suddenly, Faith was beginning to see the cracks in the armor. Then, twisting her head as dramatically as the theme of the conversation, Elizabeth said to Jacob as if Faith was not even there, "Now Jacob, that Nikita over there, she's a nice girl. You should meet a nice girl."

"Mom, this is my wife, Faith, remember? I'm married, Mom."

"Oh, I know that, dear," Elizabeth replied dismissively.

Wanting to change the topic back to something more positive, Jacob said sincerely, "I missed you, mom. I really did."

"Oh, I know, sweetheart, you and your father both. I wish you would come around more often."

Having been content up to this point to sit on the sidelines of the conversation, Faith simply had to ask, "Jacob's father? What do you mean, Mrs. Hartman?"

Elizabeth glanced at Faith quizzically, and then, as if Faith was not even present, turned to Jacob and said, "Are you sure she's all there, sweetheart? I know I'm supposed to be the crazy one around here, but even I realize that everyone has a father. Did she grow up in northern Canada or something? You know they're all a bunch of loony socialists up there."

"No, Mom, she is not from Canada. Listen, Dad hasn't come to see you in a long time. Dad died years ago when I was only eight, remember?"

"Oh don't be silly, dear," she said cavalierly. "Your father was here just over a month ago. Who do you think pays for this place? You know I couldn't afford a place like this."

For a moment, Faith almost believed her and was ready to question Jacob on the topic. Elizabeth did, after all, sound so assured of her own veracity, but her translucent eyes, the mirror image of Jacob's, told the whole story. In them, Faith saw a desperation, a sorrow so deep that it drowned her soul and left only what Faith saw before her. Faith could not imagine pulling the rug out from under her by taking the last semblance of hope she had left.

"Walter is quite generous with you, Mrs. Hartman," Faith agreed.

Elizabeth, seizing on the opportunity for a compatriot in her deluded vision, quickly shuffled her chair to Faith's side and began speaking to her confidentially, as if she no longer wanted Jacob to hear. "Well, usually. I do wish he would visit more often."

"Why doesn't he?" Faith asked.

"Well, we are divorced, you know. I know he has another family, a wife and a couple of kids, but he could at least come by once in a while, right?"

Jacob started to correct her, but Faith held out her hand to silence him, saying instead to Elizabeth, "I agree, but I can promise you that Jacob will start to come see you more often."

"You're a good girl," she said patting Faith's head lightly before pulling her head up from their private dialogue and re-addressing Jacob, "You did a good job picking this one, Jacob. She's a keeper."

"Thank you, Mom," he replied with a meaningful glance aimed at his wife.

"Would you like to go for a walk, Mrs. Hartman?" Faith asked, standing up.

"Yes, I would," said Elizabeth enthusiastically as she grabbed Faith's arm.

As they walked the grounds and read about the various rare trees that were on display throughout, Elizabeth's eyes stretched wider as if straining to let in all the stimuli around her. She seemed to be even more bewildered and lost than before but thoroughly enjoying it nonetheless.

"Don't they take you out much?" Faith asked sympathetically.

"Oh we can go out a couple of times a day, but I don't usually find any reason to go."

"Well, I'm glad you came out with us today." The rain had lifted, and a hazy ray of light shone from behind the clouds as dewy moisture reposed invitingly on the tips of the greenery around them.

Abruptly, Elizabeth broke away from both of them and rushed over to one of the trees and threw her arms around it with utter abandon. Then she turned to them and spoke as if she were giving a lecture at the local community college. "This, if you do not know, is the flowering dogwood tree. It blooms in May with pink or white flowers that are simply lovely. It really is my favorite type of tree."

"I'm sure it's beautiful, Mom," Jacob replied obligatorily.

Elizabeth's voice, for a moment, turned wistful and bright, "Oh, I wish you had come in May, Jacob. I do wish you could see the dogwood blooms; they really are so beautiful. Promise me you'll come back in May. Promise me that you'll come back and see the dogwood blossoms."

Faith interjected, "We would love to come back in May, Mrs. Hartman. We could come for Memorial Day Weekend. Jacob is usually done with school by then."

Elizabeth turned sharply and glared at Jacob, "School? What are you doing in school, Jacob?"

It took Faith a few seconds to grasp what had precipitated Elizabeth's violent reaction, but when she flashed back to Jacob's final words from the shower, she knew she had opened the wrong can of worms and that there was no shoving them back in. Shielded from Elizabeth's view, she gestured to Jacob with an apologetic, helpless shrug of the shoulders to which he replied with a mere rolling of his eyes.

"I teach, Mom. That's what I do for a living. I'm a teacher."

Elizabeth responded with a series of frenzied arm movements accompanied by a lengthy diatribe on how schools were the instruments the government used to institute social conformity. According to her primary thesis, which was further explicated by a series of tangential sub points that were only loosely related to the original premise, schools were brainwashers that taught children to subscribe to the all-pervasive social system of reinforcement through money and social status. Despite Jacob's numerous attempts to infuse himself into what was rapidly becoming a running monologue with the intermittent, "Well, yes, Mom, but..." or "I understand your point, Mom, however...", his comments went entirely unheeded, and she proceeded with her rant on how society shaped our behavior with financial rewards and punishments that all echoed back to our conditioning experiences during our school-aged years.

When she finally concluded her lecture on sociological conditioning through economics, Jacob, rankled and exhausted, asked his mother plainly, "Then what would you have me do for a job, Mom?"

Becoming as pleasant as could be, like the dramatic change during the eye of a storm, Elizabeth responded with a bright smile and a pinch on his cheek, "Oh, that's up to you to decide, dear! You have to go where your own heart leads you. I can't tell you what to do."

Dr. Thompson ate lunch with them and explained the various group therapies and treatments the Institute was employing with Elizabeth. All the while, she sat to his side, openly mocking and deriding him with childish facial gestures and a frequent grandiose rolling of her eyes. While Faith found Dr. Thompson to be a dedicated and competent professional, she could not help but smirk at Elizabeth. Through all of the sadness and pain, she still saw in Elizabeth a glimmer of vitality, a child that wanted to be rescued from the suffering so that she could laugh and play with all of the other innocent, naïve children around her.

It was this streak that also ran through Jacob. Faith knew that beneath the crusty, exterior layer of chiseled disappointment created by a lifetime of too much suffering lay a little boy who yearned to believe once more, to be taken away from the grief and bathed in the hopeful optimism that the world could be a better place. She realized now that she needed to tap into this if she was to push beyond his wall of fear and disillusionment. She must help him to envision his own happiness amid a lifetime of sorrow. Only then could he see all he had to offer to the creation of the life of another. Only then would he recognize the joy of the cycle of rebirth.

Inspired by Elizabeth's tomfoolery, she sat next to Jacob familiarly and fondled him mischievously beneath the table as she nodded reassuringly at Dr. Thomson. While she kept her posture completely erect and motionless, it was Jacob that gave her away by repeatedly pushing her hand away with pronounced movements of his own.

"Do you need something, Jacob?" asked Dr. Thompson, alarmed. He had noticed the activity, but was unable to deduce the true goings-on.

"No, sir," Jacob said uncomfortably as he shot Faith a glance that told her to knock it off once and for all. "Do you think my mom is making any real progress, Dr. Thompson?"

Dr. Thompson seemed saddened by this question, and he dropped his weighty head down towards his lap. "Well, Jacob, it sure helps to have you come see her. It's really all she has."

"Well, that's the first thing you said today that makes any sense," Elizabeth chimed in with a pointing of her bony, arthritic finger.

"I promise I'll come more often, ok, Mom? I'm sorry, really sorry." He went to her and hugged her unexpectedly with a force that made it appear as if her eyes would burst forth from her head. "I love you, Mom. I really do. I'm so, so sorry..." He trailed off there as he sobbed into her shoulder.

From that point on, Jacob would go to Hartford at least twice a year, once during the holidays when he would come bearing a fruitcake that he re-gifted from his Grandma Tess but told Elizabeth came from his father, and the other during May when he would take her for a long walk amongst the dogwood trees so that she could show him the dazzling beauty of the newborn blossoms.

Chapter 6

Sledding is for Children

He awoke that chilly morning in January of 1996 to an unusual coating of snow that blanketed the cobblestone sidewalks beneath their window. While Washington certainly has its share of humid August days, it is generally immune from the heavier snowfalls that impact the rest of the Northeast. Jacob stumbled down the stairs to retrieve the paper and considered how they might take advantage of such an occasion.

He plopped himself down at the kitchen table and laid out the paper by sections. He knew Faith would be upstairs making every effort to remain asleep, but that she would lose that battle and concede any moment now. He could hear the infancy of her stirrings. This thought comforted him, letting him know that he was not alone in this great, big, indifferent world.

"Oh, Sleeping Beauty, what would Your Highness like to do today?" he bellowed up the stairs.

The only reply was a guttural grunt that belied Faith's femininity.

"Oh, I hear you up there. You know as well as I do that you're awake."

This time the incoherent denial was louder and more anguished, followed by a desperate, "Just let me sleep."

Jacob had long ago not only accepted her morning moodiness but had come to thoroughly appreciate it as a part of who she was and why he loved her. That did not, however, prevent him from needling her about it. "That's fine. You go to sleep. I'll make some coffee and a bagel and leave them here for you when you wake up. Come on down whenever you're ready."

With this, he stood up, poured himself a second cup of coffee, and put a bagel into the toaster for her. Samwise, the ever loyal but perpetually distracted golden retriever, thinking it was time to go for a walk, relinquished his customary morning place next to Faith and rushed down the stairs barking eagerly. Jacob shushed him unsuccessfully and then walked back up the stairs and headed through the bedroom to turn on the hot water in preparation for his shower. At first, Faith feigned further sleep, but then she took one of the pillows beneath her and tossed it at the back of his head as he walked by.

He, in turn, feigned being aloof and headed into the bathroom to turn on the water. After waiting an inordinate amount of time in order to throw her off her guard, he came rushing into the room and launched himself onto the bed beside her. Clutching her to his chest, he rolled her toward him until he was on top of her. Just then the smell that was her and her alone rose to him, and he breathed in deeply, keenly aware of her essence.

"Get off of me," she said playfully as she reached up to tickle him along his sides, giggling herself.

He smiled at her mischievously and rolled her on top of him, pulling her closer as he did so. He arched his neck forward, causing his dense shoulders to strain, and kissed her lightly but sensuously on the mouth. As she kissed him back, only with firmer contact, he knew that she had tacitly understood his suggestion. She pinned him down and began to run her long, slender finger down the side of his neck. He enmeshed his hand in her long hair and tried to swallow her whole.

By the time Jacob finally got around to taking that shower, the water had run cold, a piercing reminder to turn the water off next time before making love to his wife. Still, the water energized him, called his body to wakefulness. As much as he hated it in the moment, he was grateful for its effect on him.

"Do you want me to leave the water running for you?" he shouted back out to the bedroom, not even sure if she was still out there.

"It's cold, isn't it? I could hear you in there." When Jacob didn't reply, she threw off the sheets casually and strode towards the doorway to pop in her perky, oval face. "Well, in

that case, I'm going to go downstairs and eat that breakfast
you made for me while I wait for the water to warm back up."

She stroked his short hair and turned around, but
before she could leave the room, Jacob hurriedly proclaimed,
"I'm sorry, but I didn't have a chance to butter your bagel."

"I think I'll forgive you."

He had been waiting his entire life to hear those words.

"How about we take Samwise here for a walk to the
park?" Jacob suggested. The always agreeable canine,
somehow sensing he was being talked about, perked up and
ran towards the door, nearly knocking over the coffee table in
his scampering gait.

"I thought you had a ton of papers to grade," she
responded.

Jacob hesitated for a moment as the perpetual
nervousness of work undone took over him for a moment. He
fought it off, however, and said with greater resolve, "No, it
never snows here. Let's take advantage of it. I want to spend
the day with you."

"Ok, you want to head over to Dumbarton Oaks?"

"Sure. I'll grab the leash."

On the walk over to the park, Jacob was conscious to
hold her hand as much as possible, though Samwise's pulling
at every single object of even mildly discernible interest often
impeded his doing so. He knew it mattered to her, knew that
it represented tangible thought to her, just one of the little
things that mean everything. In all honesty, he could take it or

leave it, would probably just as soon walk with a bit of distance between them. That was love, and she understood and appreciated it. Her delicate hand gave his thick, meaty paw a gentle, poignant squeeze as she walked on, smiling out to the radiant sunlight that gleamed off the snow in front of them, never even needing to look over at him. She already knew he was there.

By the time they got there, it was late morning, and the park was teeming with activity. Joggers swept past the hot dog vendor while kids who knew little of snow found ever more creative ways to amuse themselves with it.

"Hey, look," Faith exclaimed while tugging at his arm. "They're sledding over there. I haven't gone sledding for years."

Jacob resisted but could tell Faith was too excited to let this go. He followed her up the hill, sinking into the snow with his poorly equipped loafers. He looked up at her as she pranced ahead of him, Samwise pulling him hard up the hill in a desperate effort to get ahead of Faith. As they reached the top of the hill, Faith grabbed his hand and pulled him along to the steeper part of the hill where the older kids were sledding.

"Check out the tadpoles over there," she said pointing over to the smaller hill where the younger children were. A young boy with an oversized, blue puffy jacket was struggling up with his miniature legs, dragging his sled behind him like Marley's chains in Dickens's *A Christmas Carol*. A girl no more than two, whose long, tight, brown curls reminded Jacob of the girl who had sat next to him for the first half of second grade, sat on her rocket-shaped sled as her father, seemingly as encumbered as the young boy, trudged up with her in tow.

"Now, don't you want to have one of those?" she asked, whispering softly into his ear so that the nerves in his neck and shoulder sprung alive.

He wanted to think of something clever to divert her from the topic, but all he could muster was, "Do you see that dad over there?"

"Yeah, I do. He looks happy," she said, suddenly serious. She turned her head, but not her body, away and gazed out at the distant horizon as if seeking for a way to console herself.

Not anticipating her mercurial shift of mood, Jacob made an immediate effort to re-engage her. "Hey, let's go watch those improperly supervised children hurl themselves down that run of death," he said with just the right amount of sarcasm.

Faith, still pensive, noted the gesture and tried, with measured success, to resuscitate her enthusiasm. "Sure," she said.

Jacob led her over to the crest of the hill where two boys were goading one of their friends as he deliberated about whether he should ride headfirst and hit the large jump that the kids had built in the middle of the run.

"C'mon, Simon, just do it. Don't be a pussy. My sister did the same thing last year when we were out here," said one boy who was quite a bit bigger but not necessarily older than the other two.

"Yeah," said the other boy who obviously hung in deference on whatever his larger companion said. "I even saw her do it."

The head-first rider-to-be, apparently less apprehensive of the smaller boy, turned to him and snapped, "Screw you, Jerry! I don't see you doing it!"

"I'll go right after you," Jerry replied. "Christ, Simon, stop being such a puss."

Simon turned his attention back to the hill in front of him and mustered the gumption he needed. His cropped red hair was mostly hidden beneath his gray, woolen hat, but the freckles on his cheeks that were now turning crimson in anger gave him away. Suddenly, he pushed off with his feet and was racing down the hill. The sled barreled down recklessly, throwing caution to the wind that rode astride it.

"That's it, Simon," the larger boy yelled after him, pumping his thick arm into the air.

Picking up speed, Simon maneuvered the wayward sled deftly to the left so as to set a due course for the three foot kicker. When he hit it, the sled seemed to leap for delight. The jump, however, being hastily constructed, was angled slightly but noticeably to the left, and thus threw Simon from the sled almost instantaneously. He flew awkwardly even higher than the sled and came plunging to the earth with a resounding thud. The sled meanwhile, as if determined to finish the rest of the run with or without its human cargo, continued on down the hill, finally coming to rest in the small creek far below.

"Way to go, Simon," the large boy hollered down to him in encouragement. Then he turned to Jerry and said loud enough for only him to hear, "Holy shit, I never thought he would do it!"

"Hey," Jerry shouted down the hill towards Simon, "you still have to get my brother's sled all the way down there, you know."

When Simon, lying quietly in the already darkened snow, did not respond, the larger boy rushed towards him to see if he was all right. Concerned, Jacob and Faith followed close behind. Before they even reached him, they could see the crimson droplets in the snow. Jacob deflected the larger boy away with his left hand, as he kneeled and used his right arm to turn Simon over.

The thin gash above his right eye still had some blood coming from it but would probably not even require stitches. Jacob pressed his sleeve against the gash and then helped Simon to sit up. Dazed initially, Simon gathered his senses and looked around for him for a minute.

"How was it?" asked his friend, apparently no longer fearing a catastrophic injury.

"It was awesome."

"Now do you see why I don't want to have kids?" Jacob pined when they had helped Simon back up to the top of the hill.

"What? No, I don't," Faith retorted. "I really don't, Jacob. What the hell does this kid getting a boo-boo on the sledding hill have to do with our potential progeny? Tell me, Jacob, because I am failing to see the connection."

"The worrying, Faith, the constant, ever-present worrying. That's what I mean. Yes, I know, he didn't get seriously hurt. I get that. But kids do get hurt, Faith. Really hurt. Seriously hurt. All the time."

"Jacob you can't go through life that way, always thinking about the 'what if's'. I'm not suggesting that we go jump out of an airplane without a parachute, but you do have to live and accept the inherent risks that life entails. That's all there is to it." She was sympathetic to his nagging fear but was growing incrementally intolerant of it.

"No, Faith," he said obstinately. "I don't work that way. I can't just drop my apprehension because you say everything's going to be ok…"

"I never said that everything was always going to be ok," she interrupted with a biting tone.

"Ok, even worse," he continued. "You're asking me to accept that things definitively *will* go wrong, and that I should just be ok with that. Well, I'm not wired that way. Every day they take the bus to school, I will worry. Every time they go to the movies with their friends, I will worry."

Jacob was now fully engaged in the hand gestures that she had come to know signaled his mounting anxiety. Fed up with his nonsense, Faith, like a mother taking her child back to the car after making a scene in a restaurant, grabbed him by the wrist and led him over to where the boys were standing.

"Boys, can we borrow one of your sleds, please?" she asked determinedly in the boys' general direction.

"Faith, no. Come on, stop."

Faith paid him no regard whatsoever. "Boys, would it be ok if we used one of your sleds?"

"Sure. Go ahead and use mine," said the large boy, clearly unsure how he should respond to this fiery woman. "It's right over there. It should be fine for the two of you."

"Faith, no. I'm serious. Have you never read *Ethan Frome*? This will not end well, I promise you."

Faith merely glared back at him.

"I'm not going. I mean it. You can go on your own, but I'm not going."

"Oh, you're going," she spoke plainly and defiantly.

"Can't we go on the smaller hill first?"

"You're going, and I'm sitting up front."

She didn't even give him much time or notice once they were sitting on the sled. "Keep your hands and legs on the sled. I'll steer. Got it?" She waited only long enough for him to nod bewilderedly, then pushed off with her hands and exclaimed, "Ok, here we go."

At first, he was legitimately terrified. He wanted it to be over, but as the sled began to gain momentum, so did his spirit. The breeze rushed through him and awoke something that had been lying dormant inside of him, something universal and primal and yet so foreign to him. He clung to the sides of the sled yet somehow wanted to go faster, faster, faster, until he was one with all around him. For a brief moment, just as long as he dared, he removed his hands from the sides and thrust them upwards towards the glorious sky above.

By this time, Samwise was desperately stampeding after them and barking frantically but joyfully. At one point, he stumbled forward and, losing his balance, flung himself head over heels only to somehow land right back on his feet as if nothing had happened as he continued his avid pursuit of the sled.

"You better hold on," Faith hollered back, her voice barely audible as it drifted by in the blustering wind. "We're hitting that jump."

"*Oh, dear God,*" he thought, but uttered nothing.

Faith pulled up slightly on the right side of the sled, nudging it to the left and straight towards the kicker that had sent Simon flying. Proving that the wisdom acquired in reaching adulthood does, in fact, have its share of advantages, she learned from watching Simon go before her and adjusted accordingly for the angling of the jump. As they sailed through the air, Jacob swore he could hear the boys up above cheering them on. He, however, was too caught up in the moment to really pay attention. This might be the single best thing he had ever done.

The sled greeted the earth beneath it seamlessly, as if they were, like great lovers who occasionally drift apart but always come back to each other, intrinsically meant to be together. Jacob, who had braced himself for a bumpy landing, leaned back and let the sled carry him where it would. Then, just before they veered off into the creek, he grabbed Faith by the waist and pulled her off the side of the sled with him, rolling onto the soft, awaiting snow.

Ending up on top of her, he bent over the only mouth he ever wanted to kiss and placed his lips thankfully, energetically to hers. Samwise, now on the scene and wanting in on the action, slurped her as well. Then, leaping to his feet spryly, Jacob lifted her up and embraced her, saying over and over again, "Thank you. Thank you. Thank you, my beloved Faith! That was both the most terrifying and most spectacular experience of my life."

"I hope not more spectacular than making love to me," she chided.

"No, seriously," Jacob continued earnestly as Samwise eagerly paraded around their legs. "That was amazing. I get it. I get it. I want to live Faith. I want to *live* with you."

"I stopped taking birth control about a month ago."

The entire world stopped. Right then and there, the entire world paused as Jacob breathed this in and absorbed it into his consciousness. Holy shit, what the hell had she done? Should he be pissed? She had deliberately betrayed his desires and wordlessly usurped control over his own life. Should he be frightened? She could be pregnant already, and they had gone sledding, for crying out loud. Should he be hurt? She did not even feel she could discuss this with him. Or maybe, just maybe, he should be elated, elated that this woman so beautiful, so soulful, so passionate and true wanted to give him the greatest gift life has to offer. Perhaps he should be grateful for such a miraculous opportunity.

He grasped her hand and gave it a gentle, poignant squeeze. "Would you like to go home and make love?"

"I think we better bring those boys their sled first," she teased as she squeezed him right back.

Chapter 7

Delivery

Faith curled herself into a ball and stared blankly at the white wall in front of her. If only for a passing moment, she allowed herself the luxury of an empty, unfettered mind. She knew the tranquility would not last long, but she was trying to piece together the dream that had woken her twice during the night.

"Good morning, Beautiful," Jacob chimed from the bathroom. Though it broke her focused meditation, Faith was grateful to hear his voice. How was it that Jacob always seemed to know the very moment she woke? Did he have some sort of symbiotic relationship with her consciousness that allowed him unfettered access to her sleep patterns? Did he even have access to her dreams?

They certainly had been visceral throughout her pregnancy, even by her dream standards. Not once, however, did she have visions, as many women claim to, of the baby that resided inside her. Instead she ascribed the vivid nature of her dreams to the heartburn she had developed from satiating her cravings for spicy Mexican food, a heartburn that had grown more acute over the last several days.

In last night's dream, she had been trapped inside a dark and musty cavern. She had hollered out for Jacob, but he must have been out of earshot, for he never responded to her cries. Suddenly, however, a shiver of light emerged and guided her to the cavern entrance. As she emerged, she came upon an ancient river, enticing and clear. She stripped down as quickly as she could and washed the sooty remnants of the cavern from her skin. Finally, she swam to the banks of the river and dried herself upon the cool grass beneath her. The water left her refreshed but clung to her with a pervasive chill she could not shake. It had been that sensation that had roused her in the night.

"Hey, I was thinking...how would you like to go to dinner tonight?" she asked, half thinking out loud, as she was prone to do.

Jacob finished brushing his teeth and poked his head out into the bedroom. "Great idea! Soon, you know, we won't be able to go out anytime we want."

"I know," Faith rejoined. "My thinking too." She smiled at him and stood back to observe him for a moment, taking the time to truly admire her life partner. His capacity for love shone to her, and she appreciated the leap of faith he had made with her. For a moment, she was overwhelmed by her love for him as she soaked in the depth of who he really was. When Jacob followed up by asking her where she would like to go, she heard him speak, but was still somehow unable to grasp what he had said.

And then the moment was gone. "I'm sorry. What did you say? I was zoning out for a minute there."

"Pregnancy brain again, huh?" he joked with her.

She could have told him then, could have let him know that she had been thinking about him, admiring him, but she wanted this moment for herself. Sure, it would have stroked his ego, and God knows Jacob could use it, but this was her memory, her snapshot of a moment frozen in time. Some things are best never shared.

"Yeah, you know, sometimes I think I'd lose my baby if it weren't stuck inside my uterus."

Jacob pulled up in front of the deeply inset door of the Little Raven and dropped Faith off so that she would not have to walk from wherever he could find a parking spot. Under most circumstances, Faith would not have accepted such an offer. While she appreciated the chivalric intent, she wasn't that type of girl. Rather, she always wanted to walk together, preferably side by side. She would often gently admonish Jacob for walking ahead of her. The symbolism meant something to her. If Jacob went one way around a park bench, so did she. She had made a vow to intertwine their lives and make them one, and she had every intention of fulfilling both the letter and the essence of that promise. She recognized that everyone makes compromises somewhere, however, and tonight, being nine months pregnant, she allowed Jacob to drop her at the front door.

They dined at the Little Raven frequently; it was one of their favorite places in Adams Morgan. It was a small, crowded, old-fashioned Italian place with authentic red and white tablecloths and dimly lit chandeliers hanging from the ceiling. The floors were uneven and worn, giving it just the right touch of aesthetic weathering and charm.

Faith was already seated when Jacob made his way into the restaurant, and she signaled him over by extending two of her long fingers into the air. Jacob sidled past several tables, pulled out his chair, and sat across from her, as was their custom. Jacob and Faith preferred to sit across the table from each other so that they could focus their energy on each other's company. It afforded them the luxury to gaze into the eyes of the other and merely listen while their souls communed for a little while. Plus, she could always grab him flirtatiously under the table that way.

"Well, hello there, Beautiful," he said, reaching out to hold her hand.

"Ugh, I don't feel so beautiful right now." She knew she was blatantly fishing for a compliment, but she didn't care. After nine months of this, she could use all the compliments she could get.

"Sweetheart, you are gorgeous. First of all, on a purely physical level, you have kept yourself up quite well." She was not sure where this was going, but he wasn't off to a good start. "More importantly, you are carrying our baby, and nothing could be more beautiful than that. You have life itself inside of you." He reached his hand under the table and placed it on her belly. She put her hand over his and led his hand to where the baby was.

"Not long now," he said as he straightened back up after a few moments of feeling the baby kick.

"No, not long now," she echoed. The potential answer to her next question filled her with trepidation, but she decided to ask it nonetheless. "So are you excited?"

But before Jacob could answer, their waiter appeared, seemingly from nowhere. Faith had been so intent on Jacob's response that the sudden appearance of the waiter startled her, and she let out a muffled shriek.

"Whoa, didn't mean to scare ya there ma'am," he said unperturbed. "My name is Jed, and I'll be taking care of you tonight. Can I start you folks off with anything to drink?"

Jed had long, dark hair pulled back into a ponytail that was neat but hung to the midpoint of his back. About twenty-five, he had an impressively athletic build that was lean but firm. Even more noticeable, however, was his impeccably good posture, making him seem taller than his relatively average height. He even tended to stick his chest out some as he talked.

Faith did not hesitate to chime in. "Well, thank you for the introduction, Jed. This here is my lovely husband, Jacob. And my name is Faith. It is a pleasure to meet you. Now, as to your tantalizing offer for beverages, I believe my husband here would like a glass of your house Chianti. As for myself, being with child, I will have to respite myself with some of your finest tap water." At that precise moment, she had the tight, sharp pain of a contraction that caused her to bring her hand down firmly upon the table in a scene eerily reminiscent of Dr. Strangelove.

Jed, not knowing how to take this peculiar pregnant woman, and seemingly a bit afraid of her, simply said, "I'll be right back with your drinks, ma'am," and departed as rapidly as possible.

Once he was gone, Jacob leaned across the table, and whispered furtively, "I think you got poor Jed back for sneaking up on you. He probably thinks you're part of a secret pregnant woman division of the CIA where all the agents use their baby bumps as a cover for their deadly proficiency."

Her mind, however, was still centered on a few moments ago. *She* had not forgotten. "Whatever. You're not getting out of answering that question, mister. Are you excited?"

"Of course I'm excited," he said as earnestly as possible. Faith could not tell if he really meant it, but there it sat. That was his story, and he was sticking with it. She merely looked at him. "Seriously, I am," he implored.

"What are you excited about?"

Realizing where this conversation was going and what had prompted it to go there, Jacob knew that he needed to be more deliberate in his responses from here on out. He steadied himself and said, "This baby is a product of you and me, a product of our love for each other. It is a blessing, a beautiful, wonderful blessing. Sometime very soon, you and I will get to participate in the great circle of life. What could be more exciting than that?"

"*Ok, that was pretty good,*" she thought to herself. "*It even sounded genuine.*"

As she pondered this, Jed, in his customary style, appeared out of nowhere, bearing the Chianti and water. He tried his best to place them on the table and unobtrusively retire to the kitchen. Upon backing out, however, he unintentionally entangled his foot with a fellow waiter innocently passing by, causing him to fall forward violently and slam his head directly into the corner of their table.

The loud bang and consequent groan from Jed once again startled Faith, who this time let loose with a mild expletive aimed at least partially in Jed's direction. Then, seized by another contraction, she again thrust her arm down upon the table, this time volitionally. Jed, meanwhile, had grabbed a napkin from an adjacent table and was using it to stop the bleeding from a minor gash right above his temple. He was barely able to mutter, "I'll be right back to take your order," before bee-lining it for the kitchen, the napkin still pressed to his forehead.

When Jed, the earnest but hopelessly failing waiter, returned a few moments later, he had a Band-Aid applied to the cut but was still noticeably shaken by the experience. He seemed determined to persevere through these adversities for the benefit of all, but he was now clearly wary of Faith. For the entire time that he took their order, he directed his attention squarely upon Jacob, even as she directed him to be sure that her steak was rare enough to hop down and walk off the table. This peeved Faith, but he disappeared again so quickly that she was unable to slip in a jibe before his prompt exodus back to the kitchen.

Jacob, having noted Faith's anxiety, concluded that it was time for a pre-emptive strike. In order to provide her with the reassurance he could tell she needed, he needed to be proactive. "Are you still feeling comfortable with our birth plan?"

He had piqued her interest. "I am. I want to do this as naturally as possible. Are you still ok with it?"

He had not seen her be this vulnerable in some time. He reached across the table and took her slender left hand and gripped it firmly between his. He drew her in with a deep gaze and said, "I am here to support you in whatever you need at any stage along the way. While I love our ideal birth plan, I know that parts of it might need to change according to the circumstances. If that needs to happen, I want you to know that I love you no matter what and will help in whatever way I can."

"*He really is a good man,*" Faith thought to herself. "*How did I get this lucky? Out of all the schmucks and losers out there, many of which I unfortunately dated along the way, how did HE make his way into my life?*" She placed the palm of her hand on the back of his neck and pulled him towards her as she leaned intently across the table and kissed him in a way that was deliberate and passionate. "Thank you, sweetheart; that means a lot."

Jacob eased back into his seat, less guarded than moments before. "You're going to be a wonderful mother, you know."

"Do you really think so?" she asked.

"Without question," he promptly replied.

"How are we going to avoid the same mistakes our parents made?"

"Beautiful, all parents make mistakes. The key to being a good parent isn't what you buy them, the life you provide them, or the mistakes you do or do not make. It lies in giving them unconditional love, and if you provide our children with half the love you give and instill in me, they will be just fine."

She started to tear slightly but used her napkin to dry her eye, waved her hand in front of her face, and made an effort to regain her composure before the real waterworks began. For months now, even without consciously realizing it, those were the words she had needed to hear.

Faith had always known that despite his reticence to become one, Jacob would make a caring and devoted father. In fact, it was because of his hesitancy that she knew this. She understood that Jacob feared fatherhood because he knew he would feel too much, that he would have difficulty assuaging his gnawing sense of dread at the possibilities of what could go wrong. If anyone knew how the good fortune of life could turn on a dime, it was Jacob. It was this sense of uncertainty

that had made the prospect of fatherhood so daunting for
Jacob.

This thought only enhanced her admiration for her
husband. He had, as few people do, stared straight into the
face of his most significant fear and persevered. He had dared
to live in the face of all the sorrows and pains life can inflict.
"I love you, you know," she said as she made a conscious
effort to meet his eyes with hers.

At that precise moment, before Jacob could fully
reciprocate the sentiment, Jed again appeared without
warning, carrying their entrees. This time, however, it was
Jacob's turn to be startled by Jed's unpredictable
materialization. As Jed's thigh knocked into the table causing
it to shake, Jacob let out an exasperated, "Dear God, man."
Faith meanwhile, suffering from yet another contraction,
involuntarily stuck out her arm, and in the process,
accidentally punched poor Jed in the solar plexus. Knocked
breathless by the inadvertent assault, Jed lost his handle on the
two dishes. While he was somehow able to stretch out his
hand and save Faith's steak, Jacob's linguine del mare
ricocheted off the edge of the table and landed squarely in the
lap of an elderly gentleman at the adjacent table.

Jed, frantic, distraught, and still unable to catch his
breath, did not know whom to apologize to first. Finally, he
turned to the elderly gentleman picking scallops from his lap
and said, "I am so sorry about this, sir. Let me go back into
the kitchen and get you some towels." Then, in an attempt to

please all parties, he turned back to Jacob and said, "I'll get the kitchen working on another dish for you right away, sir."

While the elderly gentleman was already cursing up a storm and threatening numerous litigations, Jacob could not help but laugh at the absurdity of the circumstances. When he looked back at Faith, however, she was leaned over the table with her head thrust towards the center and her eyes tightly squeezed together. This contraction was evidently more substantial than the ones that had come before. He dashed behind her and rubbed his right hand up and down her back to soothe her. Then, he leaned over and whispered into her ear, "Is there anything I can do, or do you just want me to be quiet?"

"Just be quiet," she grunted back as pleasantly as she could.

And then, as abruptly as it had come, it was gone. Faith slowly sat up and then eased herself back into the chair, breathing deeply and with significant conscious effort. "Whew, that was a good one," she said at last, as the final ripples of the contraction subsided.

"Do you think it's time?" Jacob asked nervously.

"No, they must be more Braxton Hicks contractions. When I saw the doctor on Thursday, I was only dilated one centimeter, and while she did have some concerns regarding my swelling, she said that she thought I would go full term. You know, sort of like the fetus stuck its little head out, saw its shadow, and now there are three more weeks of pregnancy. Now, no guarantees there, but I think we still have awhile to go." She reached over and grabbed his arm to pull herself up. "I do need to go to the bathroom, though."

While she was gone, Jed brought Jacob's replacement entrée, apologizing profusely once again for any inconvenience. Jacob reassured him that it was no trouble whatsoever. The elderly gentleman, however, was not so easily placated. Even though Jacob attempted to direct his attention elsewhere, he could not help but overhear the man's heated description of the cost of the pants and his insistence upon a further conference with the manager.

As if to rescue Jacob, if not the unfortunate Jed, from being subjected to this barrage of vitriol, Faith emerged from the bathroom, using the back of her hand like the preening fan of a Victorian lady to wave Jacob back to his seat as he attempted to get up and assist her in sitting back down. "Did you miss me?" she asked seductively.

"Did I ever! You should have seen the commotion over here. Jed's actually doing his level best to rectify the situation, but crotchety pants over there keeps giving him the business anyway."

"Are you feeling bad for Jed?" Faith asked with mock sympathy.

"You know, to tell you the truth, I am," Jacob responded sincerely.

"Well," Faith finally capitulated, "I'm sure he's a nice guy, but he's not exactly my best friend right now."

"I'm sure he understands."

As they ate their meals in a mutually understood silence, Faith fought the internal battle to resist running through her baby preparedness checklist for the umpteenth time. She knew she would not have many moments like this for some time to come and wanted to savor it, but she was consumed with the preoccupation that she must have forgotten something of great importance and that they would return home from the hospital unprepared for the journey that lay ahead.

Jacob meanwhile had finally come to a place of peace in regards to the impending delivery. Somehow he had convinced himself that for once things were going to be fine, and his fears had abated. To his own surprise, he even felt a mounting excitement growing inside him.

As Faith was putting the finishing touches on her blood-red steak, Jed came over to the table, this time stomping his feet as if he were on a wilderness trek and wanted to be sure to alert bears to his presence to avoid sneaking up on them.

"Does anyone need a box tonight?" He had regained his composure and was now speaking with an almost jovial air. "Doesn't look like you'll need one ma'am," he suggested as he looked down upon Faith's meticulously cleaned plate.

Somewhat annoyed by the comment even though she knew it was just an oversight of decorum on Jed's part, Faith could not help but reply in a snide tone, "I am eating for two, you know?"

Jed, however, had sworn to himself that he would not let himself become flustered again. "I'm sorry, ma'am; I didn't mean anything by that. But since you are eating for two, can I interest you in some dessert?"

This was Jed's smoothest move of the night, though to be honest, there was hardly any competition to vie for the title. Still, he had no takers, so he departed saying that he would be right back with the check.

With Jed now safely out of distance, Jacob turned his attention back to Faith and asked her, "So what do you think about the name 'Finnegan'?"

"Are you kidding? He'd get beat up every day at school if we did that to him." Faith wanted to be sensitive, but a line needed to be drawn here with an authoritative stance. She would have invoked her veto power had she needed to.

"He could go by 'Finn'. It would be a great tribute to Joyce. You know he spent seventeen years writing *Finnegan's Wake*?"

"Slacker. You want to name our son after a slacker? No."

"Well, how about 'Tobias'? It means 'gift from God' in Hebrew."

"Why are you so convinced it's a boy anyway? It could be a girl, you know."

"I don't know," he replied distractedly. "Something gives me a gut feeling that it's a boy. So what do you think about 'Tobias'?"

"I like it. I thought you wanted to go with 'Landon'."

"Yeah, for some reason, I can't see calling my child that," he said before adopting a fake version of his own voice to simulate the future, "'Let's go to the park *Landon*'. I don't know; no ring to it. I think I like 'Tobias' better. 'Let's go to the park *Tobias.*' Plus, you could shorten it to 'Toby'."

Faith nodded her head in assent, "Ok, I can go with 'Tobias', but you have to promise to never let him be called 'Toby'."

"Well, you know his friends are going to call him whatever they want anyways. We can't control what they call him."

"Whatever. No 'Toby'."

"I can live with that," Jacob acquiesced.

Feeling the matter settled, Faith changed gears. "So what if, by some miracle of the universe, it is a girl?"

"I liked 'Amy' or 'Beckett', but they weren't really on your list," Jacob said noncommittally, "What are your thoughts?"

"If it's a girl, I would like to name her 'Aurora'." Her whole body took on the colorful glow of the borealis as the name passed her lips.

The name struck Jacob immediately, "I like it. What does it mean?"

"It means 'dawn'. The name is derived from the Roman goddess of the sunrise."

As she said this, she began to grimace and bend over in the grips of another contraction. Meanwhile, Jed, innocently enough, was returning with the check. As he approached the table, Faith seized his left arm by the wrist and said to him in a tone that was at least partially serious. "You- you cannot come back to this table. Every time you come here, I have a contraction. You must go, oh, bringer of contractions."

Jed looked over at Jacob helplessly, as if to ask, *"Is this really my fault? What the hell should I do here?"*

Jacob shot him back a reassuring smile and a subtle nod to suggest that he should disregard his wife's erratic behavior and simply walk away. When Jed was finally able to retract his wrist from Faith's death-grip, Jacob handed him his credit card above Faith's shoulder and told him he would stop at the front on their way out to sign the slip.

"Well, thank you folks," Jed said as he tried to cast as positive a light as possible on the whole experience. "I hope you have a wonderful remainder of your evening. It certainly was memorable for me." With this, he backed away and fled directly to the kitchen, probably hoping to never wait on another pregnant woman again.

When Jacob went to bed that evening, he thought nothing of Faith's contractions, especially since they had, coincidentally enough, ceased once they had escaped Jed's presence. So he was understandably perplexed when Faith woke him at one in the morning.

"I think we need to go to the hospital," she whispered towards his ear once she could tell that he had gained enough consciousness to comprehend her.

Still half asleep and probably subliminally relying on her comment at dinner that the doctor had suggested delivery was still three weeks away, he tried to turn over and asked resignedly, "Can't we go in the morning?"

"Sunshine, I think if we wait, you're going to be delivering this baby right here in our bedroom," she said as sweetly but matter-of-factly as possible.

That was all Jacob needed to hear. He sprang out of bed, got dressed, called Dr. Takasashi, and threw the bags Faith had packed weeks before into the Honda Civic they shared. Working methodically like a NASCAR pit crew, he headed back upstairs to help Faith get dressed and amble down to the car.

"How are you doing, Beautiful?" he asked her as they sped towards the hospital and she breathed her way through another contraction.

Unable to articulate a response to such an inane question at this inopportune moment, she merely glared at him to express her disapproval. Once the contraction had passed, a sense of relief settled in that, by contrast to the tortuous pressure and pain that had seized her, seemed euphoric. "Could you please try to not hit any more potholes?" she asked more as a demand than a request.

They drove on in silence for the rest of the short trip to the hospital, Jacob afraid of distressing her further. Between contractions, Jacob would drive as fast as he deemed reasonably safe, but once he perceived the telltale signs of the cresting wave of pain that he was rapidly accustoming himself to discern, he would decelerate so dramatically that they certainly would have been rear-ended had it been any other time of day.

Nothing Faith had done to acquaint herself with childbirth- no birthing class, no book, no website- had prepared her for the pain she was currently experiencing. The unyielding pressure made her feel as though she were going to tear apart. She scanned her brain desperately for every one of the numerous pain diversion strategies she had practiced regularly over the last several months. Nothing worked. The pain was too intense; it refused to be ignored.

As Jacob wheeled her up to the front desk, she had long ago determined that the birth plan was out the window. Before the stout woman at the front desk wearing far too much blush could even ask Faith her name, Faith blurted out, "I don't care what you have back there to stick in my ass, but do it now!"

Vanessa, or so her name tag suggested, had evidently been through this before. Not even pausing in her gum chewing, she lifted a thick, wrinkled finger with nail polish as overdone as the blush and said unflinchingly, "Ok, now ma'am. We'll get to that, but I do have to get some information from you first."

Faith shot back impatiently, "But I already pre-registered so that I could go straight to the birthing center."

"Yes, ma'am, but I still need to ask you a few questions."

Faith, exasperated, resigned herself to the futility of further protest and capitulated to the inquiry. When Vanessa asked for her social security number, another wave of contraction came over her, and she was compelled to employ a system of holding up her fingers to provide the requested information.

By the time they were riding up the elevator, sweat was noticeable on her furrowed brow, and she slumped over in the wheelchair like a wet towel hung out to dry. Her arms and legs had begun to swell even further, and her normally vibrant air was depleted, as her face took on a pallid, grayish hue. It was this image of Faith that would predominate Jacob's memory for years to come and consume him: this image of her as an empty, lifeless vessel floating aimlessly along the surface of the sea at midnight.

Jacob was relieved to find Dr. Takasashi waiting for them in the delivery room. She was a small, compact woman whose physical structure mirrored her straightforward demeanor as a physician. Her dark eyes were deeply set, allowing for a penetrating gaze that was generally unpremeditated. Her angled nose and chiseled facial features gave her a hardness that was reinforced by her dispassionate tone of voice.

"Dr. Takasashi, my contractions are about three minutes apart and lasting about ninety seconds," Faith said urgently.

"Well, then, we better get moving, huh?" Dr. Takasashi replied before turning her attention to the fair-skinned, dark-haired nurse who had just entered the room. "Kendra, will you start working on her vitals?"

Sprightly and cheerful, Kendra helped Faith change into her hospital robe and get into a bed that resembled a dentist chair with seemingly endless controls and displays. Faith tried to wave off help, but her effort was as languid as the gesture of her wrist. Jacob, however, refused to leave her side. Once Faith was lying as comfortably as possible, he pulled up a chair beside her and took her hand into his. He emphasized the intertwining fingers by straightening them before curling them all together. At this moment, he wanted to express to her, without words, the way their lives were enmeshed. He wanted her to feel his heartbeat pulsating through his hand and into hers to form a unified, congruous rhythm. He squeezed ever so slightly and looked at her only to find her smiling back at him with a thin ray of light in her eye that suggested an appreciative cognizance of the bond that had developed between them. For a moment, the whole world around them dissolved into nothingness and all that was left was the two of them, the center and composition of their own universe.

And then the entire world around them reemerged and came crashing down upon them.

"Dr. Takasashi, could you come here and look at this?" Kendra asked nervously.

"What is it?" replied Dr. Takasashi.

"Her blood pressure is unusually high, doctor. 180 over 120."

Abruptly, Faith, with the onset of another contraction, began to have a seizure. As her eyes rolled back into her head, and her body began to convulse involuntarily, Jacob instinctually let go of her hand and tried to hold her in an attempt to muffle the eruption that was mounting inside her.

Dr. Takasahi rushed over to Faith and helped Jacob hold her down until the seizure subsided. "Mr. Hartman, we are going to take your wife to the operating room. I am going to need you go out into the waiting room," she said sternly as she pried him away from Faith with a force that was surprising for her diminutive frame. "Kendra, go get some help and let's wheel Mrs. Hartman here down to the O.R. as quickly as possible."

Jacob turned toward her aggressively and said defiantly, "I'm not going anywhere. This is my wife. I want to know what the hell is going on with her."

"Mr. Hartman," said Dr. Takasashi resolutely, as she slid around him to position herself between him and Faith, "I do not have time to argue with you. I believe your wife has developed pre-eclampsia that may have progressed to full blown eclampsia. If this is the case, we have a serious situation on our hands, and I cannot have you in the operating room making things any more difficult and complicated than they already are."

Bewildered and unable to fully assimilate these unforeseen developments, Jacob felt he had no choice but to acquiesce and trust in Dr. Takasashi's professional care. Something in him, however, did not want to leave that room, wanted to run to her and clasp her to him, wrap her in his strong arms and refuse to let go as if that alone could save her. Instead, he backed away mutely like a child hiding from the thunder.

He was able to utter just one thing before he went out the door, "Take good care of her doctor. She's all I have."

Powerless and alone, Jacob sat in the cold, sterile waiting room for what seemed an eternity. He tried to distract himself and curb his thoughts as they spiraled further and further out of control. The thoughts that had plagued him since his father's death, the ones that he had managed to quell just long enough to muster the courage to take this leap of faith and have a child, came roaring back now with a vengeance so severe that while he sat draped over the chair, his body had a palpable nervousness to it. Somehow he knew.

When Dr. Takasashi finally stepped into the hushed silence of the waiting room, Jacob refused to move. He refused to propel himself toward the encroaching darkness. "*Let it come to me,*" he thought, "*I will not stand to greet it.*"

The words themselves he never heard. Oh, he knew the message all right, felt it drain into his soul like arsenic. The words themselves, though, he could not understand. The pressure of the gloom weighed upon his shoulders and sent him involuntarily to his knees. His eyes turned skywards, and his thoughts rose with them. "I trusted you," he began to mumble. "I finally trusted you, and you, you have fucked with everything in my life, given me things, waited for me to love them and then taken them away. Fuck you. That's right, FUCK YOU!"

Dr. Takasashi tried to reassure him. "We did the best we could, Mr. Hartman. There were no signs of pre-eclampsia during her office visit earlier this week. There was no way we could have known until she started having the seizure."

But Jacob still did not hear a word. He had bigger fish to fry; his mind was focused on the loftier implications of the situation. *"You tell people to believe in you, to put their faith in you and that you will provide for them. And this is what you do? This is how you reward faith? Well, I have nothing. You have taken everything from me! Is that a merciful God? Is that a just God? Is that a God that loves his creation? Fuck you!"*

With tears of sadness and anger streaming down his face, he rose to his feet, took a final glance upwards at the bleak and barren ceiling, then looked straight ahead and started walking for the door. He knew what he needed to do. If this was the life he was being offered, well then fuck that. Thank you very much, but he had other plans. Despite the dark thoughts dashing chaotically through his distraught mind, he was somehow just able to digest what Dr. Takasashi said as he neared the exit.

"But Mr. Hartman, your daughter is still alive."

Chapter 8

The Price of a Memory

Jacob would, until his dying day, be able to remember with utter clarity the singular moment he fell in love with Faith Colms. Some moments of his life simply stood out from the rest, leaving an indelible impression. Against the backdrop of an evening sky filled with the empty space of mundane moments and time wasted, these brilliant stars flickered brighter than the rest and filled him with the resounding echo of his own haunted past.

It was New Year's Eve 1993, the beginnings of their lives together. Six months removed from their fateful meeting at a baseball game, they were still in the throes of budding love and mutual infatuation. Both of them, though, felt themselves on the verge of something greater, something more substantial. As they peered over the edge of that cliff together, each waiting anxiously for the other to leap, what they secretly yearned to do was give the other a firm shove in the back.

It would still be several months before they moved in together and still a few more before Jacob would propose while eating wiener-schnitzel in Salzburg. Each of them, however, had begun to cling to fence post moments such as their first New Year's Eve as a couple. They seemed to be the first photos in a scrapbook they would create together.

Jacob thus wanted to mark this New Year's Eve so that when Faith looked back in later years she would be freshly bathed in these same emotions he had for her now. He wanted the memory to transcend time and space and capture this moment for her eternally, much as when Shakespeare penned:

> *So long as men can breathe and eyes can see*
> *So long lives this, and this gives life to Thee.*

So, too, did Jacob want to freeze that moment in time, to immortalize Faith in that which would endure.

Jacob's best friend from work, Grace Kerney, the plump, endearing redhead with a perpetual smile and knack for inspiring the best in others, had, only months before, moved into a two-bedroom apartment between Union Station and the Capitol with their other cohort in crime at Georgetown Catholic, Ms. Paula Conrad. Although the building had been renovated in the last couple of years, and the rent was truly more than they could reasonably afford on teacher salaries, each of them felt a draw that made the cost worthwhile.

Paula appreciated its proximity to the National Mall where she would often run on weekend mornings. She also liked that it was so close to many of Washington's best dance clubs, which she preferred to the trendy, elitist bars of Georgetown or the seedier nightspots of Adams Morgan.

For Grace, though, it was all about the view. Not that their own apartment had one, but on the tenth floor was a fire escape that led to the open rooftop. From here, one could appreciate the elegant display of pomp and circumstance that defined the District of Columbia despite its far darker, ever-present underbelly. This was why Grace had moved here, and she wanted to be a part of it.

In October, when Jacob had devoted a drizzly Saturday afternoon to helping them move, Grace took him up there to celebrate and toast their new apartment over two Smithwicks and, for her, a hurried Marlboro Light.

"I didn't know you smoked," Jacob said to her with surprise.

"Oh, only for special occasions," she said lightly as she flicked the ash over the edge of the building with a jerky motion. "Only if I'm celebrating something or really depressed."

"Huh, nothing in between?" Jacob asked.

"No, I don't want to become an actual smoker, though I do hear it helps you lose weight."

Grace went behind the cylindrical smokestack and retrieved two folded-up lawn chairs she had stashed there even before she and Paula had moved in. She handed one to Jacob, and they sat there drinking beer and talking about new beginnings.

"You should bring that chickie of yours up here. It would make a heck of a romantic date." That was the trait in Grace that Jacob was so drawn to: her endless ability to consider how she could make life better for those around her.

"You know," he said, "I might take you up on that."

It was fortunate, therefore, when he thought back to that discussion shortly after Christmas Day. It came to him in a flash: he saw the image of himself and Grace reposing in lawn chairs and drinking beers, and the entire plan came to him.

Pleased with himself, he ran back inside to call Faith, only to get her answering machine.

"Hi, it's Faith. If you don't leave a message, I can't call you back. It's that simple. Thanks." Beep...

"Ok, I've got a plan for New Year's. I'll meet you at Grace's place around ten-thirty. No need to be formal or dressy, but look as cute and sexy as you want to as long as you're comfortable. Oh, and warm, make sure you dress warm. Layering, lots of layers. I know it's not good for the instant access, but lots of layers. Ok...gotta go...uh...ok, bye."

Looking over the edge of the cliff, he wanted to take that jump with Faith, but that moment would have to wait a little longer.

As Jacob helped her onto the ladder of the fire escape, the first, and probably only, thing she regretted that night was her decision to wear heels.

"It's not like you need them, you know. Unless you derive some sort of masochistic pleasure in accentuating the difference in our heights."

"No, I just look good in them," she replied with sass.

He merely raised his eyebrow dashingly and said, "Agreed."

When Faith poked her head through the door leading to the roof, she was swept away by Jacob's romantic sentiment. He had obviously put some thought into the finer details of his preparation. Atop two warm, cozy blankets were a set of long, white candles surrounded by a veritable feast of succulent, gourmet foods. The thin glow from the candles fell lightly on the cheeses, strawberries, breads, and chocolates. Only then did she notice the warming fondue pot sitting between the two lawn chairs, each adorned with matching blankets and pillows.

"Are you hungry? The fondue pot should be ready," he asked her, a little anxious to get a more definitive reaction.

She gathered herself for a moment and considered her words carefully. "Jacob, I feel so blessed to have you in my life. I'm not sure what brought you to me, but I sure am glad it did." Then she placed her long arms around his neck, leaned over him, and kissed him passionately on the mouth.

When she finally withdrew a few moments later, leaving both of them breathless, Jacob quipped, "Well, if I had known that was going to be your reaction, I would have done this long ago. Besides, you ain't seen nothin' yet." He winked at her and led her over to the lawn chairs while he opened a bottle of French Merlot and poured a glass for each of them.

Faith had never had fondue before, so Jacob, who had prepared a pot of Gouda, showed her how to use the skewers to dip the items into the cheese. He had precisely arranged an assortment of vegetables, breads, and fruits for dipping and encouraged her to try everything. As they reclined in the lawn chairs and ate fondue with a view looking out over the city, they spoke not a word. Instead, Jacob held her hand, giving it a subtle squeeze. Then he dipped a pea pod into the cheese, allowing the strands to drip off of it copiously, and looked into her eyes as he placed it delicately into her mouth.

He made her wait for the chocolate dessert course, however: a course they would never wind up eating. He rinsed the pot and then set it on the burner to warm the chocolate. He quickly checked his watch then grabbed their glasses of wine and led her to the edge of the building.

He took a long, deep swig of wine and asked her, "Do you mind if I read you a poem?"

"Did you write it?" she asked with a trace of stunned disbelief.

"I did."

"I hope it was for me," she said with a deliberately coquettish air.

"It could only be for you."

And then he began...

You are the fireworks
That light up my nighttime sky.
Far above the world that makes up my days,
You transcend all I know
And provide brilliance and hope
Where only darkness used to tread.

I beg and plead to God
That for one brief, shining moment
The blind could see through my eyes,
Could have just an instant
To behold you as I behold you,
For then I know
That they would dwell in darkness no more.

Even Jacob could not have prayed for better timing. As he read the final lines of his poem, the city's magnificent New Year's firework display erupted behind her. With the Capitol in the forefront, the fireworks framed the National Mall. Mesmerized by the visual display before her, the greens and blues and reds as they burst forth from the otherwise vacant sky, Faith did not even notice as Jacob reached down and pressed play on the CD player he had previously loaded with John Coltrane's *A Love Supreme*. The first few notes, soulful and rich, tripped across the horizon and lifted their spirits into the crisp January air. Jacob put his arms around Faith's waist and pulled her closer to him. What she felt, however, was a distinctive shove in the back as she peered out over the edge.

She turned back to look at him and began to weep lightly. As she kissed him and heaved uncontrollably, he could taste her warm, salty tears in his mouth, and they were good. They warmed him and shielded him from the cold chill of the winter evening.

She pushed him back towards the blankets he had laid out and eased him down on top of them. As she came to rest on top of him, she pulled the blanket over them like she were closing the door behind her as she left on a trip from which she never planned to return. She shivered intermittently as she desperately struggled to remove his clothes.

Concerned, he whispered to her, "We don't have to do this. I swear it was not part of the plan. You're obviously freezing."

"Shut up, Jacob. You've done everything perfectly up to this point. Don't ruin it now by talking."

She rode him with a frenzied straining as the fireworks burst out above them and the resounding booms echoed through their chests. She was bent over him entirely so that their bodies were contiguous and symmetrical throughout, even as she lay her head down next to his so their cheeks touched softly. The positioning of her pelvis and the tight, controlled convulsions of her thrusts brought both of them to dimensions previously unknown.

While their sex up to that point had been wonderful from both of their perspectives, they had not yet found the precise rhythm to bring them to mutual orgasm. Tonight, however, Jacob was so attuned to every aspect of Faith's being- her breathing, her heartbeat, her moaning- that he was able to hold himself off with absolute mastery. When they did climax together, he felt as if this brief postponement led him to empty all of himself into her. Somehow all of his anguish and fears, the bitter pains and disappointments, the insecurities and feelings of quiet desperation, all of this left him, and the world around him was left a better place. He had fallen over the edge of the cliff, and Faith was still there to rescue him.

"I love you, Faith Colms. I really do."

"I love you too, Silly. What took you so long to say it?" She nibbled then kissed his ear before settling back into his arms and letting the warm glow of the goodness of the world wash over them.

It was this memory that played itself over and over in Jacob's mind as he drove wildly down Reservoir Road in the couple's 1993 Honda Civic. He had no idea where he was going, but he sure knew what he was going to do, and he wanted to be as far away from that hospital as possible. The memory tortured him, languished there in the darkness beyond the windshield and reasserted itself violently every time he tried to escape it. It was as if the debt collector were there to extract the never-paid price of having had the experience in the first place.

In the stages of grief, Jacob had bypassed denial and gone straight to anger. From the moment Dr. Takasashi had sent him to the waiting room, he had seen Faith's death as a very real possibility. No, denial was pointless in Jacob's world.

He was not, however, asking the typical question of the anger stage: "Why me?" He knew perfectly well why him. He also did not make the typical retort, "It's not fair." He knew well enough by now that life wasn't fair; tonight was simply another lesson in the sinister ways of fate, of Maya, of God. He was tired of being the universe's whipping boy, tired of climbing back onto the platform of the dunk tank just to be plunged back into the chilling waters of fate once again. He was tired, and he was fed up. He was through with it, through with all of it.

Hemingway had been right: life was *nada*. All that made life worth living could and would be snatched away by that thief of time, who lurks outside your window, waiting for when you fall asleep and are unable to safeguard that which is dearest to you. This was the paradox of life. God had invited him to the feast of love then left him like Tantalus reaching out for an elusive illusion that was just beyond his grasp. The pain, the sorrow, the loss of love: Jacob had had enough.

He unconsciously pounded his fist into the dashboard time after time until the knuckles started to wear raw and bleed. He turned the radio off so that he could concentrate on the weight of his thoughts, but he kept drifting back to the image that plagued him with a disquieting consistency. This memory of joy upon a rooftop near the Capitol now besieged him with torment, and he threw his arms up into the air in defiance. Free for a moment to do what it would, the car veered off recklessly before regaining its traction.

Unburdened from the concern of consequence, Jacob took two dramatic right turns and lunged the car onto the George Washington Parkway. He sped along the curving parkway as it wove along the Potomac. The Civic, unaccustomed to such use, recoiled at the demand with a begrudging persistence. It bucked and neighed with the strain. *"Not much further,"* Jacob thought.

As he rapidly approached the hairpin corner to the left with the guardrail that had seen its share of use, Jacob could not escape the sound of a deafening laughter that agonized him and pierced his thoughts. He wanted the moment back, but he knew it would not come, as it flittered away into the air like dust. *"This is what you have reduced me to. Is this what you wanted all along? To see me like this? To see my pain and sorrow like it were just a game for you? Well, I'm done with your bullshit. I will suffer your torment no more."*

He passed the exit for Chain Bridge Road and knew the turn was only a mile away. *"I may not be able to control what happens to others around me, but I can control myself, damn it."* He braced himself and steadied his nerves. The turn was right up ahead. He could just make it out as he strained into the obscurity of the pitch-black night. Pushing the accelerator pedal harder, he convinced himself that he could do this. He needed to do this, needed to end this here and now. There was nothing to believe in anymore.

Then, suddenly, the voice came to him, harkened to him through the eerie silence of the gloom. It called to him like a mother calling her young ones home for dinner after a busy day of play. He did have something to live for. The epiphany sung to him, the melodic voices of an angelic choir:

"But Mr. Hartman, your daughter is still alive."

The awareness gripped him and shook his physical senses awake. Jacob seized on the brakes and attempted to steer dramatically to the left in order to avoid the collision with the guard rail. The Civic, however, had had enough of this mistreatment and buckled under the torque of the exaggerated turn. It flipped into the air, rolling over twice before caroming forcefully into the awaiting guardrail.

Part 2: Redemption
Chapter 1

Dawn

As the morning woke and the dawn spread its fractured beams upon the tussled comforter that had been thrown askew during the long and desperate night, he turned towards the bedroom window and winced as he shielded his eyes from the blinding light of day. He had thought to lower the curtain before going to bed but had failed to do so, and now the sun's piercing brilliance disrupted the few hours of agitated, unsettled sleep he was able to muster in the wee hours of the night just before the dawn. It was only then, during what nurses on the regular overnight shift call "the devil's hour" for its uncanny tendency for producing death, that he was able to get any sleep whatsoever anymore. He rolled over and grasped a pillow over his head in a futile attempt to go back to sleep. The misery of it struck him like the rude awakening from a splash of ice-cold water on the face. He shrugged it off and resolved to rouse himself. He was, after all, still alive.

Before Jacob could get out of bed, however, she pounced on him. Morning had always been her favorite time of day, and she manifested all of that energy into the leap that sent her cascading into his unsuspecting chest. Jacob groaned mightily but then reached up to tickle her sides in retaliation. He pulled her towards his chest which had become leaner and more defined since years gone by. She frolicked with him momentarily but then settled down upon him and snuggled herself back to sleep.

"How do you do this?" Jacob thought. *"Better yet, how do you do this and I don't mind?"* Putting one of the scattered, forest-green throw pillows behind his back, he slowly pulled himself upright and reached for the remote so that he could watch the morning news with the mute button on, as he had become so accustomed to doing. As he did so, Jacob stared down at her and fixated on the one thing he had left in this world.

Her long, straight brown hair nestled over his bare chest and brought him some degree of comfort. Her compact, angular frame pressed into his sides to remind him of her presence, and he breathed in deeply. Her skin, wholesome and florid, felt good to the touch, and he ran his hands down her slender arms in an effort to pacify both of them. Her nose, bothered by one of Samwise's dog hairs, wiggled unconsciously, and he laughed quietly to himself as she lay there unperturbed. And to think this was all nearly taken from him, Aurora, his one remnant of salvation and redemption.

Where would he be now without her? She had rescued him from his vortex of darkness and dragged him to the shores of this deserted island. He clung to her even now as she lay there in his arms clinging to him. Aurora had given him a reason to live when there had been none, and the thread was a tenuous one indeed. So much of who he was, so much of the sanctity of his soul, resided in his eight-year old daughter.

Although the police investigators were never able to conclusively determine that his accident was a suicide attempt, the insinuation was made perfectly clear in their reports. Only Jacob knew that it had been that thought of his daughter that had made him turn the wheel so dramatically at the last second, recasting the head-on collision sure to kill him into a rollover accident that cost him instead numerous surgeries and months of physical therapy but only one lingering medical injury: a subtle but noticeable limp that in truth only gave him difficulty when walking long distances.

"You know this is only going to get better, right?" Grace told him with her implacable smile shortly after Faith's death. She brushed her wispy, red hair from her face as she listened.

"Bullshit, Grace. I don't need you to lie to me for chrissakes. Things are not getting better. My wife is dead, Grace. She's dead, and she's not coming back," he said cruelly as he sat back in his leather chair by the window. The baby slept peacefully upstairs.

"You have friends, you know, people who care about you," she said as she walked behind him and put her strong, wide hand upon his shoulder with a tender sympathy.

"I appreciate that, Grace. I really do," he said as his voice trailed off wistfully.

"And God cares about you. He loves you, Jacob."

Jacob stood up tempestuously and pushed her hand away. "I know you believe that, Grace, but I'm sorry, that is complete and utter bullshit. God cares about no one. You want me to believe that God loves me? My wife is fucking dead, Grace. The one woman I ever loved is gone, and you want me to believe He loves me? He's taken everything I've ever had. I ask you, is that love? Does a God that loves you make you suffer?" With this, Jacob turned and confronted her with a posture that demanded a response, like she was God's ambassador sent to satiate Jacob's blood thirst. He remembered the poor rabbi and minister from after his father's death talking to a child who could not understand, unable to explain the unexplainable.

"Sometimes," she interjected meekly. Her bright eyes were hopeful despite it all.

"Well, that's bullshit, Grace," he snapped back quickly. "He has done nothing but make me miserable, stolen from me everything I have. How is that just? How is that love? What has He done for me? What has He done other than make me suffer?"

Her response, however, was more measured. "He gave you Aurora."

It was this response that Jacob thought about now, years later as his daughter nestled against him and he felt the rhythm of her chest rise and fall with each passing breath. There was a part of him that knew Grace had been correct. He stroked Aurora's hair and reflected on the joy she had brought him.

Still Faith's death continued to haunt him. It consumed him during lonely nights that pecked at his conscious mind like vultures feasting upon the corpse of his happiness and tranquility. With her had gone the hope he had had in the world, the belief that things could be good again. He stared up at the vacant ceiling and wondered how he would face another day and the suffering it would surely bring.

Chapter 2

The Ending of a Curse

Jacob picked up smoking shortly after the accident. While it is generally unusual for someone to pick up the habit so far into their adult years, Jacob had his own reasons for doing so. Though most regular smokers are initiated during their teenage years as a fashionable form of rebellion and sophistication only to struggle for many subsequent years to break the pernicious addiction, Jacob did so with a premeditation that was truly chilling.

While he originally told himself that he wanted to start smoking only to cope with the stress of returning to work, even his conscious mind was capable of seeing through this barely plausible, thinly veiled pretext. What he in fact wanted was a death sentence, a surety of his own demise. He had, on that fateful evening, made an oath to preserve himself as best he could for the well-being of his newborn daughter until she had reached the age of maturity. After that, however, all bets were off. Smoking wouldn't take him during Aurora's adolescence, but it would doubtlessly shorten the life he had come to resent. It may not be today or tomorrow, but here was the inevitable out he was looking for.

Having never smoked previously, taking up the habit in the midst of his adult years took some doing. He asked Grace to teach him how to inhale, to draw the thick, rich smoke into his lungs so that he could feel the nicotine make its way into his bloodstream and race through his veins. His initial forays into smoking, as with most novices, were clumsy and foolish. He would breathe in the black smoke and cough as his fresh, pink lungs rejected what they immediately sensed as foreign and unhealthy. Still, he persevered, and soon he and Grace would be found taking cigarette breaks out on the rooftop of her apartment building or on the balcony of his Georgetown brownstone. It was not long before he had eclipsed Grace, smoking regularly, as much as half a pack a day as compared to her sporadic, covert puffs.

Strangely, Aurora always knew her dad as a smoker. By the time she had grown old enough and wise enough to grasp the situation, he was already a bona fide smoker with an overflowing ashtray on the glass coffee table on the balcony. While he at first tried to keep it from her, he eventually came to forgo the pretense and smoke openly, terming his cigarette breaks, "Daddy's Little Helpers". Aurora knew better.

Aurora hated his smoking, not for the foul odor or secondhand smoke she was forced to consume, but for the damage she knew it was doing to him. She would plead with him to quit, giving him long, informed lectures on the dangers of smoking, but to no avail. The problem, of course, was that Aurora was not aware of what had made him start smoking in the first place. Ironically, all her lectures served to do was reinforce his rationale and determination. The only thing he would say in his defense was, "I know, sweetheart; Daddy really should quit."

How the hell was this *his* daughter? Aurora was an eight-year old who had more composure than Jacob did, a girl who had never known her mother, yet saw and heard her father ache for her each and every day, no matter how hard he tried to hide it from her. Yet somehow here she was this grounded, directed girl with an infinite sense of respect and appreciation for all the beauty the world had to offer.

By the summer of 2004, her nagging for him to quit had become persistent. Aurora would often follow him out onto the balcony that overlooked N Street and hound him for the duration of his cigarette, droning out any minimal pleasure he took from the sensation with her pleas for him to stop. She had certainly inherited her mother's unwavering tenacity, but all her insistence was getting her nowhere.

She had employed every method known to an eight-year old girl. She would set her rigid jaw line and cite statistics she had gleaned from the internet. Other times, she would present him with grisly pictures of old men with endotracheal tubes and tell him that this would be his shared fate unless he agreed to quit. Her most effective method, however, was to dress in the long, pink sundresses that underscored her already slender frame and long brown hair that reminded Jacob of her mother. Kneeling coquettishly before him, she would ask him who was going to give her away at her wedding since he would obviously not be available. "You know, being dead and all." Yes, she had, even in her early years, mastered the art of the reproach.

Though this tactic would induce a pang of remorse, Jacob would do his best to turn away and ask sarcastically, "So are you at least going to let me pack a bag the next time you send me on a guilt trip like that?" Aurora began to realize that she needed to up the ante.

Her unanticipated opportunity came when her father's beloved Red Sox found themselves down three games to none in the American League Championship Series in October of 2004. Even at the age of eight, Aurora had long been ingrained with the ethos of the Boston Red Sox fan, and her father's persistent pessimism since the Sox's routing at the hands of the rival Yankees in game three had become unbearable. Aurora had lost her patience for her father's cynicism. Was it not Jacob who had taught her that faith meant believing that the Red Sox would somehow win no matter what the odds? Was it not he who had taught her to cheer right up until the end, such as last year when Aaron Boone had ended the Red Sox's season with a home run off of Tim Wakefield in the bottom of the eleventh inning in game seven of that playoff series? Well, where was that faith now?

Though Jacob had been letting her stay up for the weekend playoff games, Aurora had not needed to wait up for the final of game three. After back-to-back doubles by Bernie

Williams and Jorge Posada pushed the Yankees' lead to an insurmountable 17-6, Aurora accepted the fact that the Red Sox would somehow need to rally from a three game deficit in the series if they were to advance to the World Series this year.

"It's never been done before, you know. Never in the history of baseball. Never. No one has ever come back from a three to nothing hole to win the series," Jacob said as she headed upstairs to bed of her own volition.

"I know, dad," she replied resignedly. "Are you going to come tuck me in or what? I need to get some sleep for tomorrow." Aurora must have been the only third grader at Hyde-Addison Elementary School who had the responsibility to govern her own sleep patterns. She looked at him unflinchingly over the thin wood railing.

Jacob eyed her with sympathy. He knew the pain of believing and wanted to spare her that stinging disappointment. "Oh, sweetheart, you can't really believe that. Even if they win tomorrow night, they're not coming back in the series. This is the Yankees we are talking about. You know, Mariano Rivera, Derek Jeter, Bernie Williams. This team doesn't choke, kiddo. And you're talking about doing what no other team has ever done. It isn't going to happen."

"They're winning this series, Dad. Now will you please come tuck me into bed?" Something in her tone reminded him of her mother's defiance and determination.

Suddenly, it came to her, and she suckered him in. "Do you really think the Red Sox are done, Dad?"

"I'm afraid so, sweetheart," he said as he stroked her fine brown hair.

Aurora's thin lips curled into a cunning smile as she stared him straight in the eyes. "How about we make a little wager then?"

As he pulled the soft pink comforter down over her, he hesitated and asked nervously, "What do you have in mind?" Jacob knew his daughter well.

"If the Red Sox come back to win the series, you quit smoking." It was a risk, but a risk she had to take.

In the cool darkness, just beyond any light that would have revealed the look upon his face, Jacob smiled assuredly to himself. "*Gosh, she's clever,*" he thought. "*Clever and persistent.*" What had him smiling, however, beyond his appreciation for his daughter's guile was her sense of character. Most kids would be asking for the latest and greatest gaming system or a new cell phone; what Aurora wanted was for him to be healthy. "What's in it for me when they lose?"

"I'll never bring it up again. Ever."

"You promise?"

"I promise."

"All right, Aurora, you have yourself a deal, but no welching." He tucked her into bed and kissed her lightly upon the forehead.

"No welching, I promise," she said as he walked across the room and stood in the dimly-lit threshold of the doorway. Jacob knew Aurora meant every word she said, in this case as always. She started to roll over to go to sleep but then turned towards him abruptly. "By the way," she went on, "Auntie Elmo told me that you need to stop whining about the Red Sox anyway. She says that you should be happy that your Red Sox are even in the playoffs since her Cubs blew the wild card this year, and they haven't won a World Series since 1908. She says the Sox aren't the only ones that are cursed, you know. Don't you remember that poor guy that reached over for the foul ball last year?"

"Auntie Elmo" was what Aurora had been calling Grace ever since she was two and uttering her first words. With her striking red hair and rosy complexion, Grace bore enough of a resemblance to the ubiquitous Sesame Street character that Aurora latched onto it immediately. It was, however, when Grace encouraged the comparison by performing a spot-on impersonation of the high-pitched childhood icon that the association took for good. Even well into her teenage years, when most adolescents would have been too embarrassed to refer to anyone else with such juvenile affection, Aurora would call Grace by this endearing term and even ask her to do the voice, if only for a few quick lines.

"You need to stop talking to Grace so much," Jacob said meekly. "Besides their curse is based on some nutball with a freaking goat for crying out loud. A goat! Who the hell brings a goat to a baseball game anyway?"

"You shouldn't swear, Dad," Aurora said with the sanctimonious air only an eight year old can achieve.

"'Hell' is not a swear word," Jacob responded defensively.

"Auntie Elmo says it is."

"I told you to stop talking to her so much."

"She's your best friend. She's the only real babysitter I have."

"Well, just don't listen to what she tells you."

"She said you'd say that."

Jacob preferred watching the playoff games at the Rhino Bar and Pumphouse, a couple of blocks away on M Street in the heart of Georgetown. The Rhino was your typical sports bar with a treasure trove of memorabilia and signed photographs from various athletes that hung on the darkly painted walls.

The Rhino had an openly dedicated allegiance to the Red Sox, even displaying a Red Sox banner above the bar's own signage. As such, the clientele on game nights was predominantly Red Sox fans who found a home amongst their brethren. Jacob doubted he could find such a constituency even in his native Connecticut and welcomed the opportunity to watch the games with a decisively partisan crowd.

Grace and Paula had agreed to meet them at Jacob's place before heading over to watch the game. By the time they arrived, Aurora was already fully adorned in Red Sox regalia, including her favorite David Ortiz jersey and the kelly green cap Jacob had bought her when they made their annual pilgrimage to Fenway with Tobin earlier that year. Using the hair tie she customarily placed in her right jeans pocket, Aurora had pulled her hair into a ponytail and tethered it through the cap which she wore with a prominent upward tilt that made it difficult to see the red "B" above the brim.

"Are you excited for the game?" Grace asked Aurora as the latter opened the door and embraced her enthusiastically.

"Sure am!" Aurora beamed.

"Good for you," Grace said as she rubbed Aurora's hat for good luck.

Jacob, hearing their arrival, hurried down the stairs as he donned his dark blue windbreaker. "Well, I'm glad to see that you've cheered up now that Paula and Grace are here. Now when are you going to start speaking to your father?"

"As soon as you start being positive. Can you promise not to say anything negative about the Sox?"

"I'll try. How about that? I'll try."

"Didn't you ever hear that if you don't have anything nice you shouldn't say anything at all?"

"*Funny how the simplest adage of childhood can give proper context to adult situations that seem far more complex,*" Jacob thought to himself.

Then Aurora added, "And try to have fun. You could actually enjoy yourself, you know."

"Thanks sweetheart," he said with genuine appreciation. "How could I not have fun with my daughter, win or lose? I just don't want you to be disappointed when they lose, be that tonight or whenever."

Aurora cocked her head and said with emphasis, "Dad, how could I be any more disappointed than you already are right now?"

"She's got you there, Jacob," added Paula as she hiked her designer purse further up onto her arm. While Grace was wearing a Cubs cap with her typical jeans and t-shirt, Paula looked as if she were ready to go out dancing. Her tight-fitting satin blouse accentuated her fairly large breasts, while her stiletto heels raised her to an almost even height with Jacob.

"All right, you three, let's get down to the Rhino before they give away our table."

Though there had been a time when Jacob had considered leaving the city for the suburbs of Virginia, maybe even packing up and moving out West, anything to get away from the ghosts that lingered around him and haunted his dreams, he finally submitted to them and realized that they would follow him wherever he went. They did not need the physical presence of the home they had shared together to arouse the forlorn aching of his soul.

"*How could I ever leave here?*" he thought as they walked along the tree-lined streets of Georgetown. This part of the city was so vibrant with its boutique shops and restaurants. The traditional brick facades warmed him like a fire glowing in the hearth, and the stately yet varied architecture provided him a sense of grounding and rationality. Somehow he had come to feel at home here, and he knew running was not the answer.

As they walked through the front door of the Rhino and past the initial throngs of people that had congregated near the front in hopes of getting seated, they were greeted warmly by Angie, whose tight, curly blond hair hung just over her shoulders. Her petite, white t-shirt exposed a tiny, compact frame with sinewy muscles formed from a commitment to a daily exercise regimen and a good dose of manual labor.

"Got your table, right in the back here, Jacob," she shouted from across the room, as she waited for them to make their way over. Angie was not one to mind getting a little dirty, and her white shirt and faded blue jeans were both streaked with the grease of chicken wings and French fries while the cloth rag that hung at her waist reeked of one too many beer spills.

As they approached, Angie reached around the back of a patron seated at the bar in order to draw Aurora in for a hug. She kneeled down to place herself directly at Aurora's height, though being fairly short herself, she did not have to drop that far. "And how is my favorite little Red Sox fan doing tonight?"

Aurora eagerly hugged her back. She raised her small voice to be heard over the crowd but ended up with an unregulated shout that could be heard in the far back, "Just great! Psyched to watch my Sox finally come back and win one!"

Angie nodded simultaneously then raised her own voice to comply with Aurora's. "You gotta start somewhere, right? I like your attitude, sister! Some chicken fingers and a strawberry shake for you, I suppose?"

"You got it!"

Angie raised herself back up, put her arm on her hip, and addressed herself to Paula, Grace, and Jacob. "And what can I get started for you folks tonight?"

"I'll have a white Russian," said Paula first as she took off her coat and started wandering towards the vacant table with Aurora.

"I'll take a seven and seven," said Jacob.

Angie glanced at him with a flirtatious smile. "Starting on the hard stuff tonight, are we Jacob? What, are you trying to drown out your sorrows before the Sox even have a chance to play?" Her Boston accent was somehow softer, less guttural than most. Though he failed to respond with anything other than a noncommittal nod of the head, a rare gleam of felicity crossed Jacob's face.

"What do you have on tap?" inquired Grace.

"Well, let's see. We have Budweiser, Bud Light, Coors, Coors Light, Guinness, Rolling Rock..."

"Whoa, I'll stop ya right there," interceded Grace. "I'll take a Guinness."

"Coming right up, guys." Angie walked away, and the rosy good cheer of Jacob's aspect subsided. Though any self-conscious awareness of this completely eluded Jacob, it did not evade Grace's detection.

She sidled up next to Jacob and said discreetly into his ear, "She's cute. When did she start working here?"

Jacob alertly picked up on Grace's suggestion and became immediately defensive. It was apparent that he was going out of his way to play it off. "Sometime around the end of the summer, I think. Not really sure." Jacob sat down in one of the open chairs between Aurora and Paula, effectively cutting off that avenue of discussion.

"Perhaps you should find out," Grace said as she nodded meaningfully in his direction and took a seat herself. The grin on her face with the tongue rolling through it let him know that she considered his tactical positioning a detour rather than a dead end to the topic.

Paula was quizzing Aurora on her state capitols from across the table. Aurora generally had these down but often struggled with California, so Paula was sure to give it to her more frequently than the others. "Los Angeles should be the capitol of California, not Sacramento," Aurora would opine as a method of self-defense for excusing her own error. "Los Angeles has almost ten million people; no one lives in Sacramento."

Angie brought the round of drinks to the table and dispersed them to their proper owners. Giving Grace her Guinness, she leaned into the table but spoke mostly to Grace, "Right on with the Guinness. Not enough women drink real beer these days. I have a soft spot in my heart for the Cubbies, by the way."

"Really? Why?"

"Oh, my mom's family is all from Chicago, and my Grandpa Martin is a huge Cubs fan."

"I like him already."

"He's a good man," Angie said as she began to look around her. "All right, can I get you guys anything else before first pitch? Aurora, sweetheart, your chicken fingers will be right out. I told them to hold off on the milkshake until after you were done with those."

When Angie wandered off this time, Grace turned to Jacob and asked him if he wanted to have a smoke before first pitch. Both of them hated smoking indoors or in front of Aurora, so they slid outside while Paula and Aurora went back to their quizzing.

"So what the heck is up with you and Angie," Grace wasted no time in asking as they stepped outside and she lit her own cigarette before passing the lighter onto Jacob.

"Nothing, but what the hell is up with you telling my daughter that 'hell' is a swear word?" Jacob uttered as he raised his shoulder and turned from the wind in order to light his smoke.

"Because it *is* a swear word, Jacob. God doesn't like you saying it."

Jacob wheeled back around and said defiantly, "I don't give a crap what God does or doesn't like. And how the hell do you profess to know what God does or doesn't like?"

Grace had learned to endure these rages; she knew where they stemmed from and empathized. She wanted to touch his pain. "Because I listen to him, Jacob."

"Oh, here we go with that bullshit. All right, just stop telling Aurora that 'hell' is a swear word."

"I'm sorry. I didn't mean to usurp your parental role."

"I know you didn't but you gotta stop with the God crap around her."

"Fair enough," she agreed without much conviction. "So what's the deal with Angie?"

"There is no deal with Angie," Jacob said soberly. "I'm not dating, Grace. I'm sure she's a great girl, but I'm not ready for that, not yet."

Grace leaned in and hugged him affectionately, "But Jacob, it's been eight years. Don't you think it's time for you to move on?"

"I understand what you're trying to do for me, Grace; I really do. But 'move on'? Really, just 'move on'?" He sounded incredulous now. "No, I'm sorry; I'm not ready to just 'move on'. I gave my heart to love once. I am not capable of making that leap of faith again."

"That's no way to live your life, Jacob." Grace had a way of making her words ring with the empathetic echoing of great sorrow, like the cries of sailors that meet the cold and brutal seas.

"I have no choice."

"Of course you do," she said.

"I don't believe it anymore, Grace. The Buddhists are right: Desire is suffering. And I, for one, am done with the suffering. For chrissakes, I think I need that drink." He put out his cigarette and took off his windbreaker, but the odor of smoke clung to it like ticks on an unsuspecting host. He waited for Grace to do the same and then made his way back inside.

Before Jacob could put his coat down around his seat, Aurora spun away from Paula and asked like a suspicious parent, "You two were out smoking again, weren't you?"

"I'm sorry, kiddo," Jacob said, dropping his eyes to avert them from her judgment.

Disgruntled with that response, she turned to Grace. "You know, my dad is going to have to quit after the Red Sox win the ALCS."

"How so?" Grace asked.

"We made a bet. If the Sox win, he has to quit smoking."

Grace shot a cautionary glance towards Jacob who merely shrugged off the possibility of the occurrence with a dismissive shake of his head. "And what if they lose?"

"I promise to never mention it again."

Grace knew the prospects, but she looked at her and nodded affirmatively. "You go girl! Let's go Red Sox!" And with that, Grace turned to the rest of the crowd and bellowed forcefully, "You hear that, Rhino? Let's go Red Sox!"

Everyone cheered and raised their glass, but Grace was not through. She climbed up onto her chair and shouted, "I can't hear you, Rhino!" Then she turned to the crowd, put her hands to her mouth, and sing-songed in the traditional ballpark chant, "Let's-go Red-Sox!" accompanied by the mandatory stomping to that ritualistic rhythm: Ta-Ta-te-te-Ta. Soon the stomping and cheering had grown to a fever pitch, and the walls reverberated with a holy echo that seemed to have arisen from the peanut shells and ashes that lined the floor of the bar. Grace, meanwhile, merely sat down to soak in what she had started.

"You know, Grace, you really are quite loud when you want to be," Jacob yelled over the din of the raucous crowd.

"Well," Grace shouted back, "the way I figure it is this: God gave me this voice. I might as well give it right back to him, good and loud!"

Derek Lowe meanwhile was in the midst of pitching a 1-2-3 first inning, exactly what the Sox needed after the previous night's drubbing at the hands of the Yankees. Aurora punched her dad in the arm and asked him, "Did you see that? Lowe just sat 'em right down."

"All right, it's the first inning now. Don't get ahead of yourself."

By the time Angie made her way back, it was still scoreless in the second inning. "Another round of drinks for you guys?" Getting a general affirmative from the table, she started gathering the empty glasses to bring back to the kitchen. Then she leaned down to Aurora and caressed her back while she asked her, "You ready for that milkshake yet?"

"Heck, yeah!"

"How are the Sox doin'?"

"It's scoreless in the second. Lowe's pitching well. Haven't you been watching the game?"

"Too busy. I usually tape it and watch it at home."

Mark Bellhorn struck out swinging to end the second inning, and the broadcast went to a commercial, allowing Grace to divert her attention back to Angie right before she proceeded back to the kitchen. "So Angie, are you from Boston?"

Angie stood up to answer Grace. "Yeah, just moved here at the end of the summer."

"What brought you to the city of broken political dreams?"

"I started nursing school at Georgetown in the Fall."

"Good for you."

"Yeah, I know the owners here, Terry and Mike; they're my dad's cousins, so they gave me a job to get me through school."

"Right on." Grace then peered over at Jacob to be sure he was listening. Seeing that he was, she proceeded with a bit more volume. "So do you have a boyfriend? You know, just in case anyone I knew was interested."

Jacob glared at her but said nothing. He looked pleadingly at Angie, but she sent him a look that reassured him. "Actually, I do. He's in his second year of law school at George Washington. We met when we were in college but only started dating a couple of years ago. When he got into law school down here, I started looking into nursing schools around the city. That's sort of how I ended up in D.C."

"That's a pretty cool story," Grace responded with no noted disruption but a raising of her glass. "Cheers to having another great girl in the city, baby!"

Angie gestured her appreciation and headed off to get their drinks.

"Thanks for the inquisition, Grace," Jacob said, still embarrassed.

"Oh, don't get your panties in a bunch. I was just asking her about herself. Ok?"

Game four was to become yet another indelible memory in the timeless, storied lore of the bitter Red Sox-Yankees rivalry. Despite surrendering a jarring, two-run homer to Gary Sheffield in the third, Derek Lowe pitched five strong innings to keep the Red Sox in the game. Still, trailing by two in the bottom of the fifth, the Sox got clutch, two-out hits from Orlando Cabrera and David "Big Papi" Ortiz to go ahead 3-2. The lead, however, was short-lived. In the top half of the sixth, the Yankees responded with two runs of their own to go back in front 4-3. And so the game remained until the bottom of the ninth.

It was at this point that Angie came back to ask if they all wanted another round.

"I could go for another milkshake," Aurora said without looking over at her father.

"No, Aurora. That's enough ice cream for one night. Plus, it's late; we really should get going. We both have school tomorrow."

"But we have to watch the Red Sox comeback," she pleaded.

"They're playing 'Enter Sandman' in New York right now. That's Mariano Rivera, kiddo. That sound you hear is the swoosh of the door closing." Jacob wanted to come off as jovial and light-hearted, but sounded harsh instead.

Aurora, however, was not to be deterred in her belief. "But it's not closed yet, and the Sox are about to put their foot in the door." She looked over at Grace who returned her glance with approval.

"All right," he said, looking back to Angie and then to Grace and Paula. "One more round for me. You guys?"

Grace added, "I'm in, but I want a cigarette before the game is back on." She grabbed her coat and motioned for Jacob to follow her.

Paula relaxed her chin onto her wrist and slid forward in her chair. "Well, I guess I'm taking a taxi home anyway. Sure, I'll have one more." She pivoted back towards Aurora, "So what's the capitol of Alaska?"

"Oh, that's an easy one..."

"That's quite a kid you got there, Jacob."

"I know."

"She's going to be a handful. Simply wonderful, but a handful."

"I know. What's a poor father to do? Can I stunt her mental growth somehow?"

"No proven methods yet." The smoke curled away from her lips and wafted off into the thick, moist city air while the smell of garbage bags piled up in the alleyway drifted towards them. She was chilly and pulled her arms in tight around herself as she shuffled back and forth to stay warm. "So are you really going to quit smoking if the Sox win the series?"

"That's not going to happen."

"But if it does?"

"Well, yeah, of course I would. How could I not?"

"Good luck with that one." Grace took one last solid drag, flicked her cigarette down on the ground, stomped it out with her right loafer, and walked back inside.

By the time Jacob and Grace returned to their seats, Kevin Millar had already led off the inning with a walk from the indomitable Mariano Rivera. Dave Roberts, the rarely-used utility outfielder pinch-running for Millar, had then promptly stolen second base. Third baseman Bill Mueller was at bat.

"You gotta be kidding me!" Jacob exclaimed as he glanced up at the big screen television and lowered himself into his seat. Grace looked over at him and laughed her hearty, throaty laugh that never failed to add to the general merriment.

Aurora poked him again in his arm, which was slowly becoming numb from the repeated jabs. "I told you, Dad. I told you. They're coming back!"

When Bill Mueller took Rivera's first pitch, his infamous cutter, into center field and Dave Roberts slid under the tag for the game-tying run, Aurora erupted out of her seat and performed a victory lap around the table, high-fiving anyone who would return the gesture, strangers and friends alike. When she got to where Grace was sitting, Grace jumped up and joined her as if Aurora had tagged her in a game of duck-duck-goose. Jacob hoisted Aurora high into the air and twirled her around. The pessimism left him, and for a delectably precious moment, he allowed the intoxicating swells of elation to overtake him.

Putting her down, Jacob peered at his watch and could hardly believe it was nearly midnight. *"How does she still have this much energy,"* he thought to himself. She was going to need it. The game was to remain tied for another hour of tightly contested, tense baseball where each team had their opportunities but could not plate a run. When the Red Sox came to bat in the bottom of the twelfth inning, it was already one in the morning.

"Aurora, I'm sorry, but whether the Red Sox score in this inning or not, we have to leave after this. You have school tomorrow, and they're going to call Child Services on me if they see you in here at closing time."

"All right, Dad," she acquiesced without much resistance. Her physical need for sleep, though having lost the battle up to this point, was beginning to win the war with her hyped emotional state. That, and the milkshake high had worn off. She was slumped forward in her chair, and her head hung heavily in her two palms like a decorative egg in its stand. Paula was rubbing her back unconsciously, and Aurora quietly absorbed the nurturing pressure.

All it took to rouse her, however, was a leadoff single from Manny Ramirez. She craned her head forward, clapped her hands together forcefully, and projected loudly, "See now, that's what we needed. Ok guys, here comes, Big Papi."

Since his signing with the Red Sox in 2003, David "Big Papi" Ortiz had become a definitive fan favorite known for having a flair for the dramatic, especially in clutch situations. A giant hulk of a man with a jovial, good-natured smile, he had quickly become Aurora's favorite player. She clutched at her jersey and said in a voice that was now barely audible, "You're going to do this Papi. We need this."

Jacob wanted it so badly for her. He had waited all of his life to see the Red Sox win a World Series, but now he wanted this for her more than he ever could have wanted it for himself. He picked her up and stood her on the chair in front of him, clasping his arms together in front of her. His upper arms and shoulders squeezed her firmly. He started chanting and stomping with her,

"Let's go Papi!" Ta-Ta-te-te-Ta.

It was when Grace chimed in, however, that the entire bar came to life. No one remained seated. They rose to their feet and stomped in a unison that was deafening. "C'mon Rhino, I want to hear you now! Let's Go Papi!" Ta-Ta-Te-Te-Ta. "Let's go Papi!" Ta-Ta-Te-Te-Ta. It reminded Jacob of ancient warriors preparing to go off to battle. The cause was just and their purpose true. For once, just once, in the otherwise cruel and bleak world of the Boston Red Sox fan, they wanted good to prevail, for fortune to shine down on them, and it was as if they felt that they could make it come true through their collective will and belief.

When Big Papi then launched the offering from Paul Quantrill into the star-filled Boston night to end the game, it felt as if the heavens themselves had opened up to answer their call. Jacob knew that the divine could not take sides in a sporting contest. There are always two sides to listen to. There were dreams broken and prayers unanswered, equally heartfelt and worthy, on that fateful home run as well. Even the divine cannot remedy that inherent dilemma. If there is to be a winner, there must also be a loser. The divine cannot answer the prayers of all and make both happy. In bestowing glory and jubilation, it must inflict sorrow. But perhaps, Jacob thought briefly to himself, it can provide hope and joy when one needs them most. And oh, did the Red Sox fan base ever need this.

It was a role reversal of sorts. In a universe where evil, as personified fittingly in the hated New York Yankees, always seemed to prevail, here was a beacon of hope, a shining instance that there is goodness and equity in the world. As Aurora leapt into her father's outstretched arms, and a bar full of people convulsed into an infused breath of rapture, contentment, and relief, the universe seemed to be looking down on them, letting them know that their long-endured suffering would finally be rewarded.

Aurora knew then and there that this was only the beginning, that this moment merely signaled the epic transformation that had occurred, a shift in the karmic implications of the universe. Though her father would have his doubts as they played out the remainder of the series over the next three nights, Aurora's belief never wavered. She knew that Big Papi's towering home run had more far-reaching significance: the fates had been reversed, the curse had been broken, and the baseball gods had finally seen fit to deem that Jacob, Aurora, and the rest of the Red Sox faithful had suffered enough.

The Red Sox would become the first team in the long annals of baseball history to come back to win a seven games series after losing the first three, but somehow an eight-year old girl in Georgetown had known it would happen all along. On the morning after the series ended, she awoke to find a bat and ball lying on the bed beside her. Though she had no idea who Fred Lynn was, her father's note on the otherwise nondescript ball she had seen on her father's mantle but never heard him speak a word about said everything she needed to know, "You're a real Red Sox fan now."

Admittedly, Jacob was moody and disgruntled for most of the next week as he watched the Red Sox sweep the St. Louis Cardinals in four games to win their first World Series in eighty-six long years. Although it was a sweet realization of a dream he had doubted might ever come true, he was, after all, in the midst of breaking his physical addiction to nicotine. Quitting smoking was bound to make him at least a little irritable in the process.

Still, Jacob appreciated what Aurora had done for him. She had given him a reason to stop smoking, as well as resurrecting his belief in his beloved Red Sox. They watched all of the World Series games at the Rhino, and Angie would bring him his own milkshake to take a bit of the sting off when Grace would go have her smoke breaks alone.

"I'm not an eight-year old girl, you know," he would call after Angie as she walked back into the kitchen and swiped her arm out at him in defiance without looking back. "I don't need to be placated with a milkshake for chrissakes."

That would turn her around. "Yes, you do."

Aurora, seizing her opportunity, would then ask, "Sweet, can I have some of yours then?"

"No, it doesn't mean that." Aurora though, already knew how to implement the "plead to daddy" eyes. Resistance was futile. "All right, but just some of it, and I want half the whip cream this time.

Chapter 3

The Piano Reawakens

The piano had sat there for years vacant and mute. Its yearning for skilled hands to grace its keys must have been palpable. The cherry red veneer remained intact, and the luster that Jacob had brought out in the piano still shone as brilliantly as the day he had shown it to Faith for the first time. Not a soul, though, knew whether or not it had maintained its musical integrity. Since Faith's death, it had remained silent, like a nightingale robbed of its vocal chords in the midst of Spring.

For Jacob, the song had become bittersweet, a Siren's calling to elusive memories that dashed him upon the craggy rocks of his present. It beckoned him to a place he could no longer go, so when Aurora announced in March of 2008 that she wanted to start piano lessons with Uncle Charles, Jacob did not know how to respond.

"Are you sure that you want pick up the piano, Aurora? It's quite a time commitment, you know."

194

"I know, Dad, but don't you think I should learn to play an instrument? Studies suggest that it strengthens your mind." Aurora, in her typical fashion, had done her homework before going into this discussion; she never came into a battleground unarmed.

"But are you sure you want to learn to play piano? Paula has an extra guitar you could borrow. Some of the girls at school take lessons from a guy who lives over on P Street." He knew he was overmatched and was desperately fishing for an out.

Aurora had deliberately blindsided him, rendering him incapable of developing a measured response. "Uncle Charles says Mom had a true gift, a real knack for the piano. He says that I owe it to myself to see if she passed that gift on to me."

"But do you really think Uncle Charles has the time to be giving you regular lessons at this point? He does travel quite a bit."

Aurora perceived the slight tremor this discussion had invoked in her father. She felt for him and would have willingly relented, but she knew this was one of those demons he needed to confront. They had been poking their heads out from under the bed for some time now, and Jacob's strategy of burying his head in the sand was hardly proving effective in confronting them.

"Uncle Charles told me he could give me lessons after school any two days of the week."

Jacob was mute. There was no out. An uncomfortable, expectant silence hung in the air like a chord waiting to be played. Finally, unable to bear it any longer, Aurora asked, "Well, Dad, what do you say? It won't cost you anything. Can I start taking lessons?"

Unable to bring himself to sharing with Aurora the gnawing agony that he knew hearing her play would inflict upon him, he capitulated. He had been bested by a tactically superior opponent, and all that he could do now was surrender and negotiate acceptable terms for a settlement.

"Ok, but I can't be here while you play. You'll have to set up definitive, regular times for lessons and practice, and I will make arrangements to be out of the house. You do understand, right dear?" He spoke with a subdued tone, unable to look directly at her as he did so.

"Not exactly," she admitted as she lowered her own voice to match his, "but I can agree to that. Don't you think you'd want to hear me play at some point, though?"

He knew he wanted to but doubted that he could bear it.

For two years, Jacob never heard his daughter play. It was all he could do to check in with Uncle Charles and see how she was progressing.

"She's getting quite good, Jacob," Uncle Charles noted as Jacob returned home from school one afternoon in January of 2010.

"I'm glad to hear it," Jacob responded dispassionately as he sunk into his leather chair with an apple and a freshly poured glass of orange juice. He was exhausted from a long day of dealing with teenage angst and did not possess the energy for coping with his past.

Uncle Charles, unconscious of Jacob's attitude, walked into the kitchen and helped himself to one of the Diet 7-Ups that had been placed there solely for his benefit. From the other room, Jacob could barely hear Uncle Charles as he continued. "She's got her mother's gift. Those long fingers of hers are a blessing, and she sight reads like no other student I have ever had. Her melodies are truly rhapsodic. I know you've avoided hearing her play, but if she hasn't told you, she has a recital this Friday night. You really should try to make it, my boy." He strode back into the sitting room and placed his hand onto Jacob's shoulder.

"Now, Uncle Charles, you know I can't do that. I appreciate all you are doing for her, and I'm happy to know that she has taken to the instrument so naturally, but hearing her play would just bring back too many memories. I don't think I could take it."

Before continuing, Uncle Charles glanced upstairs to be sure that Aurora was not eavesdropping on their conversation from the upper hallway. "My boy, you're going to have to confront the past someday. It's been fourteen years, Jacob."

Jacob's tone remained elusive. "Not now, Uncle Charles. Not yet."

Uncle Charles sipped through his straw and eyed Jacob with sympathy. He lent his aging weight more heavily onto his cane. This was not a battle he could fight alone. He needed reinforcements. "Well, maybe someday. Someday you'll be ready to hear her play. I know she wants to play for you more than anything else."

On that Thursday following the recital that Jacob never attended, he walked home blithely through one of the heavier snowfalls of the year, suspecting nothing. Despite the significant snowfall, the winds remained silent, and so the snow fell in a heavy, consistent downpour onto the cobblestone sidewalks. It deepened steadily all around him, and his boots carved a solitary path beneath him, one not likely to be followed for some time to come. With others locked in their homes to remain safe and warm from the storm all around them, there was a hushed, muted quiet that fell upon the city.

Jacob relished such moments. There was a tranquility in the empty chaos that soothed him and brought him back inside himself. This was the time when the barren elm and birch trees, stripped of their leaves for winter, seemed to come back to life, if only for a brief respite from their long dormant state, and it was in these moments that they seemed beautiful to him once again, as if the snowflakes were their yet unopened blossoms of Spring. He stared above him into the torrent of snow that descended upon him and marveled at each wet, weighty flake. They landed on his face and melted immediately, and he licked their moist freshness into his mouth to savor them.

He pushed onwards with an ironic buoyancy to his steps. He felt alive and remembered back to the last time he had felt such a yearning to live, to the day when Faith had urged him down a sledding hill just blocks from where he stood. He could taste that memory now with each snowflake he ingested, but like the snowflakes, the memories provided no sustenance. They faded on his tongue with little impression, leaving him discomforted and wanting more, wanting something he could not have. He felt a longing for something that would nourish his aching soul. His memories brought him joy, but there was a price to pay. Fleeting and ephemeral, they reminded him that he was touching but a dream, a moment that would not return. *"Will I ever want to live like that again?"* he thought to himself. *"Will I ever find the courage?"*

He steadied himself as he removed his well-worn leather gloves and fumbled for the house keys to the brownstone. His hands shook from the cold as he struggled to insert the key into the lock. It was what lay behind the door, however, that would shake him for hours afterwards.

He entered to find nearly every member of his friends and family gathered in the sitting room. Uncle Charles, Grace, Paula, Gary, Aurora- they were all there. Even Tobin and Grandma Tess had made the trip down from New England. At first, he thought that it must be a surprise celebration of some sort, but he quickly remembered that his fortieth birthday had been nearly three years before. "*What the hell are they up to,*" he thought, becoming suspicious.

"Well, howdy everyone. Why are all of you here?"

Grace stepped forward first. "We want to talk to you, Jacob."

Everyone was standing except for Grandma Tess who had firmly implanted herself in his leather chair, preventing him even that safe haven of escape. Uncle Charles approached him and placed his thick, now bent paw upon his upper arm and squeezed tightly, as if resolved not to let go. "We're worried about you, my boy. All of us are." With this, he made a sweeping gesture with his other hand towards all of Jacob's other assembled loved ones. "That's why we're here today, because we care about you."

Jacob instinctively took a step back. "Oh my God! Is this a fucking intervention? Is that what this is? A fucking intervention?" He was angry, insulted.

Gary, always discomforted by such confrontations, tried to lighten the mood with his customary humor. "I'm afraid so, Jacob. We're not all here to cure me of my penis addiction. We all know that would be a lost cause. They'd have to give me methadone or some shit like that just to break me off the physical cravings."

Jacob's anger, however, only intensified. He pointed at Grace and then to Gary. "Besides, aren't you two supposed to hate each other?"

"What the hell does that mean," asked Gary incredulously. "We only know each other through you."

"Oh for chrissakes, she's a damn Catholic, and you're a flaming homo!"

Grace simply looked over at Gary and said smugly, "Oh, are you gay? I hadn't noticed. My 'gaydar' must be malfunctioning."

Gary returned Grace's glance with a wink and curtseyed before returning his attention to Jacob. "You need to go out and live life, Jacob. You need to get laid. For crying out loud, you haven't sex in fourteen years! Fourteen years! If I hadn't had sex in fourteen years, they'd have to put me in an insane asylum, and half of Washington, DC would be sex-deprived."

"Is that what this is all about? You want me to get laid for chrissakes?"

Uncle Charles attempted to deflect the focus back to the real issue. "No, Jacob, we want you to go out and live your life again. We want to help you get over the past, to let you know that it's ok for you to be happy again. You have suffered enough, my boy."

Tobin then said with a weight that Jacob had only heard him use a few times before, "You have to be willing to open your heart again. You have to be willing to take that risk, to expose yourself to suffering so that you can feel joy again. You're a shell of yourself right now, a shell of the great guy I have known and loved since we were little kids."

Jacob was conflicted by this profound statement. He truly appreciated Tobin's depth of sentiment, but another, darker part of him questioned Tobin talking as if from a perspective of experience. What tragedy had Tobin endured? Who was Tobin to tell him about redemption?

Grace also became serious again. "You have to give life another chance. You have to have faith that God loves you."

Jacob spoke with utter despondency. "I'm sorry, Grace, but I had that faith once, and God took that love from me. Besides, I don't see you out there fucking dating." This last part was laden with a sarcasm that contained an air of malice.

It was Grace's eyes that told him that he had gone a step too far, that he had stung her more than he needed to. Still, his anger persisted.

That feeling, however, changed in an instant. Aurora stepped forward and beamed into his eyes with such compassion, such radiating tenderness and hope. She was fourteen by now, a freshman in Grace's Catholic Studies class and soon to be in Jacob's Honors American Literature course, but she still managed the air of a child, a hopeful innocence that could fill a room. Despite the tragedy that had been thrust upon her, and a father mired in its consequence, she had a spirit that shone from the ashes and defied its darkness. Somehow she had come to accept what her father could not, and that peace and contentment showed in her countenance.

Her long dark hair and slender build were all her mother's, but her cheeks were wider, and her smile and eyes were all Jacob's. She had, in a sense, inherited the best of both of them, and she was truly lovely, something to be seen before his eyes.

"Please don't swear, Dad. I know this hurts. That's why we want to do this with you. It's been hurting you for far too long. You deserve to not hurt anymore."

By now, she was as tall as her father, and she went to him and embraced him. Her long, straight dark hair flowed over her shoulders and onto his, sending a cool, tingling warmth through his spine. Her pale, soft skin touched his cheeks, and he felt goodness once again. Like her mother had before, she drew him in with the hopes of drawing out of him the sorrow that pooled in the inner recesses of his soul. She held him and drained him and then let him go to stride over to the piano in the adjoining room.

As the first notes came falling through the room, like the snowflakes that danced just outside the bay window, he wept with a desperation and a yearning that called out for a fulfillment that would never come. Her rendition of *Moonlight Sonata* was instantaneously recognizable. It was her. It was her mother. It was all that could never be again.

And yet here it was. It was not a distant memory. It was right here before him: tangible and real. The notes drifted to him, held him above the earth like a Christmas tree ornament suspended from a branch. Aurora's playing was beautiful; it was sublime; it was transcendent. He was swept away in its current as he rode along the crests of the waves created by the rolling of Aurora's fingers across the keyboard that he had shaped as a wedding present to her mother. They carried him to a place that was divine, to a place of bliss and joy and contentment, to a place that he had not been since that day sledding many years ago.

When Aurora brought her slender fingers down with a punctuated emphasis for the final notes, it stirred in him an awakening, a drawing forth to life once more. He straightened, and his eyes opened and looked at her with an honest and profound appreciation.

Aurora rose from the piano and pushed in the bench with a stark simplicity that seemed the perfect conclusion to her performance. She exhaled with grace and good posture and then walked to her father and said, "You are always waiting for today, Dad. Always waiting for a day that is already here. It is time for you to wake up and *live today* instead of waiting for it."

"Thank you, sweetheart. Thank you."

Aurora's wide smile turned into a smirk. "Well, be careful what you wish for."

"What do you mean?" asked Jacob pensively, scanning the others for some sort of subliminal clue.

"We want you to go on a date."

"A date? With whom?"

Grace stepped forward to explain. "With Angie. I know that you remember who she is because I can still see the look that came over your face her when we used to watch the Red Sox at the Rhino. You can't hide those things from me, Jacob Hartman. In any case, I know it's been a while, but Gary talks to her when she comes into the flower store." As she gestured towards Gary, he took a step towards Jacob with a distinctively sheepish grin on his face.

"She's a mid-wife, so she sends us a lot of business just with referrals. I owe her a lot. In any case, she's been single for a while now. She had it kinda tough coming off of that guy she moved down here with. Not really sure what happened there, but I talked to her about you, and she seems to know you pretty well. She knows you've been through a lot, but she's interested."

Jacob did not know whether he should be insulted or elated. His friends, and even his daughter, had conspired to set him up without even asking him. On the other hand, this group of people had come together to rescue him, to pull the drowning man to safer shores and give him hope again. He thought back to his reaction to Faith's unexpected announcement that she had unilaterally decided to stop taking her birth control pills. He considered his possible responses then and his possible responses now, and he weighed them deliberately.

"All right, but I make no promises.

Chapter 4

A Bicycle Built for Two

They rode a tandem bicycle for their first date. Angie had never been on one before, and when Jacob said that he had never ridden one either, she thought it a grand idea. Why not try something together for the first time and see what happens? "Plus," she said into the phone with a playful taunt, "that'll put us on equal footing, don't you think?"

Jacob agreed.

"Besides, what's the worst that could happen? A broken bone or two?"

Jacob laughed along but could not help thinking of far graver repercussions that worried him more.

They decided to meet at a bike shop in Old Town Alexandria where they could rent a bike for the day. That would allow them to access the bike trail to Mount Vernon without having to ride a tandem bike through the chaos of the city.

It was a crisp, chilly morning in mid-February, but the sun shone firmly in the lower sky and promised a warmer day to come. As he sat waiting for her on a wood and iron park bench outside the door to the shop, he warmed himself with a cup of coffee he had purchased across the street. It was still too hot to drink, but the steam rose to his lungs and spread a thawing sensation throughout his body. The aroma was earthy and invigorating.

He looked up to watch as an oversized Chevy Suburban packed with a troop of young soccer players pulled out of their parking spot just as Angie steered in front of the store. She drove an older silver Jetta, and you could hear Ben Folds playing audibly behind the rolled up windows. She immediately seized on the opportunity and seamlessly parallel parked her car without even removing the plastic smoothie container in her left hand. She took a final swig of the smoothie then placed the container onto the passenger seat before exiting the car exuberantly and proclaiming, "Not a bad parking spot, huh? You know, if I do say so myself."

She reached back into the car to grab a few last minute items then locked the doors and put the keys in her pocket. She was much as he remembered her. The sprightly, blond curls belied the tight angling of her firmly-set jaw and her well-toned, muscular physique. Her eyes were bluer than his but equally luminous, and they shone before the rest of her arrived. What he most appreciated was her small mouth which was deceptively expressive, and she seemed to have a way of accentuating her lip movements in a manner that clearly spoke to her mood. She was wearing a bulky white sweatshirt and a wool ski cap as well as stretch black yoga pants that fit her form well. Something about her glowed.

"I like your parking job," he said as she was still across the road, waiting for a car to pass. "It seems as if things just come to you, fall into your lap."

"Is that so?" she asked him playfully as she came towards him. Then, taking his hand and giving it a slight squeeze, she continued, "Did *you* just come to me? Fall into my lap? Metaphorically speaking only of course. I don't want to be that forward."

The squeeze and her humor cracked any resistance in him. He remembered why he had grown so comfortable in her presence. She was an easy soul to read. She lightened him and brought him back to a self he liked to believe in. "I don't know if I fell so much as got pushed by some of our mutual friends."

Angie turned serious for a moment and held his hand tighter as she looked at him. "I want you to know, you don't have to do this. If at any point, this feels wrong or brings up too much stuff..." He looked away, but she persisted and brought her neck around to retrieve her glance into his eyes to assure him, "I want you to know, it's ok. We'll call it a day, and hey, we can even tell your friends whatever you like."

The humor allowed him to look right back at her. "No, I'm glad to be doing this, and I am particularly glad to be doing this with you."

"It's good to see you again, Jacob." She touched three fingers to his cheek.

"It's good to see you too, Angie. Should we try out this bike? I recently added to my life insurance coverage, so Aurora liked the idea and urged me not to wear a helmet."

"Let's do it."

While they both rode bicycles fairly regularly, the tandem bike was something of a foreign experience. The first decision they needed to make was who would ride up front and serve as the "captain", who steered the apparatus, and who would ride in back as the "stoker", who would have to intrinsically entrust their well-being to the general competence and decision-making of the captain. With that in mind, they both agreed Jacob would probably be better suited up front.

They decided to test ride the bike for about a block's length in the mostly empty parking lot across the street. They rehearsed a one-two-three count upon which they would take one step and mount the bike simultaneously, each person clipping in as they pedaled to keep the bike upright. It seemed a sensible plan, but on their first attempt, Jacob hesitated at the moment of going from the step to the bike. Angie mounted the bike adroitly, but Jacob was still stuck on only the left pedal as Angie began to push forward. The upstroke sent him off balance and flying to the ground.

While Angie had wanted to stay true to her ship and man it as far as she could take it, when she saw her captain go down, she knew it was time to do what she could to save herself. She leapt nimbly and pushed the bike from her as she did so. Her general athleticism enabled her to quickly spread her legs wide enough to avoid what was sure to be painful contact with the seat on the way out. This, however, caused a significant tearing in the crotch region of her yoga pants, as pliable as they may have been, all the while sending her crashing unceremoniously down to the pavement.

By this time, a couple of younger guys who had been playing basketball on the court adjacent to the parking lot had stopped playing momentarily to watch the fiasco. Angie was sprawled on the ground not far from the wreckage of the bike, her hands instinctually cupped around her exposed genital area. She had a few good scrapes but managed to eke out a tenuous laugh through gasps of pain. Jacob, relatively unscathed, ran up to her and asked if she was all right. When she nodded in the affirmative and continued to laugh, he pulled her to her feet and asked her if she wanted to give it another try.

"Oh, I don't know if that is such a good idea," she said as she looked down at her pants and then at the basketball players who were glancing over at her. She considered, but did not articulate, a series of thoughts about whether Jacob's hesitancy was significant. Perhaps the "try something together for the first time and see what happens" theory wasn't quite working out.

He leaned into her and said with confidence, "I promise I will not do that again. I will not hesitate again."

"All right, Jacob," she said with some oscillation in her voice. The fall had been humorous but was not something she wanted to repeat. "But I'm going to need to change first. I have some biking shorts in my trunk. Wait here, and I'll be right back."

Their second foray into the realm of tandem biking went far smoother. They repeated their one-two-three count, and with a single step, they mounted the bike in perfect synchronized form. It wobbled at first, as each of them frantically attempted to get themselves clipped in and pedaling, but once they were upright, it seemed to come fairly naturally. Jacob steered them in wide turns around the parking lot, making the curves narrower and narrower as they became accustomed to the bicycle's weighting and maneuverability.

The basketball players stopped again and began to cheer for Jacob and Angie as they circled with greater prowess. Angie even attempted a mock bow from her position in the back, but her righting herself almost threw them off balance and tumbling down once more. She resolved to refrain from further clowning around, at least until they had developed a better command of the bike. Jacob merely chuckled. He felt alive again. They decided to practice a few more starts, and perhaps more importantly, stops, and then headed out on their way up the tree-lined bike path towards Mount Vernon.

Once they were out of Alexandria, the path became more rural, and they were able to talk breezily as they rolled up and down the small hills that marked their way along the

Potomac. It was cold, but they rode with purpose and warmed up quickly.

"So you finished up with nursing school and became a mid-wife?" Jacob asked for a starter as they passed over a caged, wooden walkway that went out over the water and gave them a stunning view towards Maryland on the other side.

"I did. I had to go back for some further classes, but I really enjoy it. Birth is an amazing process." Angie couldn't see Jacob grimace from her position in the back, but she thought she could feel it nonetheless. "I also had some personal experiences that led me in that direction. So how long have you been at Georgetown Catholic now anyway?"

"Just celebrated twenty years. They gave me a pin and a chair."

"Ooh...a pin and a chair. I'm sure you felt special."

"Yeah, I figure if I stay long enough they'll probably feel obliged to name a building after me."

"But you're not Catholic, right?"

"No, but the school and I seem to have come to a mutually agreeable pact about all that. I don't openly question the bullshit and show up at Mass once a month, and other than Grace, they leave me alone to my own skepticism."

"Sounds like a cordial, if confused, relationship to me. I guess I just figure everyone should leave others to their own path."

"I'm fine with that."

In under an hour, they made it to Mount Vernon, the former home of George Washington that rests atop a hillside overlooking the Potomac. They rested in the grassy area out by the tourist buses before making the return trip to Alexandria where they figured they could grab some lunch in Old Town. The sun had begun to shine brightly and had managed to fight off the remaining haze of the morning. Angie reclined comfortably onto her elbow and spoke easily of herself.

"So I've been working over at George Washington for about three years now. You went to school there, right?"

"Class of '89."

"God, you're old," she said flirtatiously, as she flicked a few of the gray hairs on the side of his head.

"Oh, now come on," he responded playfully, by knocking out her elbow but catching her chin with his open palm. "How old are you exactly?"

"Thirty-three. I don't even think I'm older than you in dog years." She rolled him over in the grass and gave him a good-natured slap on the back.

"All right, well then I want to see my little thirty-three year old date back there *pedaling* harder on the way back."

"I would if you gave me any incentive up front."

As they mounted the bike to head back down to Alexandria, they began to feel more comfortable with the bike. Angie could not help herself, and she lifted her feet out of the clips and placed her legs around Jacob's waist. He swerved briefly but recovered and laughed it off. "That's awfully nice, but I don't see a lot of pedaling going on back there."

They glided down the opening hill effortlessly. The cherry blossoms were not yet in bloom, but you could look at the vacant trees and imagine the intricate beauty of the flowers. Each of them took in the blur of scenery as they sailed on down the paved pathway.

Jacob thoroughly enjoyed the bicycle built for two. Unlike his customary bike rides, someone was literally there to experience it with him. It took an inherently individual activity and turned it into a partnership, an opportunity to work together instead of apart. He felt a distinct connection, and it felt good to share an experience with someone again. Yes, it reminded him of Faith, made him think of her and what this would be like with her, but it was also unmistakably Angie, a memory he still had before him.

They arrived back in Alexandria, and Jacob didn't want to give it up. "What do you think about holding onto the bike and heading out to Roosevelt Island after lunch?"

Angie agreed, so they locked up their bike and headed for the Bilbo Baggins, a European pub and restaurant that Angie knew on Queen Street near the river. The building was a yellow cottage that looked like an Austrian villa. Inside were framed maps of Tolkien's Middle Earth that lined the dining room and wall paintings of various scenes from the *Fellowship of the Ring* adorning the tap room. While the bartender was dressed in a plain blue polo, the wait staff wore medieval garb. Their waitress, Rachel, whether due to the urging of what would certainly have to be an unabashedly sexist management or by her own volition and what could only be ascribed to a latent exhibitionism, wore a bustier that so prominently displayed her already ample bosom, that Jacob felt the need to turn his head as she walked by to avoid any inadvertent contact.

"Can I get you folks something other than water?" she inquired as she leaned in to place the water glasses on the table, making Jacob entirely uncomfortable. They both opted for water, and she left menus for them to peruse, meanwhile taking her overzealous breasts with her.

"Dear God, how do you walk with those things?" wondered Angie aloud. "And why would you put them out there like that? Do *you* find that attractive?"

While it certainly had an element of judgment in it, Jacob did not take it as a loaded question, more of a soft lob if anything. "Not in the slightest. I'm afraid she's going to hit me in the face with them. I may have nightmares later tonight."

Angie laughed through her straw and snorted some water onto the table. When Rachel returned to take their order, Jacob had to angle his seat away to refrain from openly laughing. He ordered a smoked duck salad while Angie opted for a grilled portabella sandwich.

"So can you tell me about your wife, or is it too difficult?" She had waited for the right moment to interject at least a little of what needed to be discussed at some point moving forward.

"Well, you know that she died giving birth to Aurora, right?"

"I do, and I'm sorry." She placed her hand over his forearm. "You don't have to talk about it."

"No, it's ok. It's been fourteen years. Can you believe Aurora is fourteen years old?"

"She's turning out to be quite a young woman, Jacob. I got to talk to her a bit when Gary and Grace were setting this all up."

"Oh, so I have those two to blame, huh," he said sarcastically.

"Or thank," she said coyly.

"You know what I mean," he said brightly, and he took the risk of placing his hand upon her knee beneath the table and giving it a squeeze.

She smiled at him receptively and then repeated her question. "So do you feel comfortable talking about Faith? You don't have to, but Gary has told me she was quite a hoot, an incredible woman."

"She was all that more," Jacob said with wistful reminiscence. "She looked a lot like Aurora: tall and lean and beautiful. The same long dark hair. The same damned persistence." He smiled in another direction and went on, "I think you know she owned the flower shop, but she was obviously so much more. So much more than my memories could ever do her justice."

"How did you two meet?"

"At a baseball game, actually."

"Was she a big Red Sox fan?"

"Faith didn't care much for baseball. She mostly went for an excuse to drink beer."

"Can't blame her there. Do you still think about her a lot?"

"Every day. I see her, and I long for her. I want her so much to be there, but more and more I come to accept that she cannot."

"What did you love most about her?"

"You see, that's what I learned about love from Faith. Love is about loving all of that person: their virtues, their faults, their triumphs, their vices: everything. It is about loving that individual soul so completely that you wouldn't change a thing about them because in doing so, you would alter the essence of who they are."

"I wish Brandon had loved me like that."

"Was Brandon the ex you moved down here with?"

"That's the one. He's a good guy really, but when things got hard, he split. I know it's not much condolence at this point, but at least you got to love like that once, if only for a brief time." She took his hand in hers and gave it a gentle squeeze.

The point struck home for him. While he had every right to mourn the loss of his sacred love, perhaps he should find some solace in knowing that he had even had Faith in the first place. Perhaps there was a debt of gratitude that had yet to be paid.

Lost in such thought, Jacob was caught unaware as Rachel placed their lunches on the table. She leaned over him, and as she did so, unwittingly dragged her left breast down the side of his face. She stood back up as if completely incognizant that any contact had been made and asked them if they needed anything else. As Jacob stood mute, Angie told her that they would be fine.

"I think she just dragged her boob down my face," Jacob whispered fervently after Rachel had walked away.

"Oh, she did just that all right. How was it? Was it big and fluffy like a pillow?"

"More like a large piece of rotten fruit."

She reached over the table and fed him a bite of her portabella sandwich. "Well, it's not quite rotten fruit, but try a bite of this."

Jacob liked that she shared food. It had been a long time since he had been able to do so, other than Aurora simply helping herself to whatever he was having. He felt that he could get used to this, or at least this part of it.

A chemistry was developing between them that to Jacob was reassuring. Though Angie did get a bit aggressive when it came to defending her liberal politics which were even left of Jacob's, they had an easy way of speaking to each other, one that felt simultaneously familiar and challenging, as they lingered and chatted well after they both had finished their lunches. Her pert, strong mouth provoked him and invited him to be part of a dialogue that aroused his senses and made him more keenly aware of himself.

"So when is your birthday anyway?" she asked him while kicking him lightly under the table.

"Are you asking me because you want to throw me a party or because you want to know my zodiac sign?" He drew out the last part with an enhanced skepticism and a furled eyebrow.

"I just want to know you."

"So you want to know my sign, right?" he said, calling her bluff.

"Ok," she confessed with a nervous laugh and a rare shy look away that was somehow endearing to him. "I admit it. I want to know your sign."

"My birthday is May 8th, so I'm a Taurus, but I have to warn you that I don't believe in that nonsense."

"Don't you believe in things that can't be explained?"

"I believe in things that can't be explained, but it has more to do with the absence of some great divine system of order than the existence of one."

"Sometimes things happen for a reason."

"And sometimes they don't."

The sentence came down with the weight of a hefty mallet. He had not meant to be so blunt and negative, but it had sprung out of him as a natural response. He let the comment hang there for a moment and then tried to re-orient the conversation back to the more positive strand of dialogue that had led him here in the first place. "So when is your birthday?"

"February 1st. I'm an Aquarius."

"Ah, a child of the water, a woman of causes."

"I have a few."

"I can tell."

When they paid their bill and left without further incident pertaining to Rachel's mammary glands, Jacob walked outside as he waited for Angie to use the restroom. He could feel the sun once more in the sky as it laid out its rosy fingers to greet him, and he breathed in deeply, relishing each molecule of air as it poured into his lungs and on throughout his bloodstream. His body awoke, and the vibrancy of the air filled him with nourishment and courage, such that when Angie reappeared through the door of the Bilbo Baggins, something that he would not have believed was within himself, and which he could not later hope to describe, took over him and pulled Angie towards him, as he pressed himself forward and brought his lips to hers. He kissed her with a passion that had so long lay dormant but now erupted inside of him. Angie felt for his back and pulled him closer as she matched his intensity with her own.

It was to be their one real kiss that afternoon. Though they would share a tender hug and a peck on the cheek after they had returned from their ride out to Roosevelt Island and had dinner at the Fish Market over on King Street, Jacob was so overwhelmed with the degree to which he had put himself out there that he found himself incapable of following up on the outburst of ardor that had consumed him earlier. Still, it had felt right. The moment had rendered him incapacitated, like a man struck by lightning but living to tell the tale.

Despite this, he relished the kiss and secretly clung to it for the remainder of the afternoon. He savored it later that night at home as he nestled into a bed that felt much warmer than it had in some time.

"Well, thank you for that," she said as she finally pulled away from him to catch her breath. "I must admit that was unexpected, but wonderful, really wonderful."

Angie's words seemed to come to him with a reverberating, distorting echo that forced him to take a moment to decipher and absorb them. "Well, I had been wanting to kiss you for a while now, but I couldn't with my back turned towards you on the bike."

"We could try to make that happen," she said teasingly.

He so adored this quality in her, and he gave her a punctuated kiss meant to do the same. "Sure, how many pairs of pants do you have in that car anyway? If I play my cards right, you'll be naked up on that tandem, and we would have to try a far more impressive feat while riding."

Chapter 5

Karma and a PBJ

Making sandwiches for the untold homeless around Washington had been a tradition at Georgetown Catholic long before Grace inherited the program from Sister Nancy as part of her duties as Director of Religious Studies. Every Wednesday night, the entire school community would go home and make meat and cheese or peanut butter and jelly sandwiches. Then, on Thursdays after school, Grace would enlist a group of student volunteers and distribute them in southeast DC, a few blocks from the Capitol.

While Jacob secretly felt that the program represented a colossal waste of time and effort when one considered the infinitesimal dent that these sandwiches could put in the monumental problem of homelessness in a city as large and economically stratified as Washington, he never revealed this sentiment to Grace. He was always sure to encourage the girls in his homeroom and served as a good role model, always making at least a loaf of bread's worth of sandwiches.

Until Aurora was fourteen and herself a student at Georgetown Catholic, she would assist Jacob in making the sandwiches for his homeroom, but once she enrolled as a student, she would make her own allotment, usually goading her father to make more by needling him that she was going to out-produce him. In this way, the school tradition had become assimilated as a Hartman tradition as well.

As such, when Angie asked Jacob if he wanted to go with her to a wine tasting at an upscale bar in Adams Morgan on a Wednesday night in March, he had to decline by way of an explanation of the significance of Wednesday night sandwich-making in the Hartman household. Showing no signs of being even mildly disappointed, Angie changed gears and asked him for further details about the program. She seemed quite intent about the whole process.

"So have you ever gone with Grace to deliver sandwiches?" she asked him as they lazily reposed in the plush red sofa at the Coffee Bean on a Sunday morning discussing their plans for the week. This had become something of a ritual after meeting each Sunday for a morning run on the Capital Crescent trail. Angie was often on-call on Saturdays, so Sundays had become their go-to day together, and they generally tried to make the most of it, even if that meant just sitting and chatting at their favorite coffee shop for hours at a time.

"I can't say that I have," Jacob confided.

"Why not? Grace is your good friend. Why not do it with her?"

"No reason really. I've just never considered it, I guess."

"Well, if I can switch my Thursday shift to Friday, let's go deliver this week. What do you think?"

His initial thought was to spurn the suggestion, but he suppressed the urge and reconsidered. Grace had given up asking him long ago, but here was an opportunity to spend some extra time with Angie, and he felt he should take advantage of it. "You're on. I know Grace will be psyched to have you along."

She bent over him and kissed him playfully on the mouth. Her plain white tank top hung loosely from her neck revealing the crests of her firm, petite breasts and much of the white satin bra that held them. As she rolled across and atop him, her long front curls brushed his forehead and provided the perfect visual contrast to the muted, mocha-colored walls behind her. Her strong, bony leg protruded into his side sending a painful twinge up his side and causing him to jerk his thigh back reflexively and bang his knee into the coffee table.

"I'm sorry, did I stab you with my leg? Or did I just excite you?"

"You always excite me," he jibed sexually, as they both often did, though they had yet to be intimate, "but I'm afraid that was an involuntary reflex of a different sort." And so to show her what he meant, he reached up and tickled the inside of her armpit. When she reached up to defend herself, he had strategized one move ahead of her and used his left hand as a decoy while the right deftly dashed around to the back of her thigh with a gentle pinch that caused her leg to spontaneously kick forward as she let out a near blood-curdling scream. He had not used the tactic on Angie previously, and as such had only gleaned it as a particularly sensitive spot from cumulative experience, but it obviously had a far more dramatic effect with Angie than Jacob had intended. As her leg shot forward into his groin with such unwitting force, he felt the full brunt of his miscalculation. He barely had the strength to roll out from under her and onto his side as he doubled over in the pain that is known only to men.

"Oh my God! Are you ok?" Angie asked with genuine concern but also with a barely restrained laughter just on the verge of spilling over like a dam that has reached its capacity.

Jacob laughed and coughed and felt like crying it hurt so much. As he recovered the requisite wind to resume speaking, he held two fingers in the air to signal that he would, in fact, be all right.

Angie could not start chuckling until he had fully recovered and by then much of her amusement had waned. "I'm so sorry. I'm really ticklish there, Jacob. It almost always makes my leg kick forward. I'm sorry."

"Not...your...fault," he managed to eke out in interspersed breaths.

"Is there anything I can do?"

"Just don't pick up the butter knife when we make sandwiches on Wednesday night. Aurora and I will spread the peanut butter and jelly; you just handle the bread. If that's what you do when you get tickled, I better be sure to never make you angry."

By the time Angie was able to make it over to Jacob's after work, Jacob and Aurora had each completed making their sandwiches, and Aurora was at the dining room table finishing her math homework while Jacob graded papers in his leather chair. There was a fine mist hanging in the air, and Angie arrived at the door with her hair lightly wet. Her deep purple rain jacket, however, had kept the rest of her dry.

When Jacob heard the doorbell ring, he finished scribbling down his final thoughts on a student's paper, and then sprang out of his chair to answer the door. Seeing Angie wet from the rain, he brushed off her jacket and offered to get her a towel.

"I'm fine, just a little drizzle. How are you doing in there, Aurora?" Angie asked as she poked her head around the corner towards the dining room.

"A bit busy at school but otherwise ok." She picked up her attention to acknowledge Angie but left her pencil in the book so that she could get back to her work in a few moments.

Angie stepped into the entryway. Before she had left work, she had changed out of her scrubs and into a pair of jeans and a Charlie Brown t-shirt. Her toned but thin arms jutted out from the sleeves like branches springing forth from the trunk of a tree.

Aurora, meanwhile, still in her mandatory white-collared shirt and plaid skirt from school, rose and walked into the kitchen and asked if she could get Angie anything to drink. Her cell phone rang, but she switched it to silent and returned from the kitchen with a tall glass of milk and sat at the piano with her body turned towards her father and Angie.

"Would you like to hear me play something?"

"I'd love to," exclaimed Angie as she started to assemble the necessary ingredients to make her share of sandwiches.

Aurora had come to really enjoy Angie, but the barely perceptible strain in their relationship originated from her deeply conflicted heart on the matter of her father's new girlfriend, the first woman she had ever known him with. She wanted to like Angie, and in so many ways she did. Angie had embraced her without forcing herself on her as so many potential dating partners of divorced or widowed parents do. She was so remarkably down to Earth and easygoing, so sure of herself but without pretension. Angie had an open and honest soul that had welcomed Aurora to share it with her. Most importantly, it was clear that Angie truly cared for her father deeply. Still, there was a gnawing persistence within her that tore at her and told her that she was being unfaithful to the mother she had never known. Though she knew this is what her mother would have wanted for her father, she felt that she was betraying the soul that had died in giving birth to her by abetting a relationship with Angie, especially in warming to her and letting her in.

Angie sensed this and understood. It was the same as with Jacob; it just needed time and patience- lots and lots of patience. Time and patience were two resources she had in abundance. She pulled a dining room chair over to the side of the piano bench so that she could sit down and appreciate Aurora's playing. As Aurora started into Beethoven's "Fur Elise", the notes seemed to melt together in a richly-textured tapestry woven by Aurora's skilled hands. As she reclined back further into her chair, a radiant smile beamed across Angie's pert mouth, and her face emitted a fulfilled sense of contentment. She closed her eyes and let the music wash over her as she drifted away beyond the horizon of her mind's eye, so much so that she did not even notice Jacob's presence until he placed his hands upon her shoulders and began to caress her lower neck. Rather than disrupt her euphoric state, it enhanced it, as the sense of touch came in harmony with the jubilant notes of the piano. She clasped his hands and held him tight.

They asked Aurora to continue playing while they dashed off the sandwiches Angie was to make. Aurora chose Sergei Rachmaninoff's "Prelude in G Minor" as Jacob and Angie quickly found a rhythm to their production. Jacob would take out two pieces of bread and spread the peanut butter Angie had brought, then hand them over to Angie who would place a layer of strawberry preserves over the peanut butter before cutting the sandwiches in half and placing them in the bag left over from the bread. Their operation began to move like a well-oiled machine, and at a certain moment, they both looked over at one another and smiled in acknowledgement; they were becoming a pretty good couple, a comfortable couple that complemented each other well.

After they finished making the sandwiches and Aurora went back to completing her math assignment, Jacob and Angie sat together on the couch as they talked and kissed intermittently, like teenagers out on a second date. The newness of this, the freshness of it, exhilarated Jacob as he settled into a delightful pattern of romance with Angie. It was impossible, however, not to feel a piece of Faith in every encounter he had with Angie. She continued to speak to him, a ghost that whispered to him of her absence and haunted him with an untouchable beauty that graced the very ground he tread. It left him simultaneously living in the present but somehow drawn back to the past, as the life he lived with Faith colored the world he dwelled in now. He could taste her lips as he kissed Angie, feel her skin as he and Angie caressed. Jacob stared deep into Angie's sparkling blue eyes as he kissed her in order to keep himself with her in this ever-shifting moment.

Aurora tried to forbear it and focus on the math work that simply had to get done that night, but the saccharine cooing, especially her father's, eventually became too much for her, and she rose in a premeditated huff and proclaimed, "You know, I'm glad that you guys are dating and all. God knows you both need it. But for crying out loud, get a room. I, for one, need to get some work done, so I guess I'll head upstairs." With this, she went back into the dining room to assemble her books with a touch of typical teenage melodramatic flair and headed for her room.

Angie started to get up to go after her and see what was really troubling Aurora, but Jacob cupped his arm around her. "Let her go, Angie. She wants this, she really does, but it is hard for her. She likes you, thinks the world of you, she really does, but you can never be what she most wants you to be: her mother. Just give her some time."

"Of course. Are you sure she's ok?"

Jacob stared up the stairs after Aurora. "She will be."

"Well, you know her best," she said with sympathy. She waited for Jacob to redirect his attention to her then ran her finger down the length of his neck. "I must admit, though, that I liked her idea of us 'getting a room', if you will. I'm not working tomorrow, and I would love to spend the night with you." Her eyes looked teasingly towards the staircase as a mischievous smile crossed her lips. She wanted to take this next step with him, but only if he was ready, and she knew she might need to help him get there.

A flood of memories washed over Jacob, rendering him motionless and mute. He, too, wanted this, wanted to make love to her, to lay down his bare soul before hers and have them touch in a shining moment of ecstasy, but the memory of Faith persisted in disquieting him. How could he connect his soul to another when he was still inextricably tied to her? No, he too needed more time, more time to distance himself from the vision of a joy that had been untimely ripped from him.

"I'm afraid I have to get up early to help Grace set up for Mass in the morning. Can I take a rain check?"

Angie looked at him with sad recognition. "Of course," she said with a heavy heart. She felt Jacob's pain and wanted nothing more than to ease his wounded soul, but she knew that she could only do so once he was ready. Her face grew pale and dejected, but even as a pout, her mouth was effectively expressive. She picked up his sticky notes, wrote something down, and then stuck it to his chest as she kissed him intensely before letting herself out.

Awestruck, Jacob found himself still staring at the door through which she passed several minutes after she did so. Only then was he able to shake himself to consciousness and look down at the note that read, "Rain check: Good for one free ticket to escape your problems."

As they boarded the blue and white 15-passenger van used regularly for various school activities, Jacob made sure to save a seat up front for Angie who had called to say that she would be a couple of minutes late due to congestion coming over the Key Bridge from Rosalyn. The girls packed the back of the van anyway, so the point was rendered moot, but Aurora smiled at the chivalric gesture from her father and convinced her friend, Caitlin Pierce, to sit with her up by her father in the front of the van.

Caitlin wore her shoulder-length blond hair in a bob and had large, saucer-shaped green eyes that stuck out against her pale white skin. She was veritably addicted to the new iPhone her mother had bought her as a demonstration of one-upmanship in the game Caitlin's recently divorced parents played but Caitlin consistently won. She had a tendency to be unnecessarily loud and was in the habit of overtly brown-nosing adults, but she had come to grow on Jacob who figured Aurora could do a lot worse for a best friend than an aspiring go-getter who took her work seriously and aimed to please.

When Angie entered the van a few minutes later, wearing a light pullover and a pair of hiking sandals, a couple of the sophomore girls who had Jacob in class moved forward before departing so that they could have an opportunity to grill "Mr. Hartman's special friend". No one would have contended that discretion was their strong suit. Though Jacob had explained in his awkward manner that a "friend" of his, Angie, would be joining them, they saw right through his clever ruse. They had heard through Aurora's friends that Mr. Hartman had a new girlfriend, and as Jacob was one of the girls' favorite teachers, they were eager to find out more about her. While Angie slid tactfully into the seat Jacob indicated, the sophomore girls had already pounced on her before Grace could steer the van out of the parking lot.

"So you must be Angie, right? I'm Kathryn." Kathryn Fuller was a vivacious, extroverted redhead who managed good grades on the merit of her own perseverance and her parents' persistent oversight of her academic career. Diagnosed with a number of learning differences as far back as elementary school, Kathryn compensated for her academic travails with a social exuberance that drew others to her despite her relatively plain physical appearance. She stuck out her right hand over the bench seat of the van.

"I am Angie," responded Angie with aplomb. She had been expecting this. "It's a pleasure to meet you, Kathryn."

"And you're dating, Mr. Hartman, right?" asked Whitney Blanchard, eagerly interjecting before even having the opportunity to introduce herself. Whitney had a well-intentioned heart and was capable of doing well in school but somehow had a propensity for finding herself in disciplinary situations by being in the wrong place at the wrong time, and perhaps more importantly, with the wrong people. Most teachers ascribed her personal struggles to her parents' messy divorce back when she was still a toddler but her significantly older brother and sister were both already in college. With her siblings gone, she was left alone to absorb the collateral damage. This caused her to be overly eager to make friends, and so she often found herself hanging out with those that would disregard or manipulate her decent moral compass. Kathryn, the social matriarch of sorts, had seen all of this from afar and had tried as of late to embrace Whitney and assimilate her into her social circle. Whitney, however, still needed some refinement, and Kathryn shot her a vehement glance and let out an exasperated, "Whitney!"

Angie looked over to Jacob for help, but he merely shrugged as if to tell her that he knew that she could take care of it. She fumbled for her words for a moment. "Well, yes, I guess you could say that."

"That's cool," said Whitney, nodding her head before remembering to add, "Oh, yeah, I'm Whitney by the way."

Angie could see Jacob affirming his approval with a subtle smirk, and she brightened. "Well, Whitney Bytheway, it's nice to meet you."

Whitney didn't grasp the joke, but she laughed along uneasily anyway.

Kathryn now felt the need to intercede. "What Whitney meant to say is that we're glad to see Mr. Hartman find someone nice and pretty like you."

"Well, thank you, Kathryn," Angie said with a nod of acknowledgement.

"So what's Mr. Hartman like? You know, outside of school..." Whitney asked.

"Well, *Jacob* is..." As Angie contemplated her response, the girls looked at each other to confirm Angie's use of the first name they had never heard. "He's fun. He's outdoorsy. He's got a great sense of humor. He's a good man."

Whitney nearly exploded out of her seat. "Really? He's fun? Because he's really not that funny in class. His jokes are so corny and lame."

Jacob glanced over and raised his eyebrows at Whitney before teasing her. "Perhaps, but your tardiness to my class is a pretty sorry joke as well, Ms. Blanchard." He caught Angie's eye and gave her an appreciative smile.

She smiled back before pulling the girls back in. "So what's he like in class? Does he assign a lot of homework?"

"A ton," Kathryn chimed in. "But he's pretty fair, and despite his lame jokes, he's a really good teacher. I don't know how I would have gotten through English 10 without him. He's going to be my advisor next year, right Mr. H?"

"If you'll still have me even with my lame jokes."

"Heck yeah, everyone knows Mr. H is the best!" She high-fived him and went back to her conversation with Whitney and Angie.

Angie turned towards Aurora and Caitlin on the bench behind Jacob in order to draw them into the conversation. "When do you two get Mr. Hartman?"

"Next year," said Caitlin excitedly.

Angie looked more directly at Aurora. "So are you excited for that or nervous?"

Aurora knew what Angie was doing and felt awkward at first but then began to welcome being brought into a conversation with older girls possessing social status. "It'll be weird at first, but it probably won't be much different than at home."

"I'll bet he'll give you a good grade," Whitney suggested as a potential perk.

Kathryn shook her head. "Not Mr. Hartman. He always says he doesn't give grades; you earn them. He's going to give you whatever you get. In fact, he might even be harder on you than with other students because he might expect others to think he would favor you."

"I know. Sucks, doesn't it?" Aurora said wryly.

"Don't worry, little sister," said Kathryn. "I got your back. I'll pass you down all my notes for the class, and trust me, I have tons of them."

Aurora, who had inherited her father's sense of social awkwardness despite being well-liked in general, did not often feel herself as included, especially with older students. While she was sophisticated in her tastes and mature in her thoughts and sensibilities, she still preferred activities that many girls her age had long ago deemed childish. Perhaps she simply had the maturity and foresight to relish the innocence of her youth while she still had it, but it did often leave her feeling ostracized by her peers, even if this was more her own projection than their real sentiment.

To be included now felt so exhilarating for her. For the next fifteen minutes, they discussed boyfriends, or prospects thereof, as Angie cunningly turned the tables on the girls without their notice by directing the conversation towards the one subject high school girls will never fail to act upon: themselves. Aurora even mentioned her "insignificant" crush on Jason Hardeley, though she knew her dad was eavesdropping. Angie prodded her for more detail, but Aurora demurred, even though Caitlin assured Angie that she would supply her with further information later.

Grace, in her customary ever-observant manner, also picked up on the dynamic that was occurring as she navigated the congested arteries towards southeast Washington. When they had arrived, and it was time to break them into two groups, she kept Caitlin, Aurora, Kathryn, and Whitney together along with their Senior leader, Tanya Purnell, and Jacob and Angie as their adult moderators. Grace dropped off their group just outside of the Capitol South metro station near 1st and C streets. She handed Jacob and Angie a small folding table and more sandwiches than they could imagine. Then she gave Angie a box of candy bars, before pulling Jacob to the side.

"What's with the candy bars? I thought you just gave away sandwiches?" asked Jacob as he looked back at the girls already pining away at Angie to satiate their addiction to chocolate.

"Some of the folks won't take the sandwich unless you have some kind of dessert for them."

"Well, that's ironic," Jacob said with a note of the skepticism he generally hid from Grace. "But the school doesn't pay for those, do they?"

"No, that's my contribution," Grace responded plainly. She needed to get on her way to the other location down along Potomac Avenue. "Now, I'll be back in an hour. If you need me, you have my number. If anything really bad happens, run like hell over to St. Peter's across the street."

"Shouldn't I just take the kids over to the Capitol to be safe?"

"Trust me, you'd be better off putting your faith in the church than in that ungodly whorehouse. Seriously, if anything happens, go to St. Peter's. I'll be back in an hour."

And so there they were: five Catholic school girls in full school regalia and two adult moderators. The racial divide was conspicuous. Washington always has been and always will be a city of those who have and those who have not, and that line is so ostensibly drawn by race and entitlement that Jacob maintained a keen impression of being watched. He had a sense that some folks resented their presence, and he could not help feeling it justified.

They set up shop by the escalators to the metro station along the long row of newspaper vending machines that lined the brick sidewalk. Jacob and Angie assembled the table while the girls prepared the sandwiches and candy bars. As Jacob started putting sandwiches on the table and scanned the immediate environs, he thought to himself that they were going to go home with a lot of leftover sandwiches.

That impression, however, soon turned into a prevailing concern that they would not have enough, as they were shortly overrun with a mass that had assembled on the sidewalk near the table. Clearly, these folks knew quite well the appointed place and hour for this distribution and had planned accordingly. Though the crowd flowed well into the adjoining street, they were orderly and polite as they stepped forward one by one to claim what was for many a vital source of nutrition for the day. The sole exception was a battered, older man, skinny and misshapen, who was disconnected from the rest of the crowd and shadowboxing against a non-existent opponent in the street.

Jacob watched helplessly as folks with clothes as dingy and stained as the sidewalk beneath them stepped forward to the table. He could smell the streets upon them, and it filled him with the suffering they endured as they huddled in the alleyways and under the bridges where their lot had cast them.

Angie and Aurora kept bringing sandwiches to the table while Jacob and the rest of the girls dutifully handed them out to the desperate souls who stood before them entreating them for sustenance. Jacob felt their need with each sandwich he distributed, and he wondered how he could ever fill so large a hole. With so much pain, so much needless and wasted suffering, what could he do to make it stop? He couldn't. The line seemed endless, and all the peanut butter and jelly at the local Safeway could not put an end to it.

Without looking, he reached out to hand someone a sandwich, but when the hand was not immediately forthcoming, he stopped to glance at two young children, a brother and sister, each no more than five years old, with their mother who was clinging as much to her infant daughter as the newborn was to her. The children were emaciated, and the mother had the clear appearance of drug addiction. The clothes of the two older children were tattered and grubby, but they stood erect with a sense of maintained dignity. The brother, perhaps a year older than his sister, spoke for the family. "May we have meat and cheese sandwiches, please?"

Jacob paused before reaching back for four ham and cheese sandwiches and a Twix bar for each of them. As Jacob gave them the sandwiches and candy, each of them, even the mother for whom everything seemed a Herculean effort of movement, nodded in a gesture of gratitude, and the boy muttered a humbled but audible, "Thank you." As the rest of his family walked away, the boy delayed and turned to Jacob with an ear-to-ear grin and gave him a high five. Then he turned and ran after his mother and sister. Even well after they had walked away into the landscape of their lives, Jacob thought about them, thought about the suffering they had known and what lay before them.

He knew he was powerless to make their suffering end, to take away the pain and hurt in the world. Shoot, he could not even ease his own grief and torment. But he could put a smile on one young boy's face, a sandwich into each belly that lined the streets before him. Each PBJ was a little piece of making the world a slightly better place. Sure, it wasn't much, but it was *something*. It had meaning; it was not some Sisyphean task, and he was not Don Quixote fighting the elusive windmills of homelessness. He had the power to make a difference in the world around him, even if that difference was proportionally small and ephemeral. The power of the human spirit, after all, lies not in getting the rock up to the top of the hill, he realized, but in the struggle to roll it there in the first place.

He smiled at the world around him and then looked back at Angie and Aurora who were giggling away about something and glancing distractedly over at him. Something was up. It was not until much later that night, however, that he would discover, due to the presence of a distinctively overpowering odor, the single piece of rotten deli meat that they placed amongst the papers of his grading binder. Even

then, however, he would not mind. He was too pleased that
Angie had evidently found her way in.

Chapter 6

The Freeing of the Burro

It was Angie who suggested the five-day bike trip through Spanish wine country for the first week after school was out. She had already dutifully researched a variety of trips and outfitters before presenting the idea to Jacob. He had just one requirement: They had to ride a tandem bike.

The timing worked perfectly. The weather would be cooler than mid-summer, though still hot, and Aurora would be away at a soccer camp in northern Maryland. Angie was able to get the time off from work, and heaven knows, Jacob needed the vacation.

Even stepping off the plane in Madrid, Jacob felt different, more at ease. He breathed in deeply and exhaled with a profound sense of letting go. Angie consciously took his hand as they strolled through the airport to claim his bag. She had managed to fit everything she needed for their excursion into a carry-on bag, and she teased him about having more luggage than a girl.

As they approached the baggage carousel, they saw a stout, black-haired woman with a dark complexion holding a sign with the name, "Hartman". Jacob walked over and introduced himself to the woman who said, in textbook English with a barely detectable Spanish accent, "Welcome to Espana and congratulations. I'm Lucinda, the business manager and de facto bus driver. My husband, Patrice, will be your bike guide. You must be Angie. I believe we spoke over the phone."

"That's right," replied Angie extending her hand. "Thanks for picking us up. We were planning on taking a taxi."

"No taxis for you on this trip," Lucinda responded warmly. "Normally, I'd be waiting for a few other guests to take back to the hotel with you, but your flight is coming in so late, you're the last ones to arrive. We'll get you to the hotel for a good night's sleep and introduce you to everyone else in the morning. We need to let the newlyweds get their beauty rest."

Lucinda waited for them as Jacob and Angie stood by the carousel in anticipation of his luggage. Jacob, however, could not resist covertly whispering intently in Angie's ear, "What does she mean by 'newlyweds'?"

Angie giggled and then responded, "I told them we just got married. They always give you great gifts and upgrades when you're on your honeymoon. Plus, I always wanted to be on my honeymoon, so now I sort of am." She leaned up and kissed him affectionately in what started as a playful show but turned into a lingering expression of attachment.

Sensing this, he pulled her closer and buried his face into the crevice of her neck. "All right, young lady, I'll play along. I couldn't think of anyone I'd rather be on my fake honeymoon with. I guess we're in this together now." He kissed her neck and ran his fingers through her tight, blond curls. Jacob's bag circled on the carousel twice before they finally noticed it.

"Well, you can certainly tell you two are on your honeymoon! I wish Patrice was still like that with me," Lucinda teased as they boarded the van for their hotel.

In the morning, they both felt refreshed and eager for the adventure ahead. They were supposed to meet the rest of the group in a side room off of the hotel lobby for a continental breakfast and trip briefing. As they walked into the foyer, Lucinda was waiting for them and introduced them to the Granger family next to her.

"Angie and Jacob, this is James and Nancy from Appleton, Wisconsin, and these are their two boys, Evan and Daniel. Angie and Jacob are on their honeymoon."

"Oh, congratulations," exclaimed Nancy with a good-natured, Midwestern tone. "I can still remember when James and I were on our honeymoon. He took me to Aruba."

Nancy was a plain, petite woman with a diminutive mouth that pushed forward and gave her the appearance of a small bird straining for something to eat. Her wiry, chocolate-brown hair poked out in a variety of directions, resembling a nest made of twigs. Her wide glasses with their preposterously thick lenses occupied the bulk of her face. She created quite the contrast with her husband, James, who had a grizzled, tawny beard that was only a shade lighter than the bushy hair that flowed from beneath his Green Bay Packers hat. James towered over his wife with a thick, sturdy frame that gave him the semblance of a brown bear packed with extra fat for a long winter's hibernation.

Their sons, Evan and Daniel, bore a striking resemblance to their father, as each had his deep-set, hazel eyes and substantial build. Though the two brothers were nearly the same height, Evan, the younger sibling by two years and seemingly the bona fide baby of the family, was softer and paler than his brother Daniel, who seemed at least reasonably athletic and slightly more likely to have seen the sun in the last several months. Both boys, however, had their mother's dark brown, disheveled hair.

Jacob, in his typical fashion, be it due to his role as teacher or simply because of his general mistrust of adults, directed his attention to the kids. "So what grade are you boys in?"

Daniel, who was quieter than his brother in general but more assertive when spoken to directly, answered, "I'm going to be in eighth, but my brother will be in sixth grade next year."

"That's great. I teach tenth and eleventh grade English."

"Do you give a lot of homework?" Evan chimed in as James and Nancy merely looked on.

"You know, everyone asks me that," Jacob answered as he glanced over at Angie and smiled. "I guess so, but I try to make it fun and worthwhile."

"I've never seen homework that was fun," replied Evan dubiously. "I'll bet your students don't think it's fun."

"You may be right, but I try nonetheless."

Nancy started to admonish Evan for being rude, but the situation was preempted by the boisterous entrance of Phil from Sausalito who was accompanied by his girlfriend, Pamela, and her fifteen-year old daughter, Stephanie, who seemed less than thrilled to be a part of the entire experience.

"Well, good morning everyone!" Phil shouted before he had even reached the final stair leading into the foyer. Apparently unaware that Pamela and Stephanie were still two steps behind him, he strode forward and shook James's hand robustly as he tousled young Evan's hair. "Good to see you, mate," he rejoined heartily in James's general direction, as James returned a forced smile and a nod before pulling his boys a bit closer into him.

Phil was a strapping man with broad shoulders tapering to a lean waistline. Though his chiseled physique suggested a much younger man, his salt and pepper hair, neatly cropped and treated with styling gel, spoke more accurately to Phil being a few years older than Jacob. Pamela was a stunning woman in her late thirties with long, straight auburn hair that flowed down the length of her delicately-curved back. Her torso was lean but strong, and her eyes shone with an eerie, seductive shade of green. A quiet woman by nature, her striking beauty spoke far louder than the words she usually withheld.

Stephanie, however, was far more vocal in her manner than her mother but plainer in appearance. She was athletic and fit, but thicker and more muscular than the more femininely-shaped Pamela. Her eyes were wide and pronounced but with a dark, elusive shade of brown that brooded defensively. Her lips were thick, and unless speaking, she generally held them tightly shut to avoid exposing the cumbersome braces that jutted out prominently from her cavernous mouth. Though he would only know her for a week of her life, a brief snapshot in the long series of moments pieced together to form a lifetime, Jacob would come to feel that she always appeared exasperated.

Phil turned from James as quickly as he had come and placed himself right in front of Lucinda, Pamela consistently two steps behind him and Stephanie consistently two steps behind her. "So what's the plan for today?"

Lucinda, normally an enduring, patient and good-natured soul, so well-suited to her often demanding position, had obviously already tired of Phil's pervasive and domineering personality. She ignored his question and instead introduced him to Angie and Jacob. He shook their hands firmly, looking straight and piercingly into their eyes for a moment, and then went straightaway back to questioning Lucinda. "So what's the plan for today?"

"Patrice is just finishing getting the van loaded for our drive to Abalos. Why don't we all gather in the breakfast room, and when he comes in, he can take you through a more detailed daily itinerary." In an effort to shield herself as much as possible from Phil, Lucinda began escorting everyone into the breakfast room like a highlander rounding up sheep. She surveyed the room and muttered aloud to no one in particular, "Now where are Max and Claudia? We told everyone no later than eight o'clock for breakfast."

She nodded her head in approval, however, when she saw a young German couple set off in the back corner of the room staring transfixedly into each other's eyes. Max was a wiry, bookish type with residual scars that harkened back to a troubling battle with acne throughout his adolescent years. His ashen hair was greasy and straightened to his head with stringent brush strokes that parted his hair strictly down the middle of his forehead. Claudia was more full-figured and wore large, draping clothes that made it hard to distinguish precisely how heavy she was. Her legs were quite muscular, but her arms were soft, and her cheeks were puffy. They certainly made for a perplexing couple, and though he felt ashamed for doing so, Jacob chuckled to himself that their fondness for each other was probably fortified by the fact that no one else had shown an interest in either of them. They each had a cup of coffee and a Danish before them, but the coffee had long since grown cold and the pastry would have grown stale had Lucinda not induced them to join the group for Patrice's welcome talk.

When Patrice entered the room, wiping bike grease from his forearm with a well-worn rag, Phil sat up in his chair and elbowed Pamela to pay attention, as if she had not been doing so already. Patrice grabbed a set of neatly-arranged documents from Lucinda and shuffled through them aimlessly. Patrice could not have stood more than five feet, four inches tall and wore a Castelli cycling cap that covered his bald dome on top. The rest of his body was also relatively hairless save for the few tufts of dark black chest hair that poked forth from his zipped-down bike shirt. A sinewy, vigorous figure, he had thick, well-defined calves that could choke the life from a python. As he called the group to attention, he spoke in a much thicker Castillian accent than Lucinda.

"Ok Ustedes, let's gather round and talk about the plan, shall we? Yes, that's it, let's gather round the big table here. My name is Patrice, and I will be your bike guide for our trip. I believe you have all already met my beautiful esposa here, Lucinda."

For the next thirty minutes or so, Patrice outlined the basics of the trip. As he would describe a point of interest, hotel, or destination, he would reach into the pile of papers that Lucinda had provided him. Even though they had been placed in a specified order corresponding to the chronology of his descriptions, his makeshift sifting through them earlier had left them in utter disarray, so that he now had to fumble for each picture and interrupt his speech as he did so.

Today was to be a light day with a three-hour drive to Abalos where they would eat lunch before doing a bike fitting and taking an abbreviated ten mile cruise around the local vineyards of Abalos in northern Rioja. Each subsequent day would have them biking from town to town with Lucinda taking their luggage and providing van support as they rode in a generally southwestern direction towards the sleepy town of Pedrazza in the southern part of the Rioja region.

When he completed the tour itinerary, Patrice stopped to see if anyone had any further questions.

Phil rose from his chair to ask his question. "So how many miles a day?"

"Somewhere between twenty to thirty. We average about twenty-five."

"So are there opportunities to do more?" Phil asked somewhat disappointed.

"Most of the days have optional loops as well."

Satisfied, Phil sat back down.

Nancy, waiting to be sure there were no other pressing questions, raised her hand and asked, "Are there shorter options as well?"

"Ah, si senora. We also have the van if someone really needs it." Patrice spoke with a fluid, light-hearted tongue that was jovial and endearing. Lucinda, however, shot him a glance suggesting that he should have not have broached that topic until it was absolutely necessary. There was only so much room in the van, and Lucinda could already see plenty of potential takers on that offer.

He recovered quickly, though, and asked if there were any further questions. "No? Ok, group. Now, I'd like to take a quick moment here before we hit the road for our adventure to congratulate two very lucky people. Jacob and Angie, will you stand for a moment? Everyone give them a nice, big hand. These folks are celebrating their honeymoon here with us, and Lucinda and I would like to wish you our very best for a long lifetime of happiness together and thank you for starting it here with us." Lucinda reached under the table for a bottle of Lagar de Cervera. Everyone clapped, except for Phil, who was too busy perusing the itinerary map and Stephanie, who simply seemed to care less. Nancy tugged on Angie's skirt for encouragement.

Jacob merely looked at Angie with deference and thought about what it would be like to be married to her. For once, he was able to contemplate her as an extended element of his life without any association to Faith. He stole the opportunity to kiss her intensely in front of a large audience. Angie did not seem to mind.

"Thank you for celebrating your honeymoon with us," Lucinda said as she waited to hand Jacob the bottle. "May you have a long life together."

"Ok, group," Patrice finally interjected. "Time to head to lovely Abalos. I have a feeling we could be here all day if we let those two continue to get at it. Vamanos!"

After the three-hour drive to Abalos, everyone was ready for some lunch. They checked into their rooms at the hotel and then met in the lobby dressed in their cycling clothes. The bike fitting went well, though Phil was not overly impressed by his Specialized road bike.

Jacob and Angie both remarked at the increased suspension on the mountain bike hybrid model that Patrice had brought out of the van for them. As Jacob and Angie adjusted the seats on their bike, Phil looked up just long enough to ask, "So, you two are riding a tandem, huh?"

"We did it for the first time on our first date. How romantic, huh?" As Angie said this, she brushed by Phil and gave him a flippant elbow in his flexed abs.

"I guess so."

While everyone else went in for lunch, Angie and Jacob stayed out with Patrice to fill the tires on the tandem which had deflated from lack of use. In reality, he had only lingered to get a well-earned break from Phil who had been jawing at him for most of the drive from Madrid. He pulled out a pack of European cigarettes and lit one before offering the pack to Angie and then Jacob respectively. "Either of you smoke? Don't mind if I do, do you? Thanks. You folks seem like a nice couple."

"Well, thank you," replied Jacob. "But how do you ride all the time and smoke? I mean, I smoked for a while, and I couldn't bike at all."

"It's the Spanish blood, amigo. We Spaniards are built different than you Americans. You worry too much. If you didn't worry so much, you could smoke and drink like me, amigo."

Jacob thought that there might just be some wisdom in what the man said as Patrice clasped him merrily on the back and went about his tasks, puffing away offhandedly. Patrice put away the bike pump and turned to them before resuming in his free-spirited way, "I just turned fifty-five, amigo. Before I did this, I rode professionally, even came in second in the Alpe D'Huez stage in the Tour de France one year. But a few years ago, I had to have triple bypass surgery." He unzipped his biking shirt even further to reveal a massive scar that stretched down much of his chest. "Now, I know what you're thinking: it must be the cigarettes and the vino, right amigo? But no, I got a, what do you call it in English, a...a parasite, no? The doctors, they tell me that my heart is healthy as a horse, but I have this parasite, and even with the surgery, I might die, no? And I thinks to myself at that moment, well then, it's been a good life then. I could not have asked for more. Life has given me more than I could ask for, so if this is it, well then, so this is it. Thank you, life. Thank you for all you have given me. Right amigo?"

He took a final puff of his cigarette and stubbed it off on a nearby rock. Jacob looked on him with stupefied awe, as Angie nodded with appreciative genuflection.

"The bike, she is ready, no amigo?"

"Oh, she's ready."

When they joined the others inside the quaint restaurant, Phil turned to Jacob before he could even sit down and asked, "So what do you do for a living?".

"I teach English at a girls' school."

"Huh, good for you. Those who can, do. Those who can't, teach, right?" Phil thought he was being funny, but the reaction from the group suggested that he was simply out of line.

Jacob, however, thought nothing of it. "So what do you do, Phil?"

"Well, I own a construction company that builds high-end homes in suburban San Francisco."

"Tell him about the house you designed for Barry Bonds," James interjected from the other side of the table, noticeably impressed yet intimidated by Phil.

"Another time," Phil said as he waved off James's suggestion in a patently obvious display of false humility.

"How did you and Pamela meet?" Angie asked Phil.

"We met a couple of months ago on the internet, right sweetie? We thought this trip would be a good way to test our relationship and see where we should go with it." He turned to Pamela briefly but then pivoted back to Angie and Jacob in particular. Angie amused herself thinking that she knew where Pamela should "go with it".

Stephanie, meanwhile, seemed less enthused and picked at her plate, mostly comprised of fruits and vegetables. "You've got to eat something," Pamela henpecked at her.

"Mom," she drew out with agonized exasperation.

Phil diverted his attention across the table. "So Daniel, Evan, what do you guys like to do?"

Daniel spoke first. "Mostly play video games and hangout."

Phil was disconcerted. "No, but what do you actually do? You know, what sports do you play?"

Daniel and Evan looked at each other quizzically, then Evan piped out meekly, "I...I play saxophone."

Jacob had to be refrained by Angie from bursting out laughing, though she was barely able to resist doing so herself. This mere suggestion, however, of a life unlived, of a misspent youth lost to video games and too many potato chips, sent Phil into a veritable tizzy accompanied by a proselytizing diatribe on the benefits of organized sports and a life lived with rigor and passion. Phil had been the captain of his swimming team at the University of Southern California and was a freak accident away from a trip to the Olympics. This experience and all those many others that led to his many accolades and accomplishments in the field of swimming were, according to Phil, the backbone of who he was as a man. To this day, they formed the daily regimen that made him a success in athletics, in business, and in life.

Evan and Daniel were, for their parts, stunned. They gazed on in disbelief as Phil ranted in elegant terms that were totally lost on them as nonsensical gibberish. From that point forward on the trip, Phil became their self-appointed life guru. He would tell them what they should eat and how they should train for a better life.

"You should eat those Brussels sprouts over there. They're good for you. You've already wolfed down that whole cookie," he said matter-of-factly to Evan who had pushed much of the vegetables to the side of his plate.

James and Nancy, like their children, were speechless. Evan sat quietly and waited for Phil's attention to be diverted so that he could ask his mother for her cookie. She slid it to him under the table and said, "Here you go, son." It was easy to see how Evan and Daniel were placated in the Granger household.

Patrice had watched things go from bad to worse. Phil was not just the type to make things miserable for him; he was going to make things miserable for everyone else too. "*Oh well,*" he thought, "*I still get to be on my bike.*"

"All right, everybody, vamanos!"

The ride after lunch was a predominately flat, easy venture through a series of sprawling vineyards surrounding Abalos. The countryside was composed of rolling hills covered with the region's distinctive rows of grapes and verdant pastures for farming. Jacob and Angie fell in love with the place almost immediately, its majestic scenery and sluggish, slumberous pace. As they rolled down seemingly endless, dusty roads, they chatted merrily and waved at the few passersby wandering lackadaisically down the road in the midday sun. These locals, with their skins darkened by the intense rays of the sun and with weary and often toothless smiles, would give them an energetic thumbs-up and shout after them, "Muy bien, la bicicleta de amor!"

They readily fell back into a natural rhythm of stroking that was itself simple, organic, and beautiful. Not only was the straining of their legs brought together in a free-flowing unison linking two distinct sets of pedals to a shared chain, they seemed to be in harmony with all that surrounded them as the gentle breeze rose to meet them and fill their lungs with the thick, fragrant air of Northern Spain. They sped along past intermittent poplar trees that lined the narrow road, and the intoxication filled them with an overwhelming closeness for each other.

While the compounded weight of the tandem bike was a noticeable detraction when climbing hills of any credible size, here on relatively flat ground, Jacob and Angie were able to cruise effortlessly at a good clip. As they overtook Phil, who was pedaling vigorously, he said to them derisively, "No fair, you know. You got two people pedaling that thing."

"I don't think it's a competition, Phil," Angie said with a grin, "but I may have a glass of wine sitting in me when I see you back at the hotel. Cheers."

Jacob bellowed mightily as they dug in to put some distance between them and Phil. Angie poked him in the back. "I know, what an asshole, right?"

Soon they found themselves alongside of Patrice who usually rode in back, but could go out front for this shorter leg with Lucinda providing van support in the rear.

"Ah, my favorite tandem-riding newlyweds, how are you enjoying the ride so far?" It took Patrice a moment to recover from the realization that someone had actually caught up to him.

"It's beautiful, simply lovely," Angie shouted back at him.

"You two ride pretty fast on that thing," Patrice remarked.

"Thanks," Jacob replied.

"So when did you two get married?"

Now Jacob was starting to feel guilty about deceiving Patrice. He felt like he was starting off a potentially great friendship on a foundation of dishonesty. Still, he replied, "In March, during my Spring break. We wanted to wait until now though to go on our honeymoon."

"On a tandem bike nonetheless! How romantic, amigo! I like your style, Jacob. Lucinda and I have been married for twenty-eight wonderful years now, and I don't know what I'd do without her." Jacob felt a pit building in his stomach fed by a bitter discontent that consumed him. He tried to shake it off and give greater heed to Patrice's words, but the image of a love taken prematurely lingered and distracted him. "I used to go out and party and be with all kinds of girls. You know what I mean, right, amigo?" Patrice leaned over and jabbed Jacob in the shoulder. His mind elsewhere until that moment, the gentle nudge caused Jacob to veer and almost send them toppling to the ground.

"Be careful, amigo," Patrice warned before finishing his point. "In any case, I was a rock star, you understand. I rode around the world as a professional bike racer, and the life was crazy and fun, lots of fun, but I began to realize it was empty and vacant. Where would this be when I got older? I mean, I was glad I did it, but it had no future in it. But then I met Lucinda, and I had a purpose, a meaning, you know what I mean? She was the joy that made life worth living. I see that in you two, also. I think you are going to have a very happy life together."

Angie reached forward and touched Jacob's hand, giving it a slight squeeze before tailing off. He could not look back, but as she did so, Jacob could somehow sense what her face looked like with the blond ringlets hanging down from beneath her bike helmet.

"Well, I'm sorry lovebirds, but my Spanish pride will not allow you to get back to the hotel before me on the one day I can ride as fast as I like. Adios amiogs! I'll save you a glass of wine at the hotel." And with that, he was off. It was remarkable to witness him putting it into another gear and tearing off down the road with a speed they could barely fathom. Even more remarkable, however, was the unmistakable look of bliss on his face as he glanced back at them one more time before dashing off into the wide-open horizon.

Though it had been a thoroughly enjoyable afternoon of getting to know the various personalities that made up the group followed by a traditional meal and wine tasting, Jacob and Angie were more than content to retire to their room afterwards for some much needed rest and a little time to themselves. They were, after all, newlyweds, if only fake ones.

"That was a good warm-up ride for today, but I still have plenty of energy…" Angie floated out there, hoping for a response that might provide her a stronger inclination of what Jacob was thinking. As she arched her back to bend forward and pull down the sheets, the light emanating from the nightstand lamp radiated on her shoulders and attached itself to her whole being. The contrast of light and shadow in the room allowed him to truly see her, as if for the first time, and to recognize how beautiful she really was. He stood there for a moment in just his boxers as he gazed into her before putting on his t-shirt.

This afforded her an equal opportunity to appraise the physique of the man whom she had up to now only managed mere glimpses of. His hair was now nearly entirely gray, but his torso was strong and firm, suggesting the vitality of a much younger man. His arms were lean and muscular, while his thick legs were like anchored tree trunks. *"Not bad for a man over forty,"* she thought to herself, but what always stood out were those piercing green eyes.

"Do you think I'm getting fat?" he asked her jokingly after he had noticed Angie checking him out, using a satirical falsetto to parody one of his students. He slid into bed next to her and pulled her closer so that he could embrace her from behind. He thought twice of the t-shirt and tossed it aside, prompting her to do the same. He pulled her in even tighter, trying to eliminate any gap between them so that every ounce of his flesh could meet its counterpart in hers.

She felt his hand slide across her sides and onto her midsection. As he used a single finger to line the delicate crevice beneath each of her breasts, she thought she could feel his increased arousal press against her backside. She was curious about where this was leading but interested, and she sensed a mounting anticipation inside her. She was waiting to accept him if he was ready.

Jacob ached with a physical desire for her that coursed through his veins and out his pores. He felt like a savage animal intently eyeing its prey, its senses alive and hyper-vigilant. He could feel his engorged penis pressed against her back and her subtle gesticulations that made him strain for a release. He wanted this. He needed it.

But his mind, as always, went back to Faith. He held Angie in the cool darkness where all is opened and revealed, but his hands kept reaching out into the emptiness of night for something that was no longer there. His arms seemed to stretch into the vastness of the universe, with his fingers spread out in yearning desperation, but his hands could not find what they were looking for. Instinctively, he drew away from Angie, just enough to withdraw the suggestion, and he tried to drift off to sleep, alone in the swirl of his own tortured thoughts.

Angie felt but did not look back into the quiet torrent that raged behind her. She reached back to hold him, but in some sense, he was already gone. She staved off any feelings of disappointment or rejection by reminding herself that she just needed to have patience. Time and patience.

As everyone assembled on the front steps of the hotel after breakfast the next morning, a darkened cloud developed over the southern sky. Phil and James had both noticed it and were pointing it out to others when Patrice arrived. He was not much of one for breakfast and preferred to instead indulge in an extra thirty minutes of sleep and suffice with a strong cup of coffee instead.

"So what happens if it starts to rain?" James asked nervously before Patrice could launch into the plan for the day.

As the smell of rain descended upon them, Patrice, as was his custom, attempted to lighten the mood. "We ride right through it of course, amigos. Have you never had the sweet sensation of riding through the Spanish rain? It is simply lovely, mis amigos."

"It sounds simply wet to me," retorted Evan disheartedly.

"No, no Evan," Patrice chimed. "You are missing the beauty of it. The rains here are wonderful. Don't you remember that song from *My Fair Lady?*" He looked from person to person as he began singing, but only Jacob and Angie seemed amused. *"The rains in Spain fall mostly in the plains...* Well, here we are in the plains, mis amigos, and it is going to be a spectacular ride. Today we will ride to Briones to see the Museo Dinastia Vivanco, one of the best wine museums in the world. I hope no one is wearing their good socks today because here we will actually get to be a part of the winemaking process the old fashioned way, bare feet required!"

Patrice was doing his best, but the gloom was not lifting, so Jacob, no longer capable of comprehending the negativity regarding a little rain, intervened. "All right then, sounds fun. Let's get to it." They both knew that Patrice was not quite finished with his morning pep talk, as he had not told them about the rest of the bike ride to Azofre or the van ride to Lerma, but when Jacob ventured towards his bike, the rest of the group instinctually followed suit, and Patrice was grateful for the opportunity to hit the road.

The rain held out for the majority of the morning as they passed through the hillier terrain from Abalos to Briones. With the extra weight of the tandem, Jacob and Angie hung further back and paced themselves accordingly. Plus, they would not have wanted to pass Phil again and pique his competitive spirit.

Patrice, likewise, stayed in the furthest back grouping which generally consisted of the Granger family along with Stephanie and Pamela. While Stephanie was certainly fit enough to prove a stronger rider, she had evidently only ridden a bike a handful of times in her life and had difficulty incorporating the steering and weight distribution of the bike to keep it going level and straight. She teetered back and forth across the road like the town drunk stumbling home from the pub at closing time. She had obviously been dragged on this outing involuntarily as the coincident inclusion of Phil's courtship of her mother. Though Pamela knew she would hear an earful of rage from Phil for not riding up with him, she felt guilty for subjecting her daughter to all this and rode alongside her for the better part of the morning.

Evan and Daniel, meanwhile, struggled mightily, far behind the pack. While their parents were avid bikers, it was not something James and Nancy generally imposed on the boys. Evan, in particular, his black cotton t-shirt soaked through with perspiration, slaved against what must have seemed imposing hills to a boy from Wisconsin. On the more sustained uphill pitches, Patrice would literally ride alongside him with his outstretched hand on Evan's back and help push him up the hill with the force of his own exertion. Jacob motioned to Angie to look back at Patrice as they huffed and puffed themselves up a twisting incline bordered by olive trees. They each marveled at how a man who had had triple bypass surgery could accomplish the feat so facilely.

Patrice would let both he and Evan concentrate on their cadence as they summited the uphills, only occasionally shouting words of encouragement. As they coasted along the downhills, however, Patrice would lay further off and chat aimlessly with Evan, asking him about his favorite sax players and video games that he played. As everyone pulled alongside the van parked at the Museo Dinastia Vivanco, a smile of accomplishment made its way across Evan's face. The rains had at least held off for the leg to Briones.

It was startling to see what several glasses of wine and some bare-footed grape stomping could do to energize the tone of the morning. Even the kids, who did most of the stomping, were in good spirits as they left the Museo Dinastia Vivanco to head back out on the road to Azofre, their end destination for the day. Though the storm clouds loomed even more ominously than before, the group itself was less daunted by the prospects of rain.

Phil, of course, was on his bike anxiously waiting for everyone else to be ready to go as he charged out ahead of the pack, riding ahead and alone as he generally did. Max and Claudia, who mostly kept to themselves and were rarely seen throughout the trip other than in the van or at meals, where they would sit alone together and fixate on each other's windows to the soul, were surprisingly strong riders and tailed not too distantly behind Phil. Everyone else meandered along at their own pace.

They had not been riding long, however, when the rains did finally burst loose, gentle and satisfying at first, but turning quickly to a soaking precipitation that clung to the bones. Jacob could not deny feeling quite refreshed until the skies opened up and the storm intensified. They pulled alongside the road to don their pullovers, allowing everyone but Evan and Patrice to pass them as they did so.

Jacob was just zipping his jacket up and looking out into the drenching rain that glistened and pooled in the cracks of the asphalt when he made out the figure of Stephanie's bike, shadowy from that distance as it was, swaying precipitously to and fro like an overmatched fishing boat lost amongst the waves. Then she was gone. He double-checked his vision, but he could not make her out against the horizon. He turned back to Angie as she was cinching her hood. "I think Stephanie just fell."

They raced ahead and found her lying on her side, not screaming out in pain, but merely sobbing deeply and achingly. Pamela, who had been riding a little ways ahead of Stephanie, had heard the fall and was already tending to her daughter and stroking her hair as she elevated her head upon her knee. "Oh, baby, I'm so sorry. I'm so sorry I made you do this."

Stephanie was unable to respond but sobbed even more profusely as she clung to her mother to fight through the pain. When Patrice rode up with Evan moments later, he dismounted his bike without a moment's hesitation and came running up to assess the situation. His carefree demeanor changed in an instant as he phoned Lucinda who had driven ahead in the van.

"Darling, Stephanie's had an accident. I don't think we have any broken bones, but we've got some pretty good road rash here. You better pick everyone else up and get back here. We're going to have to take her to the hospital."

By the time Lucinda made it back to them with the rest of the group, Stephanie had managed to sit upright and Patrice was applying towels to the burns and scrapes that ran high up her right leg. She had evidently fallen to her right side during the crash as the asphalt had also attacked her right shoulder through her now tattered shirt. Pamela was sitting next to her, and Patrice was crouched in front of her trying to make eye contact and ask her basic questions to check for concussion symptoms. "Do you think you can hold out for about an hour car ride, Stephanie? Logrono is only thirty minutes, but it's in the other direction, and you'd be farther from the motel if we took you there. Burgos is about an hour, but it's on the way to Lerma. What do you think?"

As Patrice was finishing his question, Phil came storming out of the van, demanding to see Stephanie immediately. When appraised of the two options, Phil blew out a humph of disbelief and ranted, "Oh for crying out loud, I think she can make it for a fucking hour-long car ride. She's not bleeding to death."

Pamela glared him and mustered the courage to not yell, but declare with significant conviction, "Shut up, Phil," before turning back to Stephanie and pacifying her, "It's up to you, baby. We can do whatever you want."

Stephanie gathered her breath but then said with strength, "I can suck it up, mom."

"You don't have to."

"It's fine, mom. I'll be fine."

Stephanie would spend the remainder of the trip relegated to the van, more engaged with Lucinda than at any other point up until then. Stephanie's only real complaint from that point forward was Lucinda's preference for Spanish flamenco guitar and her unwillingness to budge even periodically in her musical playlist. Still, Evan and Daniel pined to their parents to no avail for the opportunity to join Stephanie and Lucinda in the air-conditioned van.

Later, back at the Parador, a retreat established in the early seventeenth century for King Felipe III, where Jacob and Angie were upgraded to the actual former King's suite despite Phil's vocalized consternation, Phil, James, and Jacob shared a glass of local wine as the others prepared for dinner and Pamela checked in with Stephanie at the hospital in Burgos. Phil, still wearing his spandex biking shorts, tried to play off his conflict with Pamela and ingratiate himself with the boys.

"I mean, that's the thing about dating Pamela. She's great and all, but she comes with that daughter of hers. That girl is just as plain Jane as it gets; she never wants to do anything."

Both the teacher and the father in Jacob were provoked by Phil's comment. "Have you ever asked her what *she* wants to do?"

"That's the thing," Phil responded with a sudden defensiveness. "She doesn't want to do *anything.*"

"Wouldn't hurt to ask," Jacob said passively as he swished the wine in his glass and savored its contents.

"So how are things going to be with Pamela tonight?" James inquired of Phil collegially.

"Well, I'm probably not getting laid tonight, that's for sure, but she'll come back around. It's not like I pushed Stephanie off the bike." For some reason, though, Jacob could envision him doing it.

That night, after he climbed into bed with Angie, Jacob could not fall asleep and so paged through inconsequential emails on his phone. Angie had dozed off restfully long before, but he struggled with his conflicting thoughts and emotions well into the night. She looked so peaceful to him there in the dim glimmer of the refracted bathroom light, as her chest heaved deeply with each precious breath. He touched her there in the darkness, and her lightly freckled skin spoke to him of the life she had led before him. She was tender but strong, and her body felt like the lifeline of true happiness.

As he lifted from the bed into another space of transcendence, however, the old demons rose to greet him. They jostled him and prevented his slumber with a nagging persistence that ate at him in his own hollow hole. He wished them away once and for all, strove to beat back the current of their manifestations, but the emptiness of Faith echoed throughout the room.

He ran his fingers through Angie's hair and felt a softness that centered him. She murmured modestly but returned to her sleep with a subconscious smile across her face. Jacob fixated on that softness and felt a cool air brush past him. His eyes closed of their own will, and all he could see was blue, a tranquil blue that calmed him and reminded him of days he knew were happy, days where he did not worry what would happen next. He had a vision of himself as a young child, playing blithely beneath the warmth of the sun on a grassy beach surrounded by depths of blue. He focused on the brilliant blue where the ocean met the sky on the line of a distant horizon, and he found himself drifting wistfully into a rare contented sleep.

He awoke near the dim hours of the dawn filled not with dread but with an unnatural zeal that lifted him from the bed. Something was abuzz inside him. He strode forcefully to the antique writing desk and scribbled and erased and re-scribbled. He was a fountain that was overflowing, and the poetry spilled from him like the sweet ambrosia of the gods. It was his first poem about Angie:

Blue

There she stands in front of me
Wrapped in every shade of blue
Blue, blue, blue I say
Like twilight hours fast receeding
Across the still and sandy bay.

She is the color of that sky,
The hue of that horizon.
She is the quiet, tranquil calm
On the verge of the epiphany,
Lingering there
As the breeze sweeps past ideas and thoughts of things
gone by
Till there is nothing left but blue.

And to say that she is blue
Is to say that she is that cool softness
That floats upon the waves at daybreak,
Is to say that she is just as I found her
An unconscious babe lost at sea
Who never seemed to know.

Quietly, I lay beside her
And feel what is left that is good in this world,
Pure and unstained,
True and undisturbed.
I rest for a moment in her bosom
And return to days lying on the supple grass
My eyes gazing upon the clear blue sky
That nurtured my amazement
In its vacant profundity

For me,
She is everything Kandinsky says is blue.
She is the raw essence of its emotion,
The calm collectedness of its being.
She is the comfortable feeling
Of evenings in the dark.

After Jacob had penned the final line and done some preliminary edits, he rose from the desk and went back to a delightful slumber. He concentrated on allowing his chest to rise and fall in synchronized breathing with Angie. It soothed him and left him with a sense of fulfillment and satisfaction that he had been yearning for since Faith had left him. Though his sleep was limited by the need to rise for a strenuous day of riding through the Ribera del Duero wine region, the depth of sleep left him feeling rested and refreshed.

He awoke with a buoyancy that was readily discernible to Angie. Though she was herself still brushing off the last remnants of slumber, she walked up behind him as he was stepping into the shower and delicately kissed his lower neck. "Good morning, Sunshine! What has you up so early today?"

Jacob had not heard that name in quite some time. It made him smile, though, as he turned on whatever hot water the shower could muster. He opted not to show her the poem at that point, however; he wanted to wait until they had more time.

The ride that day took them through some of the most spectacular scenery they had seen to date. Though their route wove past majestic tree-lined mountains, they rode through a lush valley that was replete with countless vineyards stretching as far as the eye could see. The greenness of this world, as it rose to life and went about the business of its day, seeped into their skin and invigorated them as they pedaled by, casual spectators to all that lay before them.

The cycling was relatively flat, and Jacob and Angie soaked in the cool breeze as they sailed past an indifferent world. They chatted little as they each became absorbed in reflection. The silence, rather than distancing them, connected them in a still communion with nature. There was no need for idle talk; they could feel what the other was thinking.

It was only when Patrice caught up to them towards the end of the morning ride that either of them had any real need for communication. Patrice, though, just seemed to have that effect on people: you could not help but want to talk and make merry with him.

"Hey, Patrice," Angie yelled over at him.

"Yes, Señorita Bonita?"

"Why do the sheep have blue ink all over their rears? Is that how the farmers mark the sheep as theirs instead of branding them? Why do it on their bung hole then?"

Patrice laughed. "I have not heard this term before. You call it the 'bung hole', no?"

"Yes."

"Well now, since I need to be sure we are both referring to the same thing, do both boys and girls have a 'bung hole'?"

"You've got it."

"Ok then, Señorita, you will notice that only the females have these marks above their 'bung holes'. Yes?"

"Ok, I think I see where you are going with this," Angie said, a grin spreading across her face. The look on Jacob's face, however, suggested that he still did not quite grasp the insinuation.

Patrice chuckled and clasped Jacob on the back. "Don't worry, amigo; I know you are new to the game of love.

Let me explain for you. You see, the boy sheep- the farmer straps a packet on his front filled with the dye, no?" Jacob nodded. "Now, when the boy goes to, you know, make the love with the girl, he mounts her from behind, no? Well, when he does, the ink breaks open and marks the girl. That way the farmer knows which girls have been mated and which ones have not. Thank heavens all the padres of the girls I knew when I was younger did not make me wear an ink packet strapped to my chest for my dates, huh amigo? I may not be here to tell this story, you know what I mean?"

The three of them rode on together for a while laughing and discussing the sometimes plain silliness of copulation, regardless of the species. As they saw the van just ahead, Patrice prepared for a final sprint to test his competitive spirit, but before he left them, said, "Now remember you two are newlyweds, mis amigos. I don't see any markings on her yet, Jacob. I expect you to remedy this. Otherwise, I might have to trade in my beautiful Lucinda for a newer model." Then he winked at them and was gone.

Lunch was a gourmet picnic of traditional Castilian fare prepared by Lucinda herself. They lounged in the grass beneath the castle of Penaranda, with its ancient outcroppings and turreted stone walls. Even as they rode up, Lucinda greeted them with a bevy of meats, cheeses, and vegetables arranged with delicate precision across a picnic table that she had adorned with various flowers and decorations.

"This is quite the spread, Lucinda. Thank you very much," Angie said fondly as she dug into one of the sausages covered thinly in a rich grilling sauce.

Phil and Pamela had been the first to make it to the castle and were currently sitting off to the side arguing vehemently. Lucinda seemed pleased to have someone else to talk to so that she could inoculate herself from overhearing Phil's assertions that Stephanie had sabotaged their trip intentionally. "You're quite welcome, Angie. These are all my favorite dishes my mother taught me to make. The paella, for example, is a Valencian dish that is often prepared with seafood, but we lived in a village near Segovia where seafood was not so readily available, so she would make it with sausage or chicken."

"It's delicious," Angie muddled out, after putting her finger to her lips so that she could swallow the generous sampling she had just been noshing. "Much better than any I've ever had in the States."

She sat down in the grass and waited for Jacob to join her, but Pamela strode away from Phil in a huff and commenced to sit down by Angie and make small talk. Pamela needed a barrier to insulate herself from Phil's barrage, and Angie was a more inviting option for female camaraderie than the recently arrived Claudia, for whom extrication from Max seemed inconceivable. Angie had no issues with Pamela, in fact felt quite sorry for her, but the situation left her feeling edgily awkward, as she watched Phil glare in their general direction. When Jacob did make it over, he gave Angie a concealed expression of commiseration, as he sat in their general proximity but far enough off still to avoid being dragged into the drama itself.

Not long after, the Grangers rode onto the castle grounds, Evan and Daniel heaving themselves onto the ground in exhaustion and vexation. Daniel immediately proceeded to whine that he was hungry but too tired to stand up and get himself food, and he entreated his mother to bring him a plate. When she acquiesced to his pitifully delivered appeal, his brother joined the request.

That was when Phil, left with no one towards whom to direct his pent up frustration, decided he needed to insert himself into this circumstance with Evan and Daniel. "Now boys, don't let your mother do that for you. Don't you have any respect for her? For yourselves? What are you, a couple of mama's boys? That ride this morning was entirely flat. Don't be like that. Go get your own food for crying out loud."

Evan and Daniel merely stared at him mutely. Phil's draconian standpoint on child rearing was so entirely foreign to their own personal upbringing that Phil's words might as well have been futile sperm trying to permeate the cell membrane of an already fertilized egg, struggling to get in but knocking on a door that had already been shut. He stood above them, however, until they reticently rose and followed him over to the table laden with Lucinda's culinary delights, figuring that this at least would make him go away. It did not, however. As Evan began to pile his plate with various meats and cheeses, Phil set to chastising him further. "Now don't just go filling up on all those high fat foods. You've gotta grab some of those veggies and fruits also. Your body is a well-oiled Maserati, but you've gotta take care of it, put the right fuel in it. How are you ever going to play a varsity sport eating like that?"

"But I don't want to play a varsity sport," Evan responded meekly.

"Well, that's between you and your parents," Phil continued, barely pausing to consider Evan's comment. "But you've got to eat well to live well. You know what they say, 'You are what you eat.'" And with this and a hearty clap on Evan's shoulder meant to express that he was, of course, only doing this to help Evan, Phil finally walked off, smugly feeling a bit better about things because he truly believed he was making a difference in the life of two boys who clearly needed it.

Allowing Phil to first draw further off, Daniel, seeing his brother needed some relief, came over to Evan and whispered in his brother's ear, "Well, if 'what they say' is true, I think Phil is gay."

Evan smirked. "Why do you say that?"

"Because he must have just eaten an asshole."

Having spent most of her lunch anxiously conversing with Pamela, Angie wanted to be sure that for the afternoon ride to Penaranda del Duero they be decidedly in the predictable gap between the Grangers and the other two couples so that they could extricate themselves from the various group dynamics for a while. Jacob did not hesitate to assent.

The vineyards of the morning ride slowly shifted to wheat fields as they rolled along an old dirt road used principally by local farmers. Occasionally, they would spot a farmer working in the fields who would raise his hand in acknowledgement before returning to the work that needed to be done.

The tandem bike was thicker and weightier than a typical road bike and thus better able to withstand the potholes and ruts of the worn, bumpy road they rambled down towards Penaranda del Duero. They easily could have caught up to any of the riders in front of them, but they enjoyed taking a more leisurely pace for a while.

They stopped along the dusty road, the sun beating fiercely upon them, and drank to quench the thirst that seemed to arise from the road itself. They both gulped greedily like dogs drinking from their water bowl, as they sat on a dry, grassy patch along the road.

As Angie went to pass her bottle back to Jacob, she noticed a burro tied to the fencepost behind them. The burro was widely built but emaciated, its gray hair falling out like a threadbare coat that had hung in the closet for a season too long. The distinctive black trim along its ears and mane was dimmed by a covering of dust from the road, and the pungent odor of its own remains clung to the air around him. Far worse, however, were the flies that besieged him with a persistence that must have driven the poor burro absolutely insane until at long last he simply became conditioned to accept the tireless annoyance. He had learned this helplessness because the pitiful creature was tethered with no further leeway than a slight twisting motion of its head ten or fifteen degrees in either direction. As such, its only means of defense from this assault was to bat its eyes or swat its tail that was too short to reach any of its face anyway. The miserable creature had submitted itself to its fate and waited for an end to its suffering that could only come from death.

"My God, Jacob, look at that poor burro. It can't even move its head. I can't believe someone would do that to an animal. Why even have it if you are just going to torture it like that?"

As Jacob eyed the creature, he contemplated the weight of human-induced suffering and how it covered all in a layer of tragedy, much like the burro's coating of hazy dust upon his back. Jacob sighed and looked resignedly at the creature with empathy. He too had known suffering that had endured. He too had borne the burden of injustice. Jacob quickly examined the thick hemp cord that bound the burro with three buntline hitch knots. Then he gazed into the burro's sad, listless eyes that were crusted over in the corners due to its excessive blinking and whispered to it softly, "You will be free, mi amigo. If only for a moment, you too will know what it means to be free."

Angie, unable to hear him, asked, "What did you just say?"

Jacob, however, did not absorb her question and focused instead on the task at hand. "Run up ahead aways. Wait for ten minutes. When I come by on the bicycle, be ready to hop on and make a break for it. No matter what, don't stop pedaling."

Angie deciphered his intent and kissed him. He was, at first, too distracted to be much bothered, but her zeal impressed itself on him, and he suddenly comprehended just what this meant to her. She finally pulled back away from him after a last compelling press of her lips against his and said, "You're really going to do this aren't you? You crazy bastard, you're really going to do it."

"Just run down the road and wait for me. Ten minutes, I'll be there in ten minutes."

As Jacob crested the hill and came into view, the bike was wobbling from the lack of equal weight distribution created by a second rider but was nonetheless careening down the road recklessly at breakneck speed, kicking up dust that obscured the scene behind it. When the dust did settle, though, Jacob and the teetering tandem bike were hardly the most bewildering aspect of the spectacle. Directly behind Jacob came the burro running frantically. Though it was hobbled by the muscular atrophy that it had incurred over many years of disuse, the burro made desperate strides that somehow just managed to keep its legs upright beneath it. The animal, from a distance, seemed petrified but exhilarated and alive as it tore down the road in the flight for its life.

Farther back came three men in an old, beaten down pickup truck, but they were gaining ground steadily. The two men inside the truck were shouting out indistinguishable epithets in Spanish as they raised their fists into the air to curse the one who had done this to them.

Jacob pulled alongside her and shouted for her to get on. Just as he did so, the third man who had been brandishing a rifle from the bed of the pickup, let out a shot that reverberated through the thick air like a death knell. Abruptly, this became much more serious for Angie. They pedaled fiercely, but the truck just kept gaining on them. The burro, however, its stamina greatly weakened, began to tire. Though it ran with all its might, it simply had nothing left to give. It pulled up lame and collapsed in a heap along the roadside.

This left the men with a confounding dilemma: go after the man that had perpetrated the deed or procure the burro and be done with the whole affair. They opted for the latter and while the man let out one last rifle shot from the bed of the pickup, they tailed off and came to a screeching halt at the supine burro that had known liberation, if only for a brief and shining moment.

Jacob and Angie continued to ride with a wild abandon. Their hearts raced and coursed blood throughout their aching muscles. Jacob remembered the sled and what it felt to be alive, but he remained vigilantly focused on the present. No more waiting for today, it was already here. They sped off into the horizon and did not look back.

That night, when they returned home to their hotel, they never did quite make it down to dinner. As Jacob entered their room, Angie swung him around and pinned him down on the bed. She gazed deep into his mesmerizing green eyes and said with a playful passion, "That was the most romantic thing anyone has ever done for me." Jacob chuckled, but she hit him with a pillow and then went on seriously, "I mean it. That was the most romantic thing anyone has ever done for me." She leaned over him and kissed him forcefully on the mouth. "I want to make love to you, Jacob. I want to make love to you right now." She said this emphatically but was entirely tender as she laid willowy kisses down his neck and chest with each successive button she undid.

The next morning, Jacob and Angie got ahold of a blue marker and colored the back of Jacob's Camelback and Angie's riding shorts. As they descended the steps for Patrice's description of their final day's ride, Jacob flipped his Camelback around so that he wore it on his front. Patrice grasped the joke immediately.

"Very good, amigos! The marriage is now official. I am glad, for I did not want to trade in my beautiful Lucinda for anyone in the world, even you my lovely Angie."

The group was in generally good spirits as they assembled on the steps after breakfast. The sun had just begun to crest above the rolling hills and vineyards, and it spoke to a glorious day to come. They were to start the day in the hillside town of Sepulveda, dramatically situated on the edge of the Duratón Canyon Nature Reserve, where they would coast down into the valley of wheat fields surrounding Segovian towns until they reached the Casla River where the riding would become more strenuous. As they rode uphill to the medieval fortress city of Pedraza del Sierra, they would face the most significant climb they had encountered yet. One of the most stunning walled cities in all of Spain, Pedraza was nestled upon a breathtaking mountainside affording stunning vistas of the valley below. Boasting of a 15th-century castle and a medieval town square, Pedraza would be a well-earned final destination.

Jacob leaned over to kiss Angie as they set themselves to embark on the final day of their journey. She took the time to look up and in to him, as her cleats clacked against the cobblestone walkway.

"I've really enjoyed this trip together. I'll never forget it. Thank you," he said to her, as they turned towards each other with the bike settled between them. Her eyes shone as blue as ever with a shaft of light pressing against them in the early morning hours of dawn. She was everything he could have wanted, everything he could have asked for, everything he dreamed of in those lonely, desperate hours without Faith.

"I want to see you two out in front today," Phil came by and said, interrupting the perfect moment. "No more pussyfooting around out there. You've got two people pedaling that thing, you know."

"We've also got twice the weight, you know," Jacob retorted irritably. He was growing tired of Phil's nonsense.

"Oh come on," Phil said, pointing in the direction of Angie. "How much can that little thing weigh?"

Jacob merely shook his head, "Did you really just call her a 'thing'?"

"You know that's not what I meant."

"All right, Phil, you just have a good day, ok?" Jacob said as he diverted his attention back to Angie. They commenced their count together and mounted the tandem with uncanny precision, leaving Phil and his misery behind them.

And it felt just like that, like they were leaving behind all the misery, the pain, the sorrow, the weight of a far too exacting world, leaving all of it rustling in the wind that rippled past them as they rode with a fierce delight. Soaring down along the canyon into picturesque wheat fields that spread out before them like a finely patched quilt woven from the scraps of life's fabric, they relished the flurry of sounds around them and allowed their thoughts to be consumed by their organic relation to all of it. Expecting and even anticipating the challenge to come after lunch, they savored the peaceful meditation of the morning ride.

Though Patrice attempted to convince everyone to join him for a glass of wine when they stopped for lunch at a local vineyard in La Matilla, he had no takers. A general sense of apprehension hung amongst the group as they thought about the trial that lay before them. Evan and Daniel each convinced their parents to give them their flan for extra energy on the way up.

As it was, the hill did not prove all that particularly taxing to Jacob and Angie. Though it was a seemingly endless series of switchbacks that felt like walking the perpetual staircase in Escher's famed optical illusion, it was a steady incline without much of a dramatic pitch. Jacob and Angie found a consistent cadence and fell into a rhythm that sustained them as they trudged ever upwards.

"You're doing great back there," Jacob encouraged Angie from the front.

"You're *looking* great from back here," she huffed as she panted along.

"You look great from just about anywhere."

"God, you're romantic," she said. "You're cheesy as Cheez-Whiz, but you sure are romantic. Let's do this thing."

They powered through the remainder of the hill with a renewed energy that pushed them like a stiff easterly breeze blowing them home to the final dawning of human civilization. They found a common strength in each other, as they egged each other on with an enthusiasm that had become contagious.

As they passed Phil on the final stretch to the hotel, they never spoke a word, never glanced back in his direction; they just kept on going. They could barely hear him as his voice rung out, "Oh sure, save yourselves for the final hill, huh? No fair..."

The Granger boys, however, did not fare so well. On the verge of heat exhaustion as the sun beat down upon them mercilessly, they both had genuinely wanted to make it through the climb but were overwhelmed. Even with Patrice essentially pushing him up most of the hill, Evan wearied both mentally and physically and began to plead to be allowed into the van. Daniel, doing his best to challenge himself with the vigorous climb, made it further, well over halfway, before capitulating to a similar two-fold fatigue. They slunk together in the back of the van as they passed the other bikers in the group and drove into the parking lot of the stately hotel in the midst of Pedraza. The banner that Lucinda had stretched across the roadway congratulating them for their accomplishment and welcoming them to their final destination must have rung a bit hollow for the two boys, and probably Stephanie as well, but if it did, they seemed oblivious to it nonetheless.

In fact, both Evan and Daniel graciously exited the bus and proceeded to assist Lucinda in helping to stack the bikes on the red and white trailer that Patrice would drive back to Abalos while Lucinda shuttled the various parties to the airport the next day. As each rider reached the grounds of the hotel, the boys would pass the bike up to Lucinda in the bed of the pickup, and she would fasten it securely to the trailer. Angie and Jacob, being the first to arrive, complimented the boys on their effort.

Phil, of course, came soon behind them. Still embittered from having been bested on the final leg, he found his opportunity for a regained sense of self in Evan. With Jacob and Angie still well within earshot, he handed his bike to the boys and immediately set to lecturing Evan about the body's thriving upon physical exertion. Using wind as his metaphor for the free-flowing absorption of oxygen that is generated during a robust cardiovascular workout, Phil delved deep into his resources to convince the boy of a life filled with vigorous exercise, all for the boy's own good, of course. This was his final pitch, and he would know no bounds in ratcheting up the rhetorical hyperbole to seal the deal and sell this boy on an entirely reformed lifestyle. He would convince him that the life he was living was really no life at all and employ himself as a paragon of the ideal life that Evan could emulate to make himself happy. He would do what he must to change him.

"Now Evan, I saw you riding in the van. What was that all about?"

Evan hunched his shoulders sluggishly.

"You don't know? What do you mean you don't know? I know, I'll tell ya. You didn't have any wind. Do you know what I mean by that Evan?"

Another hunch of the shoulders.

"I'll tell ya. You don't have the wind of life going through you. You sit at home and play your silly video games instead of going out and experiencing life. You sit there, and you eat your Doritos, and you watch the world go by. But you got no wind, no humph to you, boy. And let me tell you something, Evan, without wind, you ain't got nothing. Without wind, you ain't got nothing at all."

Evan had had enough. He had put up with Phil's proselytizing for the better part of a week now, and he was done. He summoned every ounce of his defiance and resentment and delivered it in just one word. Like few English majors ever could, Evan found the means to convey a week's worth of frustration and bitterness with a single word that expressed Evan's outright rejection of not only Phil, but his entire blasted philosophy.

"What...*ever.*" The pause in the middle of the word allowed it to be articulated with such derision, such biting disregard and apathy that Phil, for once, was struck silent. The final syllable was so truncated by utter disgust that it left a lingering acrid taste in Phil's mouth.

"What...*ever.*" It rung in Jacob's ear long after its original utterance. It kept coming back to him in waves of hilarity. He could never have imagined such a complete dismissal, such an open mocking of an impassioned speech like Phil's, never mind in a single word. And Evan's intonation had been perfect. He was sure that Phil overheard he and Angie laughing about it hysterically, but neither of them cared. They were both just so glad to witness the universe finally rise up and give Phil a piece of what he had long had coming.

This, of course, made the farewell dinner somewhat awkward, but it was bound to be so anyway. Jacob and Angie exchanged numbers and email addresses with the Grangers and of course, Patrice and Lucinda, but the rest of the group had become irreparably splintered, and Jacob and Angie were pleased to know that their early flight out of Madrid would have them riding alone for the van ride to the airport. They said their goodbyes knowing no one else would be awake when they left in the morning.

They retired to their room and talked about where the trip had brought them. Far beyond inspiring their first true intimacy, it had brought them together in such a powerful, heart-stopping way that they each marveled at the other as they pondered just how far they had come. They lay on the bed together, reclining in each other's arms, as these reflections and the final, glimmering rays of the evening sun proliferated around them.

Jacob reached behind him into his bag and pulled out the poem he had stashed there since he wrote it a couple of nights ago. He situated two pillows under his back so that he could sit upright and then slid Angie into him. He pulled the ringlets of her hair away from her neck so that he could read deliberately and seductively into her ear. Angie sat motionless but alert as he paused dramatically between each stanza to gauge her reaction. When he finished, and the stark beauty of the final two lines washed over her, she turned to look at him, to pierce into him and see if he was real.

"That was lovely, Jacob. It really was. Look, it's making me weepy," she said as she drew a few tears from her eyes with a wipe of her finger. "Was that really for me?"

"It was really for you."

"When did you write it?"

"The other night. I woke up in the middle of the night, and the whole thing came to me like a dream."

"After we made love?"

"No, the night before that." She thought she understood.

He reached out past her and began to caress the length of her calves with a strenuous kneading motion on the way down and a light, feathery touch of the tips of his fingers as he came back up. She fell further into him, and he rested his head upon her sturdy, angular shoulder, placing his cheek softly next to hers. He angled his neck slightly as she instinctively did the same, allowing him to kiss the delicate lines of her neck. He opened his mouth wide and pressed firmly with his lips to radiate a sense of warmth and connection. Before moving on to cup her breasts with his open palms, he stopped to tickle her sides, a gesture that sent her hurtling forward, but he reached up to rein her back in, wrapping his arms around her as he did so and squeezing her tightly to him.

When he finally flipped her onto her back, he raised her shirt and lowered the waistline of her jeans so that he could place velvety kisses along the edge of her panties before running his tongue down the length of them from the inside, his tongue gently tickling her finely trimmed pubic hair. He unzipped her jeans and blew a warm, moist air down onto her nether regions that continued to tease and arouse her. He could feel the tenseness of her body, its sensitivity to touch, and he lingered around her, teasing her with the luscious anticipation of what was to come.

They each took a moment to disrobe and look fully into each other, and she was astounded by the goodness she saw in him. Jacob laid her gently down upon the edge of the bed with her legs hanging off the sides. He placed his full weight down upon her and lined her earlobe with silky, open-mouthed kisses. He positioned himself firmly against her entrance but did not immediately penetrate her, instead circling her labias with the head of his penis to stir her provocation. She, however, had had enough teasing. She reached behind him and pulled him into her with a demanding force that let itself be known.

He had forgotten what this was like, what it was like to merge one's soul with another in the darkness and mystery of night. He had forgotten the religious conversion that transpired at that moment, a transformation of the flesh into the divine and the orgiastic communion with another into the depths of being that are rarely, if ever, touched. He made love to her with a passion and an exhilaration that rendered him vacant when they were done. Every morsel of his spiritual energy had been consumed in the combustible conflagration that they had built together. Emptying himself into her, he had been baptized and was free of sin once more. He let the waters roll over him, as Angie rested her head upon his chest before they each drifted towards sleep.

"I love you, Jacob. I know you may not be ready to hear that right now, but I really do. I love you."

That, however, he had not been ready for. True enough, he had felt it, had known it already to be true, probably even felt the same himself, but to have it uttered, to have it out there like that, dangling in the air like the last precious leaf of Fall, that was too much for him. Jacob, in the pretense of falling asleep, rolled over, though he had truly been more comfortable with the weight of Angie's head nestled on his torso. Angie waited for a response, but soon realizing none was forthcoming, laid herself down upon her pillow and allowed herself to be carried off into her slumber.

Jacob, however, spent the rest of the night in tortured anxiety and guilt. How could he have let it get to this? How could he have opened his heart again, knowing as he did the inevitable outcome of the whole affair? How could he have subjected himself to the pain and the suffering again? He had seen this movie before, and he knew how it ended. Everything in this world must die: ashes to ashes, dust to dust. Whatever is loved will someday fly away, lost in the harsh winds of time and impermanence.

He had a vision of God laughing down at him from above, openly deriding his foolish human nature. God was like Lucy in the Peanuts cartoons, always convincing the Charlie Browns of the world that this time He would hold the ball down so that they could kick it, but Jacob knew that at just the moment he convinced himself that this would finally be his time, that God would pull the ball from under him and send him caroming once again into the hard truth of the Earth below, because the truth here on this Earth, the illusory knowledge suspended just out of reach like Charlie Brown's ball, is that we are not meant to rise above the Earth, not meant to kick the ball of life through the goalposts anyway. They were but a mirage, tantalizing Jacob with a vision of happiness that he could never quite reach.

Angie could feel his discontent from the moment she awoke. She felt his nervous agitation from the other side of the bed and rolled to him, asking him what was wrong. He said nothing other than that he had slept poorly and rose to start his shower. She got out of bed to follow him, but he closed the door behind him.

By the time they made their way downstairs with their luggage, it was clear that something was amiss. Jacob had shut down completely, reverting back to his ostrich mode. His non-communicative demeanor was disconcerting, and Angie desperately wanted to crack through the wall.

She would have to wait, however. When they met Lucinda in the lobby of the hotel at an hour that precluded any of them from procuring breakfast, she informed them that Pamela and Stephanie would be joining them on the ride to the airport. Pamela apparently had decided to book an earlier flight and fly out before Phil even knew she was gone. Jacob barely had time to extract a heartfelt goodbye and hug from Patrice before Lucinda summoned them to the bus.

"Ok, time to go, everyone. If you don't want to miss your flights, that is."

"All right, amigo, you take care, ok?" Patrice said extending his hand in friendship. "Remember, don't worry so much. And if you're ever in Spain again, you look us up, ok?"

Jacob promised to do so and reciprocated with a like invitation. Jacob clasped Patrice on the back and thanked him for everything before leaving the man whose advice he had already seemed to have forgotten.

"So he doesn't even know you're leaving this morning?" Angie asked Pamela as they climbed into the van.

"He has no clue," she said with a wry smile, signaling her passive way of extracting her revenge.

"Are you going to see him again?" Angie inquired.

"Not a chance. I left him a note on the nightstand. I think he'll get the hint." Jacob thought of Phil waking alone with nothing but a bedside note and, for a moment, felt sorry for him.

To give Jacob some apparently much-needed mental space, Angie sequestered herself in the back of the van with Pamela to hear all the behind-the-scenes details surrounding her relationship with Phil. As was usually the case, what went on behind closed doors vastly outstripped what was available for public consumption. Jacob and Stephanie meanwhile rode together in the front of the van, speaking little as they each looked out their respective windows and recounted their journeys through the landscape as it unfolded before them one last time.

It was not until they boarded the direct flight to Dulles Airport, therefore, that Angie was able to probe into Jacob's radical change of disposition. The first hour of the flight was fairly turbulent, and Jacob clutched vehemently to the armrests so that impressions of his fingerprints remained in the padding of the armrests even after Angie was able to pry his hand away to take it into hers. She held off on troubling him about his mood, soothing him instead by running her fingers up and down his forearm. Only when the seatbelt sign had been turned off and Jacob let out a weighty sigh of relief did Angie begin her inquiry into what had gone so horribly wrong.

"What is it, Jacob?"

"It's nothing. I just hate bumpy flights."

"That's not what I mean. You've been different since last night."

He knew that she was insinuating that her declaration of love had spurred this change. He also knew she was right. He shrugged his shoulders in silence.

Angie, however, was willing to be more direct if need be. "So last night before we went to bed, I told you I love you. Now whenever somebody says that for the first time, they have to be ready to accept that it might go unreturned. I get that, and I don't expect you to say it or even feel it for me at this point, but I was hoping you'd give me your reaction, tell me what you think about it. That's not easy for me, having it out there."

Jacob considered his next comment carefully. He leaned his head back against the headrest and thought deliberately. He caught her steady gaze and looked away. "I don't know where I'm at Angie. I simply don't know if this was a good idea."

"You mean the trip?" she interrupted.

"No, I mean us."

She was taken aback by the starkness of his comment, and she sat up in her seat and unconsciously positioned herself further away from him. "What do you mean by that, Jacob?"

"I mean that I don't think I'm ready to do this all over again, not ready to put myself out there. Does that make sense?"

"No, Jacob, it really doesn't," she said irritably but with all the empathy she could muster. "Faith has been gone for fourteen years, Jacob. You need to let that go, and I'm here to help you."

"I'm sorry, Angie, but I'm damaged goods. I've been through too much."

"Which is why you deserve this, Jacob. You deserve to be happy." She could see he was on the verge of breaking down.

"I am happy, Angie- today. But I just can't risk the pain. I can't go through losing someone else I love."

"But Jacob, that's part of life."

"A part I no longer wish to engage in." He was growing more defiant now.

She felt a deep sadness for him and reached out to take his hand. "You have to take that leap of faith again and learn to accept the terms of love."

Jacob, however, spurned the gesture, "You don't understand, Angie. You have not known the suffering I have known, felt the pain and anguish that has kept me awake for the past fourteen years."

She looked at him in warning. "Don't say that Jacob."

"It's true, Angie. It's like I said to you on our first date: Things just come to you. Happiness falls into your lap."

She started violently. "Oh is that so, Jacob? I haven't known suffering? Do you know why Brandon left me, Jacob? Do you really want to know?"

Jacob slid back defensively. He realized that he had underestimated Angie, not given due credit to her own personal history in making her the woman she was today. She was shaking with a slight tremor, and tears began to well in her eyes. He did not know what to say and so sat there mute, ready to listen.

"I was pregnant, Jacob. It wasn't right according to plan. We had wanted to wait until we were married, but we thought it an unexpected blessing nonetheless." Then she heaved forward and began to sob more profusely. "I lost it, Jacob. And as I was dealing with that shit, Brandon left me. Turns out I have a bicornuate uterus. Essentially, my uterus is heart-shaped with two 'horns', if you will, that separate. In any case, it puts me at an extremely high risk of miscarriage. Brandon didn't want a life without children, so he left me to deal with that pain all alone. I know he's just trying to be nice, but he sends me a Christmas card each year with a picture of the three kids he has with the woman he met shortly after me. All it does is remind me of the family that I'll never have. So don't tell me I don't know what it means to suffer. Don't start telling me that you have some monopoly on all the pain and misery the world has to give."

Jacob did not know what to say, what words would quiet her aching soul and mend the damage that had been done. "I'm so sorry, Angie; I really am."

She turned to him, entreating him desperately as if she may not have any more left to give. "Jacob, I just wish that for one moment you could see yourself through my eyes, as I see you. Maybe then you'd be able to believe that love is worth all the sorrow it entails. Maybe then you would see that it is the delicate compromise of life that makes it all worthwhile in the first place."

She collected herself and drew in a deep breath to summon her courage and will. "So is that it then? Is that where we stand? You can't go forward with this?"

"I'm afraid so." He regretted the words as soon as they left his mouth, but he knew that he believed them. He simply could not bring himself to take the risk to love once again.

And so they sat in silence as the plane soared above the clouds. They had left the Earth, but only for a brief while. Though he hated to fly, a certain part of Jacob did not want the flight to end. But he knew that it must. Shortly, they would land in suburban Virginia, and this adventure would be over. This chapter of their lives would be past, and they would walk back out into their individual lives, alone as they had begun. Ashes to ashes, dust to dust.

They walked together through the terminal, and she accompanied him to the baggage carousel, where she paused for a moment before leaving him, presumably forever. The bags, including probably Jacob's, were already circulating around on the conveyor belt, waiting for someone to claim them. She picked up her carry-on and slung it over her shoulder, but before she left, she said with the endearing sympathy of one who had seen the depths of his suffering and understood, "No one can make you happy, Jacob. Only you can make yourself happy and then share that happiness with others. Call me if you ever find that happiness within you." And then she was gone.

Chapter 7

A Death Foretold

Grandma Darcie died in the latter part of January the next year. Though Jacob had often heard it said that miserable individuals are more susceptible to fatal afflictions such as cancer because diseases feed on their negativity and grow in the bowels of their mean-spirited nature, Grandma Darcie had made it to ninety-seven chain smoking Pall Malls from a dinner-length cigarette holder. Her bitterness had simply seemed to crust over, providing an impermeable shell of solitude into which not even Death had dared to venture. She even got to go as almost everyone wishes to: She slid away in her sleep, the perfect picture of peaceful repose.

Jacob had to chuckle to himself regarding the irony. *"Divine justice? What a load of shit,"* he thought with a grin and an upward glance at the pale blue sky perched above. Though one could argue whether or not she deserved it, he was happy for her nonetheless.

Though Jacob was Darcie's sole heir save for a few specified charities, the court process of resolving her assets dragged on heavily and consumed much of Jacob's time away from school through the Spring of Aurora's sophomore year. The inheritance meant a dramatic upturn in financial lifestyle, but for several months, he wished it would all go away.

In large part to get his mind off his other business, he and Aurora started to research area senior communities for Elizabeth. Jacob had already called Elizabeth to tell her that he would be coming up to visit for Mother's Day, but he refrained from telling her about Darcie or the inheritance until the funds were realized. He did not want to get her hopes of leaving the Institute up until he knew it was a sure thing.

The drive to Hartford that Mother's Day morning had really been quite pleasant. As had become their customary habit, Jacob and Aurora met Dr. Thompson in the lounge area of Donnelly South 1. He greeted them both warmly and rose to shake their hands. His belly had actually trimmed over the years, but his hair had become more scattered and dispersed. "Good to see you again, Jacob. Your mother is so excited you made it up for Mother's Day."

Aurora always found the disheveled doctor an amusing facet of her visits here and enjoyed teasing him within reasonable limits. "Wouldn't have missed it, Dr. Thompson. Thank you so much for taking such good care of her."

"She sure is proud of you, Aurora," he said as he smiled at her, and she blushed mildly. "All right, well let me go get her for you folks."

They settled into the plush, muted chairs of the lounge and waited for Elizabeth to make her typical grand entrance.

As the door opened and Elizabeth burst in, she twirled clumsily for them, something more akin to a rotisserie chicken on a slowly rotating spit than the fine grace of a ballerina's pirouette. Her hair sputtered in all directions and seemed as dizzy and confused as the head from which they emanated. On completing the 360-degree turn, her right foot clipped her left, and sent her forward momentarily, but she recovered, took a step towards them, and came to rest in the love seat directly across from them, as if the entire maneuver had been her intention all along.

"So do you like my new dress?" she asked as she blew several hairs away from her face.

Jacob had been so caught up in the rest of the spectacle that he had failed to notice the green dress she had purchased for the occasion. "It's lovely, Mom. You look lovely as ever."

"It's quite becoming, Grandma," Aurora rejoined as she moved over to the love seat to sit next to her grandmother. "It shows off your neckline."

Elizabeth nodded at her appreciatively. "Why thank you sweetheart! Now Jacob, you need to raise her allowance."

"Thanks for helping the cause, Mom," Jacob said sarcastically. Aurora already knew how to manipulate without the assistance.

"Us girls have to stick together," Elizabeth responded with enthusiasm, putting an arm around her granddaughter and beaming as she did so.

They chatted aimlessly for a while before Jacob thought it was time to break the big news to her. "Mom, Grandma Darcie died recently."

"I'm sorry to hear that, son," she said with genuine sympathy.

Jacob could not conceal his consternation. "You're sorry? Why the hell would you be sorry? She hated you. She put you in here after Dad died. Why the hell would you be sorry for her? You should be doing cartwheels, for crying out loud!"

Elizabeth was solemn and respectful now. "Son, life is too short to bear grudges. We had our differences, yes, but I'm not going to dance on her grave. It will be mine soon enough."

"Good for you, Grandma," Aurora said as she took Elizabeth's hand in a show of solidarity and eyed her father dubiously.

"Ok, whatever," Jacob pushed on. "The more important part, Mom, is that she left most of her money to me and Aurora."

"Well, now that I am happy to hear! Good for you, son!"

"No, Mom, good for *you*!"

"I don't get what you mean, sweetheart."

Aurora tugged on her hand and interjected, "We're going to take you out of here, Grandma. You can finally leave!"

But instead of jumping for joy, Elizabeth appeared frightened and trembled. "But where am I going to live?"

Jacob sensed her apprehension and realized that he had probably sprung this on her a bit too quickly. Given his mother's condition, they have should have informed her more gradually, and he did his best to reassure her. "We have a really nice senior community picked out for you right near us. The people there are all about your age, and there are plenty of things to do, but you'll have the freedom to come and go as you like, no one telling you what to do. No nurses, no doctors. And you don't have to worry about anything. Now that Darcie has passed, I hold the purse strings, so you don't ever need to worry about the cost."

"But I don't want to go anywhere."

Jacob did not understand. "What do you mean you don't want to go anywhere?"

"I don't want to leave here, Jacob. I don't want to leave the Institute."

Jacob was perplexed. "But Mom, I thought you hated it here. I thought you wanted to leave."

Elizabeth looked at him sternly, threateningly, like a cornered prey that attempts a last ditch effort to convince the predator why it is better left alone. "Now listen, Jacob, I may complain about this place, and Dr. Thompson, and the staff, but I am comfortable here. They take good care of me here. I like it *here.*"

The dim, dull fluorescent light shone on her face and muted her features in a cast of artificial shadows. Jacob glanced towards Aurora, trying to see if she comprehended this any better than he did, but Aurora had already gestured Elizabeth in for an embrace, and so he had his answer.

"We won't make you move if you don't want to, Grandma, right Dad?"

"Of course not, Mom, of course not."

"Well, thank you, Jacob," Elizabeth said, relieved. "I know keeping me here is a costly expense...."

"Don't worry about it, Mom," he interrupted.

Elizabeth began to appear sheepish and pulled them both in closer. "I guess it's about time I told you something too."

"What's that, Grandma?"

Elizabeth glanced in each direction to be sure they were not being overheard and then said to them, louder than she thought she was being, "I've known your father was dead all along."

Jacob was stunned. His mother had faked it all this time. "You mean you never really had a nervous breakdown?"

"Oh, no dear, those were real. That breakdown I had after you left for college, that one was a doozy, boy. When they brought me here, I was, you know, looney tunes, like the rest of the people in here." She circled her finger around her ear and then remembered she was in a mental institute where such gestures are not deemed appropriate.

"So when did you realize Grandpa was dead?" Aurora inquired.

"Oh, I'd say after a few months. Time really did stand still for a while there."

Again, Jacob was perplexed. "Then why didn't you fight Grandma Darcie to get the hell out of here? Why didn't you want to go back to living your life again?"

She looked at him with looming sorrow, compounded by being harbored all those years deep within her soul. "I was comfortable here, Jacob. Life was simpler here."

As they walked back to the parking lot in the escaping hours of twilight, Jacob and Aurora strolled amongst the dogwood trees and consoled each other. Jacob could commiserate with his mother's suffering, but it was the self-inflicted aspect of it that troubled him so. This whole time he had attributed her misery to the external force of his father's death and Grandma Darcie's subsequent torture of her, but in the end, it had always laid with her. What bereaved him most, though, was his inability to help make it stop. For years, he had waited for this day, waited for the shining moment where he could walk across these grounds and hand his mother the key to her freedom. Little did he know, she had held it in her breast coat pocket all along.

He dwelled on the absurdity of life: its hypocrisy, its paradoxes, its mutually exclusive contradictions, but also its love, its humor, its ever-fanciful whimsy. He surveyed the scene around him and noticed the dogwoods were blooming. His mother had been right; they were simply stunning in their full array of color and light. The white blossoms shone brilliantly against the contrast of the fading light of day, their yellow centers emitting a sense of hope and charity. He sensed the renewal all around him, and he knew he was being offered a choice.

Chapter 8

A Near Miss

"All right now ladies, who can tell me what part of speech dominates the first quatrain of this poem?" Jacob was, after all, a grammar nerd at heart.

"Verbs," answered Chelsea Sinclair, the thin redhead widely considered to be the second smartest girl in the sophomore class at Georgetown Catholic. Her efforts were more substantial than Meredith Klein's, but her natural abilities, especially in the linguistic arts, simply did not compare. Meredith, however, only engaged when she deemed the discussion to get "really good".

"Exactly," Jacob agreed. "And what type of verbs are they?"

"Action verbs, violent ones at that," Chelsea concluded.

"Good, and what kind of sound device does Donne employ in the first quatrain?"

Jacob scanned the rest of the room to find someone different to call on. This time, it was Aurora who answered.

She knew her father loved noting the use of alliteration. "He uses a guttural alliteration with the repetition of the b sound: 'breathe', 'bend', 'break', 'blow', 'burn'. It's like he's beating you over the head with it." Aurora had grown into a perceptive student of literary analysis. Her freshman year with Ms. Ford had honed her writing skills and provided her with the confidence to speak more in class, but it was in Jacob's course that she had really developed an eye for language.

They were discussing John Donne's "Holy Sonnet 14", and Jacob was trying to establish the point that Donne's violent language was a direct expression of his frustration and deeply conflicted relationship with God. "Right, with that in mind, what is Donne asking him to do here?"

Cheryl Pitlance, the tennis player who aspired to little more than find herself a wealthy husband who wanted tons of kids, chimed in before anyone else could. "He's asking God to beat him."

Jacob turned to her position in the back corner of the room. "And why would he want that?"

"Because he's bad?" she asked more than answered.

"Precisely," said Jacob wheeling back to the rest of the class. "So let's get to the second quatrain and see what he thinks he's done wrong. He says 'I… Labour to admit you, but O, to no End.' What does he mean by that?"

Chelsea, not wanting to be outdone, responded, "He wants to take God into his heart, but he can't."

Jacob strode back towards the white board in front of the room and picked up a blue marker from the tray beneath. "So in the next line, what is keeping him from God?"

"Reason," came the rejoinder from Jadelyn Smith. The excessively popular and stunningly beautiful sophomore rarely did her homework, but she engaged in conversations to try to appear interested in the class.

"And what, Jadelyn, is the opposite of reason?"

"I don't know."

He walked towards her in the second row and pointed the marker out as if to give her a bridge to cross. "If I ask you to believe in something, but I tell you that you can't see it, hear it, or anything else for that matter, what am I asking you to have?"

"Faith?"

"Exactly," Jacob said. He dashed back towards the front of the room and wrote the two words on the board, becoming more animated as he continued. "We have a dichotomy of faith versus reason. 'Reason' is believing in what our five senses tell us is true, but 'faith' is believing in that which reason tells us does not exist or is untrue. The two, Donne is telling us, are mutually exclusive. So why is he so conflicted with God?"

The rest of the class was scribbling down notes, but Aurora's head remained erect and she quickly commented, "He wants to believe in God, but his reason is preventing him from doing so." As she said this, however, she began to grow pale.

Jacob, too absorbed in the complexities of the class to notice, pivoted back to the class and drew them in together, like a huddle for a football team. "So here's the real kicker for Donne. You see, Donne never wanted to be a man of the cloth. When he eloped with his one true love, Anne Moore, her father was irate and had King James pressure Donne into taking Anglican orders. He was a widely popular preacher, but in 1617, Anne died giving birth to their twelfth child."

Jacob paused here to compose himself so that he did not divulge too much, giving Amy Reisenbach, the typical class clown, just enough time to inject her generally inappropriate humor. "Twelve children? No wonder the poor woman died in child birth!"

Though Jacob glared at her to attune her to his displeasure with the interruption, he was glad to have some added levity to allow him to move on. "So, in any case, Donne then writes the Holy Sonnets in 1618."

Aurora put her hand to her head. "Dad, I don't feel so well."

At that moment, however, Meredith Klein, now interested, inserted herself into the discussion. "Wait a minute, I get it. Donne cannot believe in a God that takes his wife, the thing he loves most. When Anne dies, his faith has been broken, and reason consumes him, telling him that a just God would never have allowed Anne to die."

"Dad, I really don't feel well." Aurora stood up out of her seat weakly.

"Which is why he asks God to 'divorce' him from his 'enemy': reason," opined Chelsea, apparently oblivious to Aurora. "He wants God to take him and 'imprison' him with faith."

By now, however, Jacob was no longer listening. He had noted Aurora's condition and had seen enough to be alarmed. He rushed towards her as she took a step forward, but he was a moment too late as she collapsed to the floor with a thump that reverberated throughout the hallways of Georgetown Catholic.

As he rode next to his daughter in the ambulance rushing towards Georgetown University Hospital, the very place where he lost Faith fifteen years before, the anger and resentment rose in him anew. Everything he had ever loved had been taken from him, everything but this. *"How could this be just?"* he thought, the tremors of anxiety already overpowering his conscious will to mitigate them. He saw God holding the ball aloft after yanking it away from in front of his expectant foot as he sailed precipitously into the awaiting hands of fate.

The sirens wailed as they sped down roadways unseen by Jacob as he hovered above his supine daughter, praying to nothing in particular for the well-being of his last remnant of happiness. The silence, however, was deafening, echoing even louder than the pulsating alarm of the ambulance. He wept, but there was no one there to hear him, and the stale air of the ambulance made him feel as if he were going to his grave alone, buried in a vacuous coffin.

When they arrived at the hospital, a horde of awaiting ER staffers surrounded Aurora and wheeled her into the operating room without delay. The flurry of activity left Jacob overcome and bewildered. All he wanted was to be next to his daughter, to lie down with her and hold her as he had done when she was still a child, but he was led instead to a waiting room, while the staff prepped Aurora for surgery. They told him he would have to wait, wait for the outcome fate had prepared for him.

He sat alone on the cold, sterile bench feeling helpless and isolated. The only other people in the waiting room were a young Hispanic couple anxiously awaiting news of their infant son who had somehow managed to ingest radiator fluid. The couple comforted each other in a remote corner of the room, straining for an update each time a nurse walked down the adjacent hallway. He had never known these people before, and probably never would again, but he thought it odd that these circumstances had brought them here together, and he commiserated with them from afar. He knew their pain, and he observed them carefully as his troubled heart ached for what might await them.

"Might". That was the key word. "Might". Who knew, after all, what would befall us in this life? What power did any of us have, Jacob thought, to shape our destinies? What could we do to insulate ourselves from the harrowing episodes of tragedy that are the inherent course of human life?

Jacob realized that he had let "might" rob him of the sole realm of dominion he had over his own life. The only power he really had was the power to choose, the power to choose life for as long as he awoke with the morning dawn. Each day, he had that choice, and for far too long, he had allowed "might" to pilfer the one decision he had the sovereignty to determine.

He thought back to Patrice's reaction to his surgery and to the life he had been granted. *"Life has given me more than I could ask for, so if this is it, well then, so this is it. Thank you, life. Thank you for all you have given me."* Patrice had implicitly understood that life extends no promises, just transitory joys we can accept or reject. Jacob realized that he had rejected far too many of the joys in hopes of a promise that was not being offered. His daughter lay on an operating room table, and it struck him that she was all he had left. He could accept and embrace his love for her, but if he did, he did so on love's terms.

A precisely-coifed resident from Mumbai walked into the waiting room and called Jacob's name. He informed Jacob that Aurora had suffered an episode of ventricular tachycardia, a life-threatening quickening of the heart's rhythm caused by a congenital abnormality in the electrical impulses of the ventricles. Aurora was stable, but the next couple of hours would be dicey as they implanted a cardioverter defibrillator, or ICD, to monitor and prevent any future tachycardial events. The device, about the size of a cell phone, would be surgically implanted into Aurora's chest so that it could detect an increase in heart rate and deliver precisely calibrated electrical shocks to restore a normal heart rhythm in the case of a future attack. The surgery had its inherent risks, but it was the only way to ensure her long-term health. The intern promised to appraise Jacob as soon as he knew anything more.

Jacob settled back into the bench to absorb what he had been told. There was nothing he could do but wait. He soothed himself with the memories he had of Aurora, of the days and moments that he had been blessed to have had with her. He hoped for many more of those moments to come, as he prayed too for the young Hispanic couple in the corner. Then, he curled up in his windbreaker and allowed himself to fall asleep.

It was hours later when the sacred hand awoke him, gently caressing his exposed right arm that protruded from beneath the windbreaker. It beckoned him back to the here and now with a light touch that reminded him of what it meant to be human. She was seated beside him on the bench, dressed in the blue jeans and Tom Waits t-shirt she had thrown on as soon as she heard the news. Her jaw was firmly set, but her skin was soft, and he meandered back towards sleep with the calm reassurance of her touch. Her words, however, reminded his conscious of the gravity of the situation before him.

"She's going to be all right, Jacob."

He stirred, but could not fully grasp the meaning of what she had said. Suddenly, he sat upright to bring himself to attention, and so she repeated herself. "Did you hear what I said, Jacob? Aurora is going to be ok."

She was staring straight at him now to gauge his receptiveness. This time, however, he had heard her, and the depths of his jubilation were restrained only by his need for further clarification, an assurance that what he had been told was certain and true.

"What did the doctor say?"

"He said the operation was a success. Her heart rate is currently normal, and they implanted the ICD without complications. Aurora should be able to go home in a couple of days."

Then, Jacob was puzzled. "He talked to you about all of this? Didn't he want a family member?"

She afforded herself a moment of levity and giggled. "I told him we were married. We have, after all, been on our honeymoon."

Angie was as resplendent as ever. Like the blossoms of the dogwood tree pressed against the evening twilight, she radiated a presence of the divine in this otherwise lifeless environment. The blue of her eyes shone brilliantly and instilled in him a warmth that he knew was real. He reached out his hands to run them through her tight, blond curls. "It's so good to see you. I can't tell you how much I missed you."

"I missed you too, Jacob."

"Why did you come back?" he inquired as a tear made its way down his grizzled cheek.

She tried to look at him but had to turn away to answer. "I love you Jacob. I couldn't let you go through this alone."

"How did you even know?"

"Grace called me from the school. She was coming if I didn't."

He did not need to know anything else, didn't care to. All he knew was that she had come back to him, that he had the choice one last time, and this time he knew what his answer would be. He stroked her cheek with the back of his hand and began to weep openly as he imbibed its tender grace.

"Are you happy, Jacob? Are you finally happy?"

He knew everything the question suggested, everything it entailed. He thought to himself that it was funny that it was the most simply constructed questions in life that were the most complex and had the most far-reaching ramifications. Jacob, however, had been contemplating this one long enough. He had been thinking about it his entire life.

"At this moment, Angie, I am happier than I ever thought I could be. I have no idea what life may bring going forward, but I am happy right now, and that's all I need to know."

She smiled brightly at him and embraced him. It felt good to have him in her arms again. Her hands traced the solid musculature of his back, and she felt grounded, like she had gone back to her childhood home to live for the rest of her life, a place filled with memories and self-knowledge. "You see, Jacob, that's what all the suffering was for: this moment right here, to make this moment mean something."

Life is full of binary opposites, but Jacob smirked at the thought that humans can only understand concepts through their corresponding counterparts. Heroes would not seem so wonderful if they had no evil to fight. How could one understand the encompassing presence of darkness without the piercing brilliance of light? How would we ever come to measure or appreciate happiness without the suffering we must endure?

Jacob understood the implication of what she had said, and he thought to himself that if this were true, he must be the happiest man on Earth given the depths of suffering he had witnessed. Suddenly, however, it all seemed worth it, all of it: the star-crossed, lonely nights, the desperate yearning of a grief-stricken heart, the palpitations of fear, the feeling of an unjust crucifixion upon the altar of a mocking, deriding God. All of it gained the meaning that had heretofore eluded him. He rejoiced at the thought, for it was through all of this that he was standing here right now with his fingers pressed deeply into Angie's hair and his mouth, anxious to experience every last part of her, frantically covering her with kisses.

It was not without trepidation, however, that Jacob would suggest several months later that they try to conceive a child. They spoke frankly and at great length with Angie's ob-gyn, Dr. Sporato, so that they understood just what the miscarriage rates were for a woman in her mid-thirties with a bicornuate uterus. Still, he was unwavering in his determination to at least try to have a child with Angie.

"Are you sure you want to do this, Jacob?" Her face was crimson, and her knees trembled ever so slightly from nervous energy as they sat in the same sitting room where he had discussed having a child with Faith. "You heard what Dr. Sporato said. The likelihood of a miscarriage is remarkably high. Do you really want to go through that? Do you really want to risk that potential heartache?"

He breathed deeply and exhaled. "I love you. I am willing to take that chance." His lucid green eyes remained fixed and resolute.

It was then with an immeasurable joy, commensurate only with the extent of the suffering he had borne, that he witnessed the sweet miracle of life as Angie brought their child into the world, a world filled, yes, with pain and sorrow, but filled too with hope and salvation. He heard the cool softness of the rain outside the window, and it brought him a resounding contentment. As Jacob held his newborn son, Finnegan, in his hands for the first time, he smiled at his beautiful wife and reveled in the bliss that she had brought him before he looked to the heavens and said simply, "Thank you."